The STAR PROTOCOL

Copyright © Ramon Marett and Simon Marett 2019

The right of Ramon Marett and Simon Marett to be identified as the authors of this book has been asserted by them in accordance with the Copyright, Designs and Patents Act 1998.

All rights reserved.

All rights reserved. No part of this publication may be reproduced, stored in or introduced into a retrieval system or transmitted, in any form, or by any means (electronic, mechanical, photocopying, recording or otherwise) without the prior written permission of the publisher or unless such copying is done under a current Copyright Licensing Agency license. Any person who does any unauthorised act in relation to this publication may be liable to criminal prosecution and civil claims for damages.

The STAR PROTOCOL

THE MARETT BROTHERS

First Published in 2019 by Fantastic Books Publishing
Cover artwork by Ramon Marett

ISBN (ebook): 978-1-912053-15-5
ISBN (paperback): 978-1-912053-14-8
ISBN (hardback): 978-1-912053-13-1

To Karen and Becky our wonderful wives.

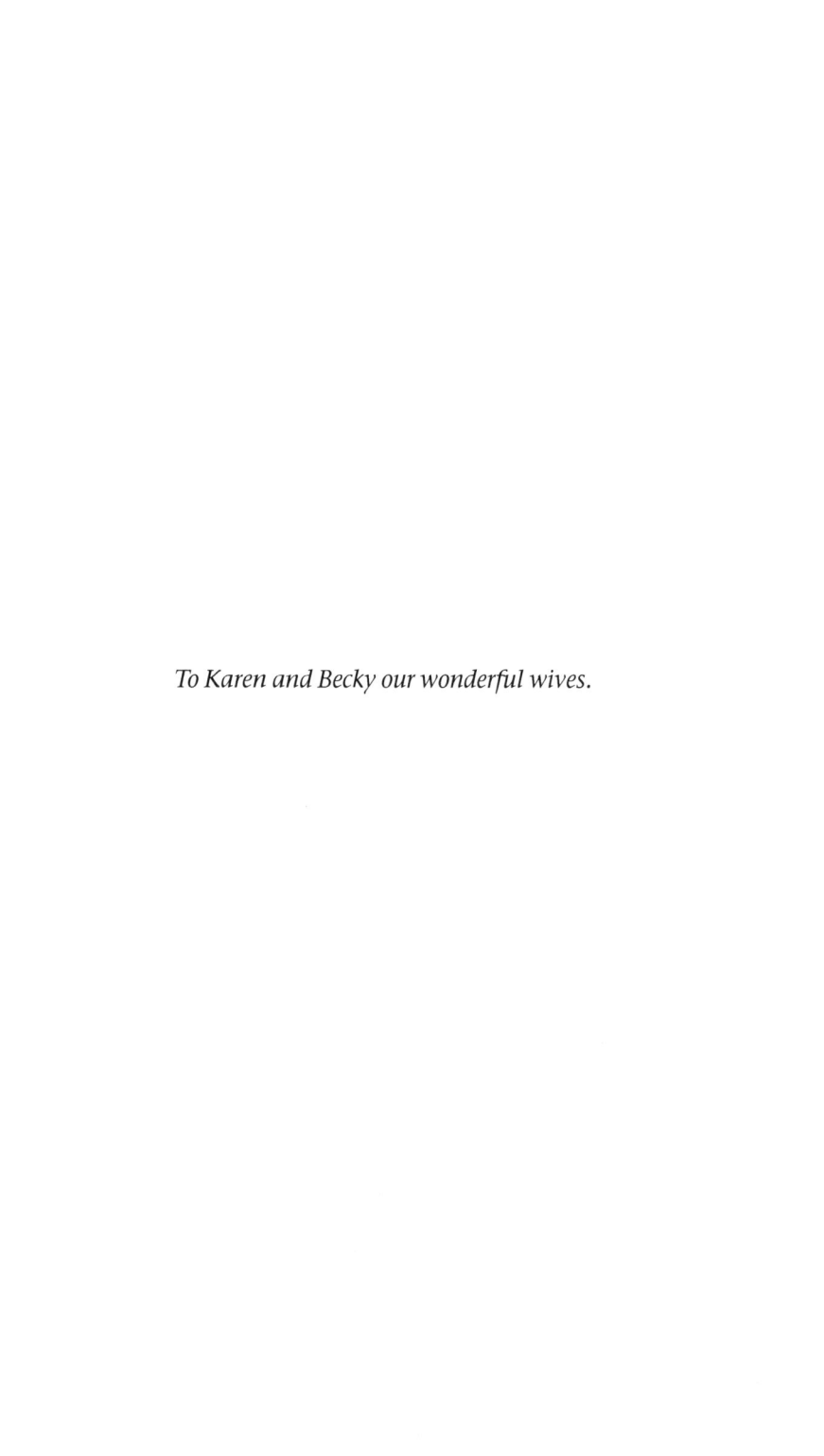

ACKNOWLEDGEMENTS

In no particular order other than the rather well known alphabetical one:

Joffy Bradford eventually.

James Coates for listening to every idea under the sun and giving his sage advice on all of them.

Stuart Fuller for knowing his whisky from his bourbon.

Dan and Gabi Grubb for being the most supportive and enthusiastic publishers one could hope for.

Andy Smith and the Dragon Archery family for inspiring us to shoot straight for the stars every time.

Anne-Marie Strand our fantastic editor.

Sandi Wood for her artistic concepts.

Hugo Zundel for editing our first draft and pointing out the many, many plot holes (you'll find none now, thanks to this guy).

Simon's D&D group, Anthony Trueman-Jones, Andy Wearne, Pete Bruford and Phil Bruford, who helped hone Simon's story telling skills over the years.

CHAPTER 1

Bullets whizzed past Dash's head as he dove for cover. 'God-dammit,' he muttered as fierce rounds impacted around him, spraying chunks of razor-sharp rock and grit out in all directions. He hid behind one of the larger weather-worn boulders and brought up his assault rifle. Torrid Iraqi desert heat was unforgiving. Salt-filled beads of sweat trickled down his forehead, stinging his eyes. An old wound in his leg ached. He braced his back against the side of the outcrop, wiped his brow and risked a peek around the edge of the boulder. One eye closed, his weapon nestled secure into his shoulder, Dash scanned the landscape of sand and rock and searched for a target. Heat haze rising from the desert floor warped the scenery before him. Seeing no immediate threat Dash glanced over at his Delta Force buddy, Will, who had taken up a prone position, lying as flat to the ground as possible. With the scope on his high-powered sniper rifle Will stood a much better chance of finding the source of the bullets.

'Anything?' asked Dash as he pulled down his scarf, which had covered his beard. A swig of warm canteen water did little to his dry mouth.

'Nothin' but sand and dust. Where's our spook?' Will replied.

'Dunno. You know what spies are like. We split up …'

'Wait. Target acquired.' Will had been double checking

the area, magnified through his scope. With a satisfied grin, he gestured ahead.

Dash peered down his own scope once more and noted a new trail of dust being kicked up as their target moved; the air, still and dry, not even a gentle breeze to disrupt the motion of the dirt cloud. The assailant might as well have been holding a giant red arrow pointing at himself. His heading, the ruined temple of Ur.

'If he gets into that building we're going to have a nightmare flushing him out.'

The old temple, or ziggurat, impressed Dash; a massive structure, an epic work of construction as magnificent as the Pyramids of Egypt, rising out of the sand, a three-step pyramid with a daunting flight of steps leading to the first level. Two further sets of stairs ascended in opposite directions at right angles to the main flight. More in common with the Incan monuments on the other side of the world than anything here in the Middle East. Dash surveyed it, knowing that only the foundations remained of what had been at least a hundred feet in height, and that it was still a long way to the top of those stairs.

'What about our spook? We headin' on without him?'

Dash couldn't locate the MI6 agent they had been assigned to escort. He studied the landscape one more time before turning to Will. 'John knows what he's doing. Let's move.'

The two soldiers left the relative safety of the rocks and sprinted towards the pyramid. Dry baked earth cracked under their steps sending dust billowing up into the arid air. Their desert combat fatigues would offer some protection, blending in with the surroundings, but they had to run across open ground now. Besides, Dash was sure the target was more interested in getting away than trying to shoot at them again.

They were almost upon the ziggurat when Will shouted, 'Top of the stairs!'

Dash glanced upwards. 'Got him.'

A figure darted inside the ziggurat. On the left hand staircase, about halfway up, was the MI6 agent, bounding after the target they were all chasing.

Dash ran after Will who had taken point, his sniper rifle slung across his back, his assault rifle out in front of him. Cautiously ... this would be an ideal place for an ambush, the two soldiers raced their way to the top.

Waiting for them was the British spy, John, heaving with exhaustion. Sweat poured off him only to evaporate as it hit the sandstone floor. Unlike the two soldiers, he was dressed casually; pale grey chinos, a dark blue polo shirt. He stood out a mile in this landscape. A pair of aviator-style sunglasses completed the image. Dash glanced at his shoulder harness holsters for the two pistols; Sig Sauer P232s by the looks of them.

'Thought I might have been able to cut him off,' he said, stopping to take a breath.

'Which way did he go?'

'Around the corner.' John pointed to a long outer wall which was holding in a mound of earth and sand.

With caution, they stacked up on the corner forming a single, wall-hugging line. Dash, in front, glanced round, greeted only by another long pathway to the next corner. Drawing his assault rifle up to his chin he crept around. This was going to be a textbook operation; the target was running out of hiding places. Will followed close behind, covering him, with John last, looking out behind them with his two pistols ready. Halfway down the path Dash held up his fist, a sign for them to hold position. In front lay a rough-hewn entrance with a pale light emanating from inside.

'Taking a peek,' said Dash. He shot his head round to check down the new hole, trained eyes spying everything he needed to evaluate the situation in a split second, and back again. 'Passageway going down, long way down, and a string of lights hooked on to the right-hand side of the wall. The excavation is recent. Any idea whose it is?'

'Nope. Any sign of the target?' asked John.

'Negative.'

'Well, what we all waitin' for?' said Will.

Dash couldn't help grinning at the contrast of Will's southern drawl against John's clipped British tones. 'OK let's go.'

He turned, gun still up ready to fire. With nothing but a weak impression of light in front of him, Dash led his team down into the ziggurat.

In the calm waters of the Gulf of Oman, not far from Dash's position, a United States Nimitz class aircraft carrier cut through the rippling waves on patrol. A young ensign in the operations room kept eyes fixed on the screen in front of him. It displayed live footage from the camera of a Predator spy drone. Its focus was Dash's team, call-sign Trident, as they entered the structure. He had been the eyes-in-the-air for the three-man team since the start of the mission three days ago and, unless anything drastic happened, Dash had the target cornered.

It'd soon be time to pick them up. A Black Hawk helicopter stood ready for the go signal and an F/A-18F Super Hornet twin seat multirole fighter aircraft was airborne, ready to assist in case the ground unit requested air support. The ensign handled the flight stick, untethered from the nuisance of turbulence in his safe position on board ship, and kept his eye on the monitor. He flew his drone into a slow circle high above the ziggurat and zoomed the camera closer in on Dash. All seemed fine until he spotted a cluster of people and vehicles moving in on the structure from the same direction Dash and his team had come. He increased the lens in further to try to identify the group. Locals, maybe. He counted over twenty, but these 'locals', he noted, were carrying AK47 assault rifles and some had RPG's.

He stared at the armed men, a cold chill had hit him, then he cursed himself for taking too long to inform his Commander. 'They must have waited until Trident entered the building, sir.'

'Get me Trident on Com-Sat,' said the Commander. 'And contact the Captain on the bridge. Inform him of the situation. They may need air support after all.'

Dash and his team made their way further into the temple through the cut passageway. The rock was sharp and the floor uneven. Will stumbled as a loose stone gave way under foot. 'Y'all havin' as much trouble as me?'

Dash was about to say that although the light was little it was still too bright for their night vision goggles when, from some place further below a female voice cried out in surprise, and then his sat-phone flickered to life.

'Trident this is Pitchfork. How copy? Over.'

Perfect timing, Dash rolled his eyes and shook his head at Will, sure he had seen him jump. He let his assault rifle rest over his shoulder, took the sat-phone from his pocket and answered, 'Pitchfork, this is Trident. Solid copy.'

'Be advised, Trident, hostiles on route to your position.'

'Copy that. Trident out.'

He turned to Will, handed him the sat-phone. 'Buy us some time.'

Will nodded and readied his sniper rifle. 'Roger that.'

'Never easy is it,' said John. He smiled as Will ran back to the surface of the ancient building. Dash caught the gleam in John's eyes and brought his rifle back up. 'OK, let's go.'

At the bottom of the passageway, Dash identified a large doorway. Light spilt from the room beyond. Shadows blocked it at erratic intervals and the faint, but unmistakable sound of a struggle echoed out. Alert, they progressed towards the noise.

The sight which greeted them was one of mayhem. Dash evaluated the situation with haste. Next to the doorway, a woman, late twenties, in loose brown shorts and a white vest lay sprawled on the floor. In the centre, the man they were after had an elderly chap by the throat with a pistol to his head.

He eyed the young woman on the floor, her horror, obvious. A quick nod to John, then he let his assault rifle hang on his shoulders and drew his more accurate sidearm. John holstered one of his pistols, and held the other with both hands. Dash took deliberate, slow steps into the room and put himself between the woman on the ground and their target. One potential problem out the way, but he wasn't sure the old hostage would make it.

John, who had tried to flank the man, spoke to the target in Arabic telling him to lower his weapon. The man turned to John but had the sense to keep the old man as a human shield, presenting as small an object of himself as possible.

Dash took the opportunity to scan the room once more, confident John had this covered. He saw a camera on a tripod in one corner, and some ancient-looking tablets scattered across the floor. They were covered in strange inscriptions. Brushes, mini pick axes and a small notebook lay by the woman's feet. Archaeologists. Must be.

The ground moved. He tensed and looked around. It hadn't been enough to knock anything over, and he wasn't about to lose focus on why they were here, but the solid stone floor beneath him had definitely moved.

Will ran to the top of the slope and out towards the exit, shielding his eyes from the blazing sun. The heat hit him with a blanket of scorching air almost smothering him. He cursed Dash for sending him back here as he felt the sweat on his forehead. Then sounds from the desert below distracted him from the temperature. He set up the sniper rifle, resting the barrel on the crumbling sandstone wall and peered through the scope. Through the haze he identified five pick-up trucks, kicking up a mountain of dust behind them which meant they were travelling fast; two had large calibre machine guns mounted on the rear.

Not good. Did he engage now at a distance, risking revealing his position too early, or did he wait for them to get closer; easier to shoot but a danger of being overrun?

Decision made.

He took aim on the driver of the lead pick-up. The suppressor on the end of his sniper rifle would muffle the noise and reduce muzzle flash. With luck his position would remain hidden, for now. He pulled the trigger. A round spat out of the barrel, travelled over the baking desert, and smashed through the truck's glass windscreen. The pick-up careened to the right, crashed into a ditch and flipped end over end coming to rest on its roof. Satisfied, Will waited. The other trucks stopped.

Will fired again, his target, a commanding officer pointing and issuing orders. A puff of red mist exited the rear of the man's skull; the figure next to him froze as his Commander dropped to the floor. A fatal mistake. In less than a second he too slumped to the ground.

The area in front of Will erupted in sparks and cracks, parts of the wall he was using as cover, disintegrated. One of the soldiers with some initiative, or blind panic, had grabbed the reins of a heavy machine gun and fired in Will's direction. Will rolled to his right, crouched low and took up another firing position. He lined up on the soldier, finger poised, when a sudden glint of light flashed in front of him. Gut instinct took over. He ducked as an enemy sniper, concealed in one of the many dry ditches took a shot, the bullet whistled through the air where Will's head had been but a second before.

He rested his back against the wall, aware the enemy was now making its way towards him. Once again he weighed his options. Surgical precision now no longer necessary, he strapped the sniper rifle to his back and readied his assault rifle for a more direct approach.

Then, thundering above the pyramid appeared two thuggish Hind helicopter gunships, rattling the ground and blocking the sun. One of the airborne brutes pivoted mid-air and brought its Gatling gun to bear. The down draught of the rotor blades whipped up a storm of dust that billowed off the side of the building. Will used its cover and raced towards the entrance, weaving as he went. Every muscle burned, screamed and begged him to slow down, but even through the noise of the helicopter he could hear the motivating impact of large calibre rounds chewing up the path behind him. He leapt to the relative safety of the open passageway and spun around to witness a line of bullets rip past him.

He opened up a comms link to Dash. 'Ivan's come to play.'

The young ensign on board the US carrier heard Will's crackle over the sat-phone. 'Pitchfork, this is Trident. How copy? Over.'

The Captain, who had been called to the Ops room earlier, sensed the urgency in Will's voice and picked up the phone himself. 'Trident this is Pitchfork. Solid Copy.'

'Requesting air support at my location. Over.'

The Captain had seen the arrival of the two Russian-made Hind helicopter gunships on the monitors in front of the Ensign. Silent Rain, the F/A-18F on patrol was airborne and ready to help but before the Captain could respond to Will's request, one of his radar operators spoke.

'Captain, AWAC has detected five MiG-29's inbound, thirty-one miles out.'

'Captain,' piped another sailor. 'Message direct from the White House, the Russian President denies having troops in Iraq. We are cleared to engage any hostile force.'

'That was quick,' said the Captain to his number two. 'How did they know?'

'Do I re-task Silent Rain?' asked the sailor.

'No sailor, you do not. That's what they want us to do,' said the Second in Command.

The Captain nodded and spoke into the sat-phone. 'Trident. Air support inbound your position three minutes. Will hand you over to Silent Rain. Pitchfork out.'

Dash was getting impatient. This standoff had gone on for too long and John couldn't talk the tight lipped man down. Their target was getting wound up and with nowhere to go, the enemy had found himself in a no-way-out situation. Dash heard Will's communication crackle in his ear piece. 'Ivan's come to play.'

'Russians?' said Dash and looked straight at the enemy. The man flinched and Dash saw recognition in his eyes. It was all John needed. Whilst the target was distracted, the British spy fired. The bullet passed right by the hostage's ear and through the target's head.

'Russian?' said Dash, again, this time the question directed at John, who shrugged and went to help the old man up.

'Wait!' the woman screamed.

Both men froze. Dash glanced around at the woman,

who had not stood up. John dropped to one knee, his pistol trained on the exit. Dash looked at the woman. She was obviously concerned about something and it wasn't the dead guy. 'What is it?'

'The floor. It's unstable.'

Dash tried to evaluate the situation. The old man was inching on all fours back towards the far wall.

'John, see if you can …' Dash was cut off as the floor shifted, and this time they all felt it.

After speaking the words, 'Requesting air support at my location. Over,' Will had stared at his sat-phone with growing frustration. He'd spoken directly to the Captain; where was his confirmation? Why the delay? The thundering of enemy helicopters didn't help. 'No, it's fine. I'll hold,' he muttered.

Then, at last. 'Trident. Air support inbound your position three minutes. Will hand you over to Silent Rain. Pitchfork out.'

Will had no time to relax though. He could hear voices coming from the edge of the stairs, the language, Russian, no mistake. With his assault rifle up, firm against his chin, he peeked around the corner of the doorway, eyes straight down the barrel of his gun.

One Hind had turned away from him to get a better angle for troops on board to grapple from the four ropes thrown out of the helicopter. Two soldiers were on their way down so Will wasted no time, opening up on the nearest one. His weapon fired a three-round burst felling the soldier. Whipping round, the other one raised his weapon a fraction too late as another three-round burst hit him square in the chest throwing him off the rope.

The pilot slewed the helicopter around. Heavy fire destroyed the final protection Will had. Someone on board shouted and pointed down at the Delta Force veteran. With the Hind hovering menacingly above him, a tinge of despair washed over Will. He raised the assault rifle knowing damn well it wouldn't do any good against the bullet proof underside of the metal beast.

A glimpse of something small … a streak of white smoke impacted the side of the chopper. An instant later it exploded in a dazzling fire ball.

The sat-phone sprang to life. 'Trident this is Silent Rain. Apologies for the delay.'

Will allowed himself a moment to smile, delighted to see a Super Hornet banking in for another attack run. 'Hot damn, your timing is perfect.'

'Copy that. Glad to be of service. Will stay on station for as long as possible.'

'Roger that. Trident out.'

Will grinned in satisfaction as the burning helicopter began to come down, and continued to watch until a realisation killed his grin. The flaming Hind, with all its unused ordinance, headed straight for him.

'Ah, for crying out loud.' He sprinted down the corridor.

As he burst into the room Dash and John were in, he yelled at their shocked faces, 'Get down!'

Too late. The shockwave blasted through, vaporising the insurgents outside and causing the old temple to shake.

Then, the floor gave way.

Dash blinked, shaking off the dirt in his eyes. 'This damn desert,' he muttered, feeling the weight of rocks on top of him. It was still dark, but he could recognise the woman, just. It was clear she was a bit dazed, but thankful to be alive. Dash focused on her in the hope of shaking off his own mild concussion. She had managed to haul herself up free of the rubble. He watched her take a moment to absorb the situation as dust drifted from her body. She looked cut and bruised, but otherwise OK. Doing better than him at least, what with these rocks on top of him.

'Dad,' he heard her call out, noting her English accent. Her eyes must have adjusted to the sliver of light as she had started to pick her way through the rubble. A large section of the floor was untouched forming a huge circular space, clear of rocks. Dash winced and groaned when he lifted one of the heavy rocks off himself. The noise attracted the woman's attention and she hurried over.

'Here let me help you.' She reached down and grabbed Dash's arm. His strong hand grasped back and almost pulled her off balance as he got to his feet.

'Thanks. Name's Dash. Sorry about the mess, but we'll get you outta here.'

He watched as the young woman appraised him. What did she see? A bit rough round the edges, but not bad looking, he hoped. And maybe his presence made her feel safe.

'Thanks for saving my father and me,' she said. Dash nodded. He'd been doing his job. 'My name's Cassandra.'

'Pleasure to meet you, Cassandra. Let's see if we can't locate your father.'

'I have the old man!' John shouted from somewhere across the room.

'Who are you calling old? Young upstart!' boomed another voice.

Cassandra laughed. Dash saw a huge wave of relief flood through her. 'He did save your life father,' she called into the darkness.

'Yes, and almost killed me again. I blame him for the fall, you know!' He then lowered his voice. 'I am very grateful, young man, but you know … one's pride and all.'

'What were you doing here in Iraq anyway? You OK by the way? Nothing broken?' Dash heard John ask.

'Just a few cuts and bruises, nothing serious. We were lucky to hit that object.'

'Object?' said John.

'You didn't feel it, young man? It was like a slide. We hit something and slid off. You didn't feel that?'

'You were in the centre of the room when the floor caved in. Maybe you hit a support beam or something.'

'Well, I'm a lucky old sod then, aren't I?'

Dash could see them now. It was clear to him that John decided there and then that he liked this wily old fox. Sporting a well-trimmed beard and slicked back hair the old man had strength enough to survive the fall, and still had his sense of humour despite being held hostage; yes, the sort John would like.

'My name is Professor … well no, my name is Alexander, but I'm a professor. But … but my friends call me Alex.' The old man held out his hand, which John shook and both men laughed.

'Why are they laughing?' whispered Cassandra.

Dash shrugged and picked up his rifle. 'Come on. Let's go into that central clearing there.'

They stumbled towards the middle of the chamber where the going got easier when they were clear of the fallen rubble. Dash and John called for Will.

No response.

Then Dash spotted him standing, holding his rifle across his chest, staring up. His buddy had put on night vision goggles.

'Hey, Will, we've been shouting for you,' called John.

Will turned to the group still with his NVG mask on and pointed up. 'Have y'all bothered to look up?'

They all did.

'Can't see anything,' said Dash.

'Yeah, hardly any light. Try putting your night vision on.'

Dash unslung his backpack and found his NVG, flicked a switch to activate them and held them up to his eyes. 'You've got to be kidding me.'

'That was my first thought,' said Will. 'Guess we found out why the rocks and crap didn't spread out across the whole floor.'

'You've got to be kidding me.'

'Yeah OK, take a minute. Took me awhile to let it sink in.'

'What! What's going on?' said Cassandra, holding her father's hand with a tight grip and trying to edge away from the centre.

'Flares?' asked Will.

'Flares,' nodded Dash.

They removed their NVGs and struck a couple of flares, scattering them about the room. Once all were ignited the room lit up with a reddish hue which flickered and cast long shadows. Above the group, the light reflected off a perfect chrome disk.

Dash, Will, John, the Professor and Cassandra stared up at the metallic object. No one spoke. Jaws were dropped.

'That's … big,' whispered Will. Thirty metres in diameter at least, thought Dash, which put into perspective the size of the chamber they must be in.

Dash felt the underside as he got closer to the middle. A ripple of rainbow light spread out from his point of contact highlighting the edges of an intricate network of hexagons. Like a bee hive or snake skin. Cassandra and the Professor both had a go and touched the metal. The spectacle continued, like dropping a small stone in a pond.

Will scanned the perimeter and told them that four squat landing pads were standing the saucer-shaped object up, but it was John who discovered an extended ramp that led into the machine. And he was the first to say it. 'Christ, a flying saucer!'

Dash and Will chuckled.

'Well Professor, what do you think? Find of the century?' said Dash.

'The legends are true … All the myths about them are true,' whispered the Professor.

'We don't know that, Father.'

'What else could it be? I knew something was here.'

'We're in Iraq. It could be what the Americans thought were the WMDs, or this could even be American. Who knows what they've got out here?' Cassandra clearly wasn't believing her own eyes, or at least wasn't prepared to agree with her father before exhausting rational ideas first.

'Yeah, it's not ours,' injected Will.

'Not ours either,' said John.

Cassandra frowned at John. 'No offence but how would you know?'

'No offence taken, but those two ...' John pointed at Dash and Will. 'American Special Forces, Delta Force, and I'm from MI6.'

Cassandra nodded, giving John a sideways look as though happy to find a fellow countryman. 'OK, well until we examine this in more detail it's going to be hard to prove it is them,' she said, aiming the sentence at her father.

'But this is the proof we've been looking for. I'm sure it's one of theirs,' said the Professor.

'Whoa, hold up. You know what this is? Who it belongs to?' Dash stared at them.

'Well not exactly. We're here searching for clues, I never expected to find ... but ... I might have a good idea who it belongs to, yes.'

'I'm game. Give me your best shot. I don't think I'll be surprised with anything you have to say at this point.'

Cassandra folded her arms and shook her head. Dash could see she wasn't eager for her father to embarrass himself in front of strangers. But the Professor came alive as he spoke. His back straightened, his khaki clothes seemed a better fit, and his blue eyes shone with triumph. 'I believe this is ... or once does ... or still does ... or is ... does ...' The Professor took a deep breath and gestured up at the flying saucer. 'I believe this vessel belongs to the Anunnaki.'

'The who, now?' said Dash.

'Yes,' said the Professor. 'Ancient Sumerian texts read that there were those who came down from the heavens, beings who created the Sumerians themselves, six thousand years ago. The Sumerians worshipped them as gods and referred to them as the Anunnaki.'

'Aliens?' Will muttered, lifting his weapon and re-scanning the chamber.

'So, what do they look like then, these Anunnaki? Little? Green?' Dash asked, ignoring Will.

'They are supposed to resemble lizards, if you believe the pictures and carvings,' said Cassandra with her arms still folded, a slight scowl across her face.

She reminded Dash of Lara Croft, with her Khaki shorts, desert boots, and long dark hair. Attractive and like the character she spoke with a British accent, but you'd think her father was giving up national secrets with the scowl she was giving him.

'Some of these lizards, according to the Cuneiform written by the Sumerians described the Anunnaki as shape-shifters and they were masters in genetic manipulation,' said the Professor.

Dash was about to ask another question, genuinely curious, when he heard John's voice coming from behind him with an odd echo. 'Hey guys, you've got to check this out.'

'Where are you?'

John's head popped down from above the ramp. 'Where do you think?'

A soft white strip of light wrapped the circumference of the saucer. A strip of light also lit up the middle of the underside revealing a concave part of the ship with a massive booster rocket nestled inside. The kind of rocket exhaust that reminded Dash of a space shuttle. And there was a powerful hum in the air. If a piece of mechanical hardware could ever be described as alive it was now.

'What the hell?'

'Rescue team will be here shortly. Thought I'd go and see what's up here before it's too late. I must have found the light switch.'

'What does he mean by too late?' asked the Professor.

'Once the military sees this, it'll be the last time any of us do,' Dash told him.

'Oh,' said the Professor, looking at his daughter with big questioning eyes.

Dash caught the look. His head was going to ignore it, but his gut decided first. 'What the hell! Let's go see what Britain's finest has broken.'

'What's with these spooks? Can't take your God-damned eyes off them for second,' Will murmured to Dash.

They all clambered up the ramp, greeted by John's grinning face. Behind him was the polished silver entrance into the ship.

Dash was last up the ramp, hesitating before climbing aboard. It occurred to him whoever owned this piece of hardware might not be far away.

'I think this flying saucer works,' said John.

Dash groaned as he got to the top. 'Why, what have you done?'

'Let me show you. Hey Alex, you're going to be impressed.' Dash saw Cassandra smile at John's use of her father's first name.

Past the doorway, the ship opened up into a smooth oval room, a long table at its centre; everything the same silver as outside. As Dash entered, chairs appeared along the sides, rising from the floor. He stared at the strange curves, seats like rearing cobras.

His gaze took in the walls, lined with equipment and

screens. He followed John along a short corridor that led to the cockpit, just two chairs here but plenty of standing room. A blank silver sheet stretched across the domed space. Above it, offering a one-hundred-and-eighty-degree view, was a window. He scrutinised it, curious about its constituent parts, myriad circular pieces held together by thin transparent struts.

There were joysticks at each seat. 'Manual control for lateral thrusters?' John suggested tentatively.

'No obvious yoke for manual control elsewhere,' Dash responded, turning back to the oval room and scanning its height. Up above was a mezzanine floor. Access by staircase, he noted. His gaze tracked higher. Over everything lay a huge clear dome.

'Will, over-watch, rear.'

Dash felt a churning in his stomach. This was off mission. He hated the feel of his heart beating fast through his thick army issue clothes. Will nodded at his command and knelt at the back of the ship, his weapon pointed downwards, out of the ramp. He could rely on Will, but having civilians here was making things awkward. How the hell did two archaeologists even get permission to be here?

'This is amazing.' He heard the Professor's voice. The old man had wandered into the cockpit.

Dash followed him.

'That's not all,' John was saying. 'Touch the silver sheet in front of you.'

The Professor's trepidation was obvious as he reached out, carefully wiping away a layer of dust, and tapped the long sheet. Instantly the cockpit lit up. A black screen replaced the metal, showing a column of chevrons at one side, pointing north, and a simple circle at the other.

Blue writing appeared to hover an inch above the metal pane that ran from one seat to the other. Circling at the middle of the console was what looked to Dash like a blue holographic image of the Earth.

'This writing, I recognise it,' said Cassandra. 'It's a form of Cuneiform.'

'Those are words? It all looks like little arrows and a bunch of lines to me,' said Dash.

'No, no, Cass is right. This one ...' The Professor pointed at a red symbol. 'It means door or gate ... gateway.'

Dash studied the "word" the Professor was talking about. 'Looks like a fish trying to eat a rocket,' was his conclusion.

'I'd surmise that it would close the outer door and bring the ramp up,' the Professor went on. 'Thus, closing the gateway.'

'Try it. Let's see if you're right,' said John.

'Hold on,' Dash interjected. 'Before we do anything, we need to know we can shut this off?'

'Of course, just tap the metal part of the console twice,' said John.

'You've only been in here five seconds. What are you, an expert in flying saucers at MI6?' Dash raised one eyebrow at John, though appreciating his optimism.

'I've flown many a fighter plane in my time. This isn't much different.'

Dash flashed him a this-is-very-different look.

'I don't think it's a good idea,' said Cassandra.

'The worse that could happen is the door won't close, some safety feature or something, right Alex?' John winked at the Professor.

'Yes, quite so, my good man, and Cass shame on you. Where's your sense of adventure?'

'Suppose we won't get a second chance once the rescue team gets here.' Dash knew he was trying to convince himself more than the others.

'Who's going to do it?' called Will from where he was still covering the exit of the saucer.

'Alex, you would like the privilege, I assume,' said John.

With the glee of a child finding a new toy under a Christmas tree, the Professor reached down and touched the symbol. A low vibration started to spread around them. The ramp retracted and a door slid across the open exit without a sound.

'Door closed.' Will stated the obvious.

'I was right,' said the Professor.

'Not bad Profess …' Dash trailed off as the hum increased.

'That just dudden sound good,' called Will.

Without warning, one of the other symbols started to flash. It pulsed faster and brighter than the others. The buzz became a loud, ever-increasing whine.

'The faster it flashes, the louder that sound is getting,' said Cassandra.

'Red is a bad sign,' said John.

The Professor put his hands over his ears. The ship began to shake, vibrating violently as the noise increased. Everyone grabbed something to steady their balance. Dash watched transfixed as Cassandra sat down in the pilot's seat and touched the red flashing symbol. A grinding motion shivered through the vessel. All Dash could think of was landing gear retracting, and right behind that thought came the realisation that the vibration they'd been feeling had become smoother. They were no longer in a craft standing on the ground. They were hovering in the air. Then, to his dismay another symbol started to flash red.

'Think it's time to shut this down,' he said.

'OK,' said Cassandra. 'How?'

'Double tap an empty part of the console?' suggested John.

Cassandra tapped the metal console twice with her finger and was rewarded with a sudden loud buzzing noise which echoed throughout the ship. All the symbols on the instrument panel started flashing red.

'Well, that was a bad idea,' said Will.

Cassandra tapped the metal once and the console went back to blue, apart from the original red flashing symbol, and the buzzing stopped.

'Now what?' John said.

Dash took command. His gut told him this was dangerous; a situation he had allowed to happen.

'Professor, take a seat in the centre room. John, Will, get that exit open. I'll sit here and help Cassandra.'

He heard her murmur, 'Cass,' as he lowered himself into the co-pilot seat whilst the others followed his orders. He watched to be sure the Professor went where he was told and saw that as he sat, the seat moulded around his body, adapting to his contours. The reshaped chair then turned to face the wall, upon which a miniature console slid out and flickered to life, the holographic display looked similar to the one in the cockpit with the same symbols glowing vibrant blue.

'These consoles are workstations of some description,' the Professor called back.

'Great,' shouted Dash. 'Don't touch anything!'

Reaching over, he ignored his own advice and touched

the red light. A shutter slid over the windows, closing their view of the outside. The dome window at the top of the centre room was covered with shutters too. Another light started to flash next to Cassandra. She looked to Dash for guidance. He could see she was shaking more than the ship was.

'It's one button after another. Let's see what happens. Maybe it's just a power cycle,' he said.

She touched the red symbol with a tentative finger. Both the pilot's and co-pilot's seats moulded around them whilst the image of Earth was replaced with a red triangular object. Unrecognisable letters, or numbers more like, were changing every second on top of the hologram. A countdown.

'I really don't like this,' said Dash. 'Will! Get that damn door open. We need to get out of here.'

Will and John had been searching for controls, or even a simple lever to open the outside door and extend the ramp, and found nothing. Dash saw that the urgency in his voice had encouraged Will to draw out his pistol and shoot at the door. The bullet ricocheted around the room, causing a brief panic as they all tried to dive for non-existent cover.

'Y'all alright?' Will asked.

John put his pistol away, looking glad he hadn't been the fool to fire first.

'Will?' asked Dash again. Then the red hologram flashed a couple of times and went blue. A ship-wide, soothing voice said something in a language none of the occupants could understand.

Then sunlight lit up the cockpit as the ship took off, out of the ziggurat.

The F/A-18F was still on station, circling the building below waiting for a sign the ground unit were OK. The Predator drone had gone back to base to refuel and the F/A-18F pilot had just been informed the rescue team were ten minutes out when the structure below erupted, like a volcano. A huge cloud of dust boiled up from below. The base of the structure exploded in all directions sending stone blocks high into the air and from out of the dust cloud a huge silver disk shot past the fighter plane.

The pilot yanked on his flight stick, banked into a tight turn and gunned the afterburners, chasing the unidentified flying object whilst activating his nose mounted camera, wishing he had one more set of hands so he could rub his eyes.

The co-pilot spoke into his radio. 'Pitchfork, this is Silent Rain come in.'

'Silent Rain this is Pitchfork.'

'A UFO has launched from the structure and we are in pursuit, I repeat we are in pursuit.'

'Come again, Silent Rain?'

'I repeat we are in pursuit of a UFO.'

'Please confirm last.'

'We're chasing a God damn flying saucer!' yelled the pilot in exasperation.

'Confirmed. Silent Rain, you have permission to engage target.'

'Roger that.'

The pilot selected a Sidewinder missile and attempted to lock on to the silver ship.

Cassandra saw two more symbols light up red. She turned to get out of her seat, wanting no more responsibility but Dash held out a reassuring hand. 'We'll sort this,' he said.

Cassandra eased herself into the pilot's seat, stared at the two symbols for a heartbeat then flashed out her hand pressing both as quick as she could. The first one she touched made the window shutters deactivate and they slid back revealing cloudless blue skies. The second symbol returned to blue but didn't do anything.

'At least we didn't blow up,' said Dash.

The pilot chased after the UFO, his heads-up display already had a red box around the vessel, with a diamond target closing in too, a beep, beep, beep rang in his ear as he went for missile lock, when a beam of white light lanced out from the unidentified ship and hit his plane. The controls went dead and alarms sprang to life as the engines died. Not giving up without a fight, he tried to wrestle with the controls but no success, his plane was in a flat spin unable to keep itself airborne without any kind of thrust.

The pilot yelled into his radio. 'Eject, eject, eject!'

The canopy blew open and both pilot and co-pilot were propelled from the plane as the ejection seats fired them into the air.

CHAPTER 2

'We've left Earth's atmosphere,' said Dash, leaning back in his seat.

Will appeared between Dash and Cassandra, his hands gripping the seats. 'I couldn't get the damn door open.'

Dash didn't answer. He stared into the depths of space, a million stars peering back at him.

'What a view though, huh?'

'What a view?' said Cassandra. 'We've got to get out of here, now. That view … that view is our death.' She started hammering as many buttons as she could press on the console. Nothing happened. It was like the system had completely shut down. 'We're going to die.'

'We're not going to die,' said Dash. 'Will, search the ship, escape pods, space suits, anything.'

Will nodded.

'And get John up here. Let's see if his flight experience can help with any of this.'

'Oh my God, Dad,' said Cassandra and got out of her seat.

'Hey, wait a minute, you're not floating. You should be floating. We're in space,' said Will.

Cassandra shook her head, as if that wasn't worth caring about right now, and she headed down to the main oval room.

'Ah was just saying,' said Will.

'You're not worried?' asked Dash, gesturing to the view out of the window and at their predicament.

'Hey, she doesn't know you like I do. You'll get us out of this, Sergeant.'

That was the first time Dash had heard Will call him by his rank in a long time, although Master Sergeant was more accurate. 'Just find me something, a radio will do.'

The Moon, a small grey circle in the night sky was getting larger with deliberate, controlled measure. John turned up and sat next to Dash. 'They're not doing well in there,' he said.

'It appears our destination is the Moon,' said Dash.

'Right. Well let's make sure that doesn't happen.' John grabbed one of the little joysticks down the left hand side of his chair. Dash had the same set of eight stub joysticks on the right hand side of his chair.

'What are these?' asked Dash.

'I'm hoping they're a manual override for the thrusters.' John tapped one to the right, and the craft moved laterally to the right, but his smugness was short lived, for when he let go the craft automatically returned to its previous position and course.

'Keep at it,' said Dash. 'I'm going to check on the others.'

Dash took the few steps down into the main room going over the events which had led them here. Trying to make sense of it all. Assuming the spacecraft was older than the ziggurat, why would it come to life and strand them in space or on the Moon after just a couple of button presses. Cassandra, he could tell, was doing her best to stay calm, but she was feeling the same fear they all were. Dash wasn't even sure if he could keep it together, his rib cage felt so tight across his chest he thought anxiety itself would kill him. The only person appearing to enjoy himself was the Professor.

'Think about it,' the Professor was saying to Cassandra. 'We're breathing air. This craft was on Earth. Whoever it belonged to, they must need the same atmosphere we do, besides I'm not so sure we are going to land on the Moon anyway.'

'What do you mean?' said Cassandra.

'Well my dear … um … you too Dash, I took time to study the console in front of me, and I believe we are on a flight path which takes us away from the Moon.'

'Are you sure?' asked Dash.

'I can examine our trajectory on the screen.' The Professor pointed at his console.

'When did that screen appear? Our consoles have gone dark in the cockpit.'

'When you shot down the plane following us. One of my symbols started to flash red so I pushed it and the screen came up, showed me exactly what was happening behind us. It was a good shot,' said the Professor.

'Oh no!' cried Cassandra. 'The other symbol, it didn't appear to do anything.'

'Don't worry dear, the pilots ejected to safety, these things happen.'

'To us Professor, not to archaeologists,' said Dash checking over the Professor's console. 'I reckon you've got a navigation set up here.' Dash worked at the console controls bringing up another image of some kind of triangle, more through luck than judgement.

'Yes, navigation; my thoughts too. I have a good knowledge of Cuneiform sir, and this is all similar.'

The Professor went back to the console and manipulated the information on screen before turning his attention to the table in the centre of the room. A moment later it lit up and a three-dimensional hologram appeared. The Moon was there, a small blue flying saucer and a large red triangular object. There was a thin blue line from the centre of the flying saucer to the centre of the red triangle, curving around the Moon.

'That is where we are going,' said the Professor, his finger interfering with the red triangle hologram.

'A hologram of something red, doesn't bode well,' said John, coming into the room.

'Actually, it's a three-dimensional volumetric light,' said the Professor. He was met with blank stares. 'You see a hologram can only be viewed from a couple of angles, this is not technically a hologram but a three dimensional … you know what, let's call it a hologram. It's not important.'

'John's right though,' said Cassandra. 'What is that? A space station? Another spaceship? It's probably derelict, given how old this ship must be.'

'Given how old this ship is, it's still working fine,' called Will. He was on the mezzanine floor leaning over the hand rails, 'so it might not be derelict.'

'Professor,' said Dash. 'What's the likelihood we'll find air on that ship?'

The Professor didn't answer.

'That's what I thought. Will, get me a God damn radio.'

'There's nothing up here Dash.'

'Alright, I'll try the sat-phone.'

The sat-phone replied nothing but static. They all knew it was never going to work, even a bullet couldn't make its way out of this ship. 'OK then, Professor, see if you can talk to this ship; get it to turn off its autopilot and return control to us.'

'Or see if you can scan that red ship? Life signs or air even?' suggested John.

'I can do that,' said Cassandra and sat at another console next to her dad. The console turned on when Cassandra faced it and the chair conformed to her seating position. She had a black, glass-like panel at keyboard level and two rows of two monitors in front of her. The black panel showed a number of icons as Cassandra hovered her shaking hands over it. Dash checked his own hands, they were shaking too so he rubbed them together hard and hoped no one noticed. He still had this gnawing pain in his chest, never had he felt anxiety like this before. Never had he been in a spaceship. Hell, he'd never even trained for a situation like this. Cassandra sat still in her chair facing the screens, water welling up in her eyes, though Dash could tell she was doing her best not to cry. He grabbed John's arm as he walked past. 'Go help Cassandra, you seemed to pick up the ship controls quicker than most.'

'I'll give it a shot,' said John. He didn't sound confident.

Dash joined Will on the mezzanine.

'How they all doin' down there?' asked Will. Dash leaned over the rails. John was kneeling by Cassandra attempting to access the computer system. The Professor had his notebook out and could be seen scribbling away with his pencil.

'Honestly? I think I'm bricking it more than anyone else. I don't know if it's crazy optimism or ignorant scientific superiority, but the Professor is convinced we'll be fine.'

'John seems to know his way round.'

Dash chuckled. 'You'd think he'd flown one of these before, the way he handled the controls earlier.'

'And he was the one who got the engines started,' replied Will.

They both took a heartbeat then set curious eyes on John.

'Nah,' they said in unison. No time for conspiracy theories now.

Dash and Will took the time to explore the small ship. Behind them on the mezzanine floor was a door which led to the power plant room. Moving further into the main room, they stumbled on a tall door set flush to the wall, almost hidden. Inside had a lift which went down one floor to a storage section with maintenance access to the main rocket engine and the four undercarriages.

Three hours passed and Dash found himself in the cockpit contemplating their journey so far. Adapt, improvise and overcome, those are the laws a soldier lives by and Dash had failed. He caught a whiff of perfume before Cassandra sat in the chair next to him. She released a long sigh and leant her head back on the seat.

'Did you get the computer up and running? Are we heading to another ship?'

Cassandra stared at him with a tired gaze.

'Is there air?' asked Dash again.

'No Dash.'

'No air?'

'No, we didn't get the computers to work. What did you expect? This is an alien spaceship, I barely know how to use my phone!'

She was right of course, what had he expected, but for

the moment, the impressive, panoramic view outside grabbed his attention. 'Your dad was right.'

One thing was clear about the Moon. Dash called back to the others. 'Comin' round to the dark side of the Moon. You were right Professor, we're not going to land on it.'

'What's that?' said Cassandra.

Dash gazed past the cover of the Moon's shadow. Floating there like a dark blot against the back drop of space, a triangular shape. A thick wedged ship, like a B-2 Stealth Bomber but with no fuselage or tail. And big, much bigger than their craft.

'You should have power in there now,' called the Professor from the main room, and whilst he was saying it, the console did indeed boot up. A slow turning blue triangle in the centre of the console turned yellow almost immediately, then Dash caught another yellow blinking light on Cassandra's side. She instinctively touched it, but the yellow flashing refused to stop.

'That's new.'

'Yeah and we're slowing down.'

'We might be docking with whatever it is,' said Will. Dash glanced back, waiting for Will to elaborate, only to see the soldier, John and the Professor had left their consoles and were gathered around the central table.

'If I can read this telemetry right, which I'm not sure I can, we're headed for what appear to be some big hangar doors,' said the Professor.

'I agree,' said Will.

'Doesn't seem like that from where I'm sitting,' said Dash, examining the ship in front of them. A ship with no apparent door of any description, let alone one large enough to accommodate their craft.

'The ship in front of us certainly appears seamless,' said the Professor as if he'd been reading Dash's mind. 'But I'm convinced an opening will appear soon.'

'Either that, or we're on course to ram it,' added John.

Dash got out of his chair. 'I think I know what's going on, Cassandra I need you to stay here and when that yellow symbol turns red, tap it. Professor I need you to keep an eye on our course in case I'm wrong. John, kit up. Will, full tactical gear, but leave your sniper rifle here.'

'Care to fill us in, boss,' said John who then checked his ammo. He'd only used one bullet so far. Will tightened the straps on his Kevlar vest.

'Since we took off we've been on autopilot and I think the Professor is right, we are going to dock in that ship and I don't want to be caught off guard.'

Dash pulled out his sidearm and turned to Cassandra. 'You know how to use one of these?' he said, handing her the gun.

'No,' said Cassandra shaking her head. 'I'm a scientist not a soldier.'

'This is a Colt M119a1, seven round magazine with a bullet chambered.' He turned the gun side on and pointed. 'This is the safety, press that lever and you're ready to go, point it at the enemy and keep pulling the trigger.'

'OK,' she said, and Dash heard the unease in her voice.

'Besides, if anything hostile is on that ship, they'll need to get past us first.'

Will slammed a magazine into his assault rifle. 'Amen to that.'

John, armed with two pistols, gave one to the Professor. 'Don't worry Alex, no one gets past us alive if we don't want them to.'

'I don't believe anything hostile is on that ship, John,' replied the Professor.

Dash was kitting up when Cassandra turned her head. 'The symbol is flashing red.'

'OK here we go. If I'm right, when you press it, hangar doors will open, and we'll land. If there's air on that ship I'm guessing our ramp will automatically descend.'

'That's a big if,' said Will.

'We've got air on this ship, but we're about to find out if the Professor is right. OK Cassandra, do it.'

Cassandra tapped the flashing red symbol and this time it turned to the familiar blue. Ahead, in the cold, hostile environment of space, two massive doors along the hull of the shadowy ship opened like the black maw of a shark preparing to eat its prey.

'Doors are opening. We were right,' confirmed the Professor.

'Get ready,' said Dash. 'Will, take point.'

'Got a hankerin' to get off this ship anyway,' said Will.

The flying saucer glided without a sound into the dark hangar. On her console the landing gear symbol started to blink. Cassandra deployed them and, like a leaf falling from a tree, the saucer landed with hardly a bump. As soon as another symbol started to flash she pushed it, shutting down the propulsion system.

'The ramp hasn't extended,' said Dash.

'No, but the symbol for it is flashing. What do you want me to do?' asked Cassandra.

'Good question, either we do nothing and hope, or we risk it and pray there's air in there,' said John.

'It's very dark in here, I can't see anything,' said Cassandra.

Command had hard choices, and this was one of them. *When you're in command, command.*

'Do it,' said Dash. 'Ready night vision.'

Cassandra hesitated for a heartbeat and pushed the symbol. The back door slid open and the ramp started to descend. There was no drop in pressure and no air was sucked out of the saucer; a good sign. Before it had fully extended the three Special Forces men were running down, Dash and Will in night-vision goggles. Will ran ten feet from the ramp and took a knee, the military art of crouching with stability, with haste. Dash and John did the same, peeling off left and right. All three scanned the hangar bay.

'Anything?' said Dash.

'Negative, no movement,' replied John.

'No movement here, but there's another ship like ours about fifty feet away,' said Will.

'John, cover our ship. Will with me.'

John moved off into the darkness.

Dash viewed the lightless surroundings; his night vision goggles bathing everything in a bright green hue. His heart should be racing but he was a Delta Force commander on recon patrol. The mission was all that mattered. If anyone … any*thing* … appeared to be hostile, he'd adapt to it. He led Will to the other flying saucer, assault rifle tucked into his shoulder, aim straight down the scope. Will covered behind, assault rifle up, aware of all directions, ready for ambush.

As they approached the second craft, they both slowed. On seeing the landing ramp extended, they entered the ship, Dash examined the first room whilst Will, took the cockpit.

'Clear,' said Dash.

'Clear,' replied Will, moving back to Dash who was already walking down the ramp out into the hangar.

'Let's assume this flying saucer works, and not touch anything,' said Dash.

'Hey, it's not ma fault we're here, I'm not the spook who decided to have a "let's see what this button does attitude".'

Will was right of course. Dash knew it was John who had discovered how to turn the ship on, but that probably hadn't mattered, and the result would have been the same. 'We were all curious, I probably would have pushed the symbol anyway.'

The second ship in the hangar now secure, they walked back to the craft they had arrived in, the soft glow of the lights radiating out of the ship, a bright harsh illumination in their night vision goggles. As they approached, Cassandra and the Professor walked down the ramp to greet them.

'Where's John?' they both said in unison.

'Not again,' groaned Will.

'Relax I'm right here.' John walked out of the shadows.

Dash hadn't seen John until he had spoken and it unnerved him.

'First things first,' said the Professor. 'We need to get to the bridge of this ship to determine what if anything we can do. It would also be helpful if we found a light switch.'

'The sooner we can contact Pitchfork and let them know what's going on the better,' said Dash. 'We'll split into two groups, stand a better chance of finding the bridge.'

'Have you seen any horror films?' asked Cassandra.

'Let's hope there are no mad axe-men on board. You're with me Cassandra. John, Will, you're with the Professor.

Call-sign is Trident Two. Cassandra and I are Trident One. Keep in contact. Report anything out of the ordinary.'

'You're kidding right?' said Will. 'Ah reckon this whole place is outta the ordinary.'

'You know what I mean.'

Cassandra went to hand her gun back to Dash.

'No, you keep hold of it.'

'Quick radio check,' said John.

Dash nodded. The three Special Forces men put in their ear pieces and tested their radio transmitters, located their throat mics, spoke into them and did a thumbs up to indicate they could hear each other.

'Do you want me to power down the ship?' said Cassandra.

'No, leave it on in case we have to get out of here in a hurry,' said Dash.

'If we can work it out,' added John.

'OK, let's go,' said Dash.

They all moved towards the logical exit of the hangar. Cassandra had a hand on Dash's shoulder, the Professor had his on John's and John on Will's.

As they walked towards the far end of the room, Dash's night vision picked up a light source; faint at first but brighter the closer they got. An oval doorway. Taking off his goggles, Dash said, 'Check this, its blown inwards, back into the hangar.'

Dash approached. Unlike the silver metal of the saucer, the material around them was black with silver flecks. It reminded him of highly polished granite but metallic.

'This was a big door,' said Will.

'You can see the outline, about four-foot-wide and ten, eleven-foot-high, I'd hazard …' said the Professor.

'I'm more concerned about what made this hole. They obviously weren't welcome,' said Dash.

'Let's hope whoever made it are long gone,' said Cassandra.

Dash looked through the opening. He wanted Cassandra to be right, that whoever made this hole was long gone, but his gut said otherwise. They'd barely been on this vessel ten minutes and already he was preparing for combat. It felt wrong, but Dash was no diplomat. Combat was what he knew, and he knew it well. 'I'm sure they are,' he lied and stepped through the opening into a massive nine-foot-wide by fourteen-foot high corridor.

'OK, light enough not to need the goggles.'

They all cautiously stepped into the corridor, weapons ready. A shallow glow dipped into recesses above. The walls glinted and winked as the light bounced off every silver speck.

They made their way down the dim passage. Dash stopped, held up a fist, halting everyone in their tracks. They could see the passageway split further down, but that wasn't what had stopped him.

'Doorway to my left,' whispered Dash.

'Blown in like the last one,' noted Will.

'Stack up.'

They all hugged the wall behind Dash, with John at the rear.

'Taking a peek.'

Dash quickly looked around and snapped his head back.

'Another corridor like this one, looks like it leads to another blown out door,' he said.

'I guess this is where we split,' said Will.

'OK, I'll take Cassandra left here. You take the rest and carry on.'

'Roger that,' said Will.

'Stay in touch. I mean it. No-one gets left alone in here.'

Will nodded to Dash and they clasped arms. 'Good luck.'

'You too, buddy,' replied Will.

CHAPTER 3

Dash stepped through the doorway into a new corridor followed by Cassandra. Ahead of them, fifty feet down, another blown in door and a room beyond. With a caution born from years of training Dash readied his gun and beckoned Cassandra to follow him. His gaze darted from place to place noting the shadows sucking in the weak illumination.

A small figure darted past the doorway in front of them. Dash froze as Casandra stifled a gasp.

He put his finger to his mouth. 'Come on,' he whispered, taking a firm hold of her hand. 'Stay behind me.'

A mess of metallic tables and consoles met his eye. Screens flickered on and off, charts and graphs lay everywhere. Panels had been torn apart. Metal frames and pipe work hung from above. The consoles trailed thin fibre optic filaments. He stumbled as loose wires caught round his ankles, hard to see through the thick mist that carpeted the floor.

No sign of the small figure. If he hadn't heard Cassandra react to that brief flash of movement, he might believe he'd dreamt it.

He could feel her moving nimbly behind him, just the racing pulse at her wrist giving away her fear. God alone knew what was going through her head. Even he was way beyond his comfort zone now.

Her free hand pointed to the centre of the room.

Standing in the middle of the room rising from the black floor, an operating table, perhaps. At one end various tendrils of different metals hung like a dead octopus suspended by a pole. He imagined lying on the slab with all those tendrils alive, slivering like snakes about his body. Up his nose and into his ears. He shuddered. Guns and bullets, he could cope with, weird operating tables were a bit much. What a horrible torture room, he thought.

'This must be their med bay,' said Cassandra.

Yes, that made more sense.

'Over there,' Cassandra whispered and pointed.

At the far end Dash could see a set of stairs against the wall which led to a small balcony. Looking down at them from the shadows was what on first glance appeared to be a small child. Although its features were all distorted and hard to distinguish in the light, it was about four foot tall, dark grey skin, a thin childlike body and a large head. Too large to be human. The creature had no discernible ears although it did have what appeared to be nostrils, no nose but two vertical slits close together under the eyes and a small mouth. Its large black opaque eyes bored into Dash. Dash became hot and sweaty, hate emanated from the alien's eyes. Dash pointed his weapon at the creature.

'Incoming!' He yelled.

The ground around him erupted, sending him into the air, shrapnel and sand leapt up around him, slicing into his body, small cuts all over. The shockwave sent him flying, the wind knocked out of him as he landed. Dazed and confused he tried to get up but collapsed back to the ground, his right leg useless.

A pair of strong arms grabbed his outstretched hands.

'I got you buddy,' said a familiar voice above him, and dragged him into a gully.

Dash gritted his teeth. Protruding from his right leg was a large chunk of twisted metal shrapnel, glowing orange and red, wisps of smoke rising.

'Contact left!' cried another voice.

Sounds of gunfire echoed around him.

After what seemed like an eternity, his hazy eye sight returned, clawing his senses back to him. He was in Afghanistan fighting the Taliban, his four-man Delta Force team had walked into an ambush and were now fighting for their lives.

'Dash, you OK?'

That voice.

'Right leg's busted, Will.'

'Can you shoot?'

'Oh yes.' Dash hauled himself up on his rifle and lay on his belly.

The Taliban were coming up over the next gully and running at them. They had also circled round to their rear. Dash and his men were trapped, and they knew it.

'Air support's five minutes out,' said Will.

Dash let off a burst of rounds and saw one of the Taliban go down, but two more combatants took over the position of the dead enemy. They weren't going to last five minutes.

'Contact right!'

One of the American soldiers swung his machine gun around and fired it from the hip, downing another two Taliban but caught a bullet for his efforts. Dash's four man team were now three.

'RPG!'

Everyone dove to the dirt. This time the rocket flew past and exploded harmlessly behind them.

'Make 'em pay for every inch lads,' called another voice.

They resumed their firing positions, but ammo was getting low.

'Where is that God damn air?' shouted Will.

'Keep them pinned down. It's our only shot,' said Dash in command.

'I'm out!'

Dash grabbed a spare mag and threw it to the Delta member. There was another blast, followed by screaming. The dust settled, and his buddy was clutching his wrist, his hand blown clean off. Then a grenade landed at the feet of the soldier. Dash dragged himself towards his comrade, but too late. The grenade exploded. The ringing in his ear drowned out all other noise. He'd gone off mission for an enemy mortar they'd spotted, but at what cost? The radio hissed and cracked, louder than the ringing in his ear. For once, air support was early.

'Pop smoke, air has arrived!' said Dash.

Will grabbed a smoke grenade and with an almighty throw lobbed it at the Taliban, whilst Dash did the same behind them. Red smoke billowed out on the battle field, marking the target drop. The roar of jet engines pierced the shouting and gunfire when one of the Harriers swooped in low. His heart was beating so fast with adrenaline, Dash experienced everything in slow motion. Two bombs later and the world around him turned into a fiery hell, and he screamed.

There was more gunfire, this time to his left. He saw Cassandra, surrounded in flame, but untouched by its heat. The Colt handgun he'd given her held in both hands firing ... at the balcony above them.

Realisation came to Dash and he pointed his assault rifle where the alien had been but saw nothing.

'You back with me now?' asked Cassandra.

'Yeah, I was in Afghanistan for a moment.'

'You had been staring at that alien for about five minutes, and I thought something was wrong, so I fired a few shots into the air, hoping to scare it off.'

'Appears you did enough. Thanks Cass.'

He saw her surprise at the familiarity of this new diminutive; felt surprise himself that it had slipped out.

'Was it reading your mind or something? It looked like it was reading your mind.'

'I don't think so, more like it was searching for who I was, gauging me. Like flicking through a book and stopping at a page that interests you.'

'Was it trying to communicate?'

'No, I have a pounding headache, I felt my memory was being ripped from me, I got a sense from it, I didn't matter, I was nothing to it, just an insect to be swatted and studied.'

'That doesn't sound good.'

'It wasn't. If you hadn't of fired, God knows what would have happened.'

'We should tell the others.'

Dash pressed his throat mic. 'Trident Two this is Trident One. How copy? Over.'

'Trident One, Trident Two solid copy,' came Will's voice, filtered through static.

'Just had an encounter with a little grey alien, paralysed me and tried to rip into my memories.'

'Copy that. Alien hostile?'

'Affirmative, treat as hostile combatants.'

'Copy that Trident Two out.'

Dash smiled, professional as always. He had just told Will about a mind reading alien and Will had taken it in his stride. 'I'll check out that balcony, you stay down here and see what you can find. Make sure we stay in visual sight of each other. I don't like the idea we can be pinned down just by looking at them.'

Cassandra nodded, and searched the immediate area around her trying to find anything of use. Dash held up his assault rifle and went to the stairs, determined not to get caught out this time. If a grey alien popped out again he was going to put a bullet through its head.

As he ascended the stairs he also kept a watchful eye on Cassandra. Should the alien appear anywhere near her he wanted to get it first. His attention back on the black, silver flecked stairs, as cautious as he could be, Dash climbed up and on to the balcony. No alien … no sign of it either. Picking his way, he proceeded along the balcony until he came to the end. The Grey alien was nowhere in sight, but a hole in the ceiling, too small for him to clamber into, was where it must have escaped.

'Damn,' said Dash to no one in particular.

'What is it?' called Cassandra from below.

'Our little friend went through a damaged air duct of some description.'

'You've seen the film Aliens?'

'Yeah, don't remind me.'

As Dash started along the balcony, returning to Cassandra, something wet and glossy made him stop and double back. Black liquid on a hand rail. He took out one of his gloves, put it on and touched the liquid. It had the same sticky quality as blood. 'Looks like one of your warning shots was a bit closer than intended,' said Dash.

'Why?'

'Fresh blood, if you want to call it that, not red like ours but black.'

'Oh God, is that good?' said Cassandra eyeing an undamaged console.

'If they bleed it means our weapons are just as effective on them as on us,' said Dash making his way back down into the room.

'This console isn't damaged, and I don't think it's been tampered with.'

'Leave it,' said Dash. 'We need to get to the bridge.'

'Then let's go through there.' Cassandra pointed to another blown out door.

'Good call. Stack up behind me.'

Cassandra was getting used to some of the military terms, and hugged the wall behind him ready to enter the corridor beyond. Her gun pointing toward the door they had entered from. Dash knew she must be checking in case the alien had circled back on them somehow. Impressed, he allowed himself a small smile.

CHAPTER 4

Will led John and the Professor round a curved corridor to a door so violently blown apart parts of the frame and wall were missing.

'Something went on here,' said Will as he stepped over the twisted metal. His words echoed ominously throughout a large room, a good twenty metres long. In the centre stood a pedestal made of the same silver alloy as the saucer, complete with small hexagon tiling. The Professor, intrigued, raced over to the object. Will tried to grab him but missed. 'Professor, wait …'

The Professor reached the structure no problem. Will came in a moment later. 'Don't run into a room like that, Professor,' he ordered and shook his head in disbelief.

'He's right, Alex,' said John.

'Sorry, John. I got excited when these lit up.'

Around the sides of the pedestal, four holographic keyboards glowed bright, cutting through the darkness. But it was the strange, hovering symbols the Professor was pointing to.

'Cuneiform?' asked Will.

The Professor nodded.

'Can you read them?'

'Oh yes, my boy.'

'Good. We need to find a way to contact Pitchfork,' said Will, though the Professor wouldn't have a clue that

Pitchfork was his and Dash's command carrier in the Gulf of Oman. 'Or anyone on Earth for that matter.'

John nodded towards the opposite end of the room. Another entrance had been forced open. And to their left, another door stood intact.

'Stay here.'

Will headed to the damaged doorway. He stepped over the threshold to be met by an eerie silence. He peered up unable to picture the ceiling; darkness engulfed the place. He took a knee and waited for his eyes to adjust. It was a curved corridor, the same size and shape as the one they'd gone down to reach this room, though bent in the opposite direction. With plenty of damaged doors and scorch marks, this ship had been subject to more than just an attack. The boarders must have been searching for something, something valuable enough to rip through the whole ship to get at. With nothing noticeably dangerous he shouted, 'Clear.'

'OK Alex, we've got to move. How are you getting on?' said John, still pointing his pistol through the scorched door frame where they had entered. The Professor stroked his stubble-covered chin, and breathed heavily through his nose. John put a kind hand on his shoulder.

'It's OK, Alex. This is alien text. You're not going to learn something complex like this straight away. Let's continue to search the ship.'

'This here,' said the Professor ignoring John's words. 'The word *House*, on ancient clay tablets back home, is similar, almost the same.'

The Professor gestured to a symbol, a right angle, like the corner of a picture frame. 'And this one ...' he pointed to the next symbol '... cartography. Map, maybe?'

Will came back into the room and John motioned for him to join them. As if on cue, the two symbols started to flash. Red.

'Red is bad, isn't it?' said the Professor.

'Seems to mean something imminent,' said John.

'Should I press it?'

'Any idea what the symbols mean?' asked Will.

'Home map,' said John. Smug.

'I think,' added the Professor.

The Professor touched the symbol and the pedestal lit up. A holographic image of a triangle spaceship appeared. It spun round at a gentle pace and had a transparency to it, a three-dimensional internal blueprint. The hangar they had landed in, their flying saucer and the other one already there when they had arrived. The main doorway out of the hangar was shown in red, blinking on and off. In fact, most of the points of access were blinking with red dots.

'Schematics,' said Will. 'That's what "home map" means. Schematics of this ship, and ah bet those are all damaged doors.'

The Professor pointed to the flashing lights. 'If we do assume red is bad, not that I like to assume …' He pointed to another section on the hologram. '… but there is a room two decks down from here lit entirely in red.'

A familiar sound rang out from somewhere else on the ship. Loud bangs which made the Professor jump. Four gunshots in quick succession. John ran back round the corridor they had come in from, pinching a quick glance down the direction Dash had gone. 'Nothing here,' he called back.

Will ran to the intact door. 'Any chance you can get this open, Professor?'

The Professor froze for a split second, like his mind was so dedicated to working out the hologram controls it couldn't even allocate functionality for movement. Then he tried to pick up the hologram and move it around. That worked. He traced a path from the hangar bay, round a curved corridor into a massive room. Two doors were red, one was white. The Professor pressed the white door, and its real-life counterpart opened.

Will was met with a long corridor, over a hundred metres. At the far end a blue shimmering light, but no sign of Dash. Gunfire, thought Will, meant a problem. He grabbed his mic, but before he spoke, Dash's voice came through his ear piece. 'Trident Two this is Trident One. How copy? Over.'

'Trident One, Trident Two solid copy,' replied Will.

'Just had an encounter with a little grey alien, paralysed me and tried to look through my memories.'

'Copy that. Alien hostile?'

'Affirmative treat as hostile combatants.'

'Copy that, Trident Two out.'

Will glanced at the Professor who had clear bemusement in his eyes. Will realised the Professor had only caught his end of the conversation and was hanging on the word, 'alien.' John, who had listened in on the conversation stepped in and answered Alex's un-asked question. 'Little green men. Only this one was grey.'

'Right,' said the Professor, unfazed. He pressed the red room two decks down on the hologram and the image of the ship zoomed in until the selected room was shown, this time as a red outline. Now the room glowed blue but a huge sphere in the centre flashed red.

'What is that?' asked John.

The Professor shrugged. 'I might be able to decipher some more of these symbols given enough time.'

'It looks important, I'll go check it out,' said Will.

'That a good idea?' asked the Professor.

'The quicker we sort out what's going on the better.'

'What about the "hostile" aliens?'

'What about them? If I see one I'll kill it, I've been in worse situations by myself.'

'OK,' said John. 'I'll stay here with Alex.'

'Show me how to get there,' said Will.

'According to the schematics here, if I'm correct, there should be a lift on your right as soon as you step through there.' The Professor pointed to the open door. 'Once you're in, descend two levels and you'll see a corridor in front of you, head down it and take the first left. It'll lead to a door which should be the lobby area of this room with the red sphere in.'

'Got it,' said Will.

'You sure?' said the Professor.

Will peeked round the corner to make sure the coast was clear, glanced back, smiled and nodded at the Professor and disappeared though the doorway.

John positioned himself, so he could keep an eye on all three doors. The Professor reached into his pocket and removed a scruffy looking notebook with an elastic band around the cover, opened it and pored over his notes.

'So,' said John. 'What's your story?'

'Hum, what?' said the Professor, not looking up.

'How come you and your daughter ended up in the same mess as us?'

'Ah yes, well, that's a long story.'

'We're not going anywhere in a hurry.'

'Yes, quite,' agreed the Professor. 'Well, I ended up becoming an archaeologist because of an old school study I did on aliens and UFOs. Something I did as a child, I must have only been about eleven or twelve. I thought the project would be something fun to do, nothing serious but I ended up spending hours at our local library. Fascinating. It's a pub now. The library. Serves the most wonderful ale.'

'I took you for a wine drinker.'

'Oh no. A good ale and a warm fire, that's me.' The Professor drifted off for a moment. 'Well, I wanted to see them for real. UFOs. So, I made sure I did well at school and went to on to Cambridge.'

'They've got a degree in alien studies, have they?' joked John, to which the Professor rolled his eyes.

'All across the world the same iconography appears in civilizations separated by thousands of miles. Oh, there are differences, but they represent the same thing.'

'Interesting,' said John.

'Exactly what I thought, so I started to dig around a bit, pun intended, and concluded it all linked to the Anunnaki.'

'You mentioned them when we found the saucer.'

'Yes, or Anunna, a race of gods for want of a better term. Not that I believe in a God.'

'After what I've seen today I have a very open mind. Carry on, Alex.'

'These gods are said to have descended to Earth around six thousand years ago, although it's quite possible they were here long before that. It's still unclear as to what they wanted though. They helped the local population build massive structures, like the temple of Ur where you rescued us. But why? What possible, genuine, truthful reason would they do it? My research has shown they also helped build the pyramids of Egypt, the ziggurats of the Incas and Aztec's, which all have striking similarities you know.'

'So little grey men built the pyramids then,' said John.

'No,' said the Professor, flicking over a couple of pages in his note pad. 'From what I can tell, they have various forms, but none like the alien Dash described. Most of them take on a lizard-ish, appearance. Humans or humanoid anyway, albeit for the scales on their skin. There are others though, a branch of the species perhaps, who one might describe as bipedal geckos standing at least nine foot tall.'

The Professor showed John a photograph stuck in his notebook of an ancient carving on a sandstone wall. It was indistinct but now he had said it, it did appear like a lizard standing on two legs.

'That explains the big doorways,' said John, fascinated by what the Professor was saying.

'And some,' said the Professor finishing off his sentence, 'some are meant to be shape-shifters.'

John double checked the safety was off on his pistol. 'Are they hostile?'

'There's a lot of speculation in that area. My belief is no. In general, I think they are benevolent and they were trying to guide man but for what reason, I couldn't tell you.'

'How would they guide us?'

'If you accept the possibility some of them could shape-shift, which I do, then they could easily infiltrate the governments of today. In the past they could have been wise men or priests, people with power to influence others. I would bet good money on Leonardo Da Vinci being one of them.'

'Really?' said John, sceptical this time.

'Yes, a great painter, sculptor, musician, architect, mathematician, engineer and of course inventor. Some of his inventions were way, way ahead of his time.'

John took a suppressor from his pocket and started to casually screw it on to the end of his pistol.

'What's that?'

'A suppressor, or what people call a silencer. It reduces the sound of a bullet coming out the bad end of a gun barrel. But it also gets rid of the muzzle flash, leaving the target clueless as to where the shot came from.'

'Ah, interesting. So, what's what your story then, John?'

'Typical to my type I suppose,' said John. 'Parents died early in my life. I am an only child, so went from foster care to foster care. Soon as I was old enough I enlisted in the Royal Navy. From there I went into the Royal Marine Commandos, then to SAS selection, which I passed. After a while some of my abilities shone through and I was recruited into MI6 and they put me to use.'

'I don't think there's anything typical about you, John. There's a lot more to your story than you're telling I think.'

'We all have secrets, Alex. You got lucky digging in Iraq of all places.'

'True, true. Well I for one am glad you're with us. I feel a lot safer with you around.'

'I like you too, old man.' John gave the Professor a friendly wink.

'Old man indeed!' The Professor pretended to ruffle his feathers. 'If I was thirty years younger I would have shown you.'

'I believe you would have,' laughed John.

Will reached the elevator. It opened, so he stepped in and found himself in a glass cylinder around twelve feet tall, at his best guess. The familiar holographic touch panels, dotted throughout the ship, lit up with three symbols. *Even I can guess what these symbols do*, thought Will and he tapped the one to descend.

The floor changed to a lattice of fine silver spindles like a spider's web. He could see straight down between the gaps. There was no bottom, no apparent destination, further down appeared to be nothing more than an endless expanse of nothing. 'Well Professor, you better be right about where this elevator goes,' he muttered.

Will refused to drop his eyes down. He did not want to witness the floor rushing up to meet him. Instead, he checked his weapon.

The next floor down approached, but the lift didn't appear to be slowing. Not his stop.

Standing there, as if waiting for the lift, a small grey humanoid followed his descent. Large black eyes bored into him.

Will raised his assault rifle and almost pulled the trigger. The alien was smiling, or appeared to be, but when Will didn't shoot, the smile turned to a sneer and then the floor passed by. So that was his first encounter with an unknown species. Was it taunting him into shooting out the glass possibly killing them both? Was that what it wanted?

When the lift stopped, Will blew out a breath. He wasn't condemned to an eternal descent to nowhere. The door opened to reveal a single long corridor just as the Professor had said. Edging forward, he came to the door he was after, and put his hand on its rough, steel edge, cold even through his gloves and thick like oak.

'I'd love to get me ah hold of the gun that did this,' he murmured, caressing the charred blast marks. Inside was smaller than the map room, and more like a lobby as towards the end an open archway led into a much larger area with a faint shimmering light reflecting on the ceiling, caustics, the kind you get in swimming pools or anywhere light is reflected off water. With his gun up, he moved forward.

Everything seemed fine, but 'everything' could be deceiving. About halfway in Will heard a sound above and behind him. He spun around aiming his gun. Nothing. 'Getting paranoid?' he whispered. He backed away. A bit. In case. The dark walls and dim light were not ideal conditions.

He turned around to continue onwards and for a split second thought he saw a small dark Grey humanoid with a large head, standing just in front of him, staring with malevolent eyes, but it was another trick of the light.

Stepping through the archway, muscles tense, every sinew rippled, senses on high alert, he felt as he had many times before. Going into a hostile situation he had learnt to trust his training with his own enhanced instincts.

The room was huge, bigger even than the hangar bay. The object that required such a large space was a huge silver ball, suspended in mid-air between two massive cones, like exhaust jets, vertically positioned. One above and one below as if pointing to the sphere. Around its base, like a moat around a castle, a shimmering blue liquid pierced the gloom, creating patterns that danced across the ceiling and bounced off the ball. Not too far from him, another console blinked with several red symbols. And up in the darkness were pipes, ducts and thin fibre optic cables. It was a mess. Someone or something had begun to dismantle this room piece by piece.

Movement. No more than a flicker but enough for Will's instincts to kick in. He leapt aside as a green beam of searing hot energy shot past him. It caught the side of his stomach, burning through his fatigues and skin.

He rolled and recovered straight into a crouch with his weapon ready to bear on whoever fired on him. A quick flash of grey, a small figure running to the other side of the exhaust jet. Will moved the opposite way, to catch his target.

As he rounded the corner of the massive exhaust jet, he caught sight of the grey alien. It wore pieces of metal, glove-like, and held its small hands close to its chest, palms together generating a glowing green ball of fire. The creature flung both hands out in Will's direction and the green energy sped towards him.

He sidestepped again and felt the heat of the beam as it trailed past.

When he looked back, the alien was gone. Will carried on around the corner and had almost gone full circle when the hairs on his arms stood up. He spun around to see fibre optic cables shoot out from the ceiling. His assault rifle was knocked out of his right hand as the filaments engulfed his arm. He went to grab the cables with his free hand, but more snaked across the floor entwining both his legs and lifting him off the floor.

From out of the darkness, the dark grey skinned alien

emerged, its thin lips parted to a smile. It stared straight into Will's mesmerized eyes.

Will glanced up into the blue sky noting the two Harrier jet fighters banking round for another strafing run on the remaining Taliban; the bombs they had just dropped burned the land around them. Black smoke billowed into the air; the reek of burning earth and flesh reached his nostrils and thoughts turned to Dash who, battered, bleeding and exhausted was crawling over to him. His other two squad mates, his friends, lay dead.

'I failed us, Will,' said Dash.

The sat-phone flared to life. 'Blackhawk inbound on your position, ETA five mikes.'

Will acknowledged the call. Five minutes. This gully would be their grave if they didn't hold out. As if to affirm his thoughts gunfire raged all around him, dust and sharp stones erupting everywhere. He grabbed Dash and yanked him into his gully.

The Harriers roared, raining down a stream of anger, chaos and death with their cannons. It wasn't enough. Either desperation or sensing impending victory, the Taliban charged Will's position.

He saw the first one through the receding smoke, and fired a burst. The Taliban fighter went down but was replaced by two more. Automatic gunfire rang out louder than before. Dash, valiant as ever, moved to help but his leg gave way and he fell back into the gully. Will watched in an almost trancelike state as Dash pivoted and fired his assault rifle, one-handed at the enemy almost upon them.

Will bellowed with anger. No, this was not going to be his last fight. Today was not a good day to die. And he launched himself into the oncoming enemy soldiers. The first two were caught by surprise, not expecting a direct assault, and died still gazing at this lunatic running at them. Will then went down to cover in a small insignificant dip, on one knee, his assault rifle nestled into his shoulder. He focused down the barrel of his gun shooting anything that moved. Bullets tore past him, one catching him in the shoulder, but he ignored the pain and continued to fire, vaguely aware of the two British fighter jets coming in low ahead of him. The pilots had done all they could, if they fired now they would risk taking out Will and Dash as well as the Taliban.

Will fired his last round, dropped his rifle and whipped out his sidearm. Too late. An enemy soldier had him in his sights. But in an instant the soldier's head snapped back. Will glanced behind him and saw the smoking barrel of Dash's gun. Dash had crawled out of the gully to help his friend.

Will and Dash knelt together, firing off round after round, knowing death was seconds away. Then the Harriers were upon them again, the British pilots had known they couldn't fire but they had come in so low to the ground that the down draught from the jet engines flattened everyone to the floor. The Harriers couldn't hang around though, this close to the ground they were susceptible to rocket propelled grenade fire. It pained Will to watch them leave but as they peeled away from each other they revealed something far more impressive. The Black Hawk. The mighty. And by God, it was flanked by two Apache helicopter gunships, the flying tanks, the angels of death, their chain guns roared to life laying down a sheet of lead around the beleaguered Special Forces team. Hellfire missiles streaked out annihilating anyone close to the team. The Taliban broke and ran. Will tried to stand up but out of the sand fibre optic cables wrapped round his legs. His arm was trapped too. He pulled at it with the strength of a man who had been subjugated to about five minutes of intense adrenaline.

The cables tore off his arm and Will was hanging upside down on board an alien spaceship.

The grey alien gritted its teeth and snarled, full of contempt. Will snatched his sidearm from its holster and in one fluid motion brought it up, pulled the trigger twice. A double tap. The first bullet went through the creature's throat and out the other side. The second shot caught it full in the eye. It was dead before it hit the ground. A heartbeat later the cables keeping Will prisoner released their grip. He fell to the floor, rolled gracefully and stood, went up to the dead body and to be certain, shot two more rounds into its head, splattering its brains across the floor.

He walked over to his rifle and sat down next to it, took a cigar from his top jacket pocket, lit it with his Zippo and activated his throat comms. 'This is Trident 2-1. Tango down.'

CHAPTER 5

Dash glanced down at Cassandra's hands though tried not to make it obvious. She held them both clasped tight around her pistol, shaking. She hadn't said much since their brief but dangerous encounter and she stayed close to Dash, close enough for the scent of her perfume to cut through the stale air. The med bay had another room off to the side, a prepping area or research lab, with two exits to the right from where they'd entered. One of the doors, like most of them on this ship was blown open, so Dash was able to step through and continue the exploration. When he did he met a long corridor which went off about a hundred metres to his right, but a few metres to his left there hummed a blue energy source blocking a main set of doors. Trying to lighten the atmosphere and ease Cassandra's nervousness, Dash spoke with an air of nonchalance. 'Ooh, shiny.'

Cassandra followed, her eyes drawn to the blue shimmer.

'Wow. I'd guess this is a force field?' said Cassandra, clearly glad to be thinking of something other than a little grey alien. 'We know there's limited power because of the lights, but a few of the consoles appear to be working.'

'I agree. Also, right there is the only door we've seen which hasn't been blown wide open. So, whatever they were using to cause damage on this ship, didn't affect here,' said Dash.

'Question is how we get past it?'

'No idea, but I bet the bridge is behind this door.'

'Makes sense. The place where everything is commanded from is going to be more protected.'

Dash pulled his combat knife from its sheath. 'Stand back,' he said and gently tossed it.

A bright light flared up when the knife hit the force field, like a magnesium strip set on fire. Vaporised.

'Nuts,' said Dash. 'That was my best knife.'

'A bit impulsive wasn't it?'

'Suppose so. I thought it'd bounce off, didn't expect it to vanish.'

'It didn't "vanish", it disintegrated.'

'Yeah, let's not touch it.'

'Good idea,' said Cassandra. 'Search round, there must be a way to turn it off.'

'Wouldn't the Greys have thought of that?' said Dash.

'Greys?'

'It's what I'm calling them, the mind reading freak who attacked us,' said Dash. 'They remind me of all those documentaries about aliens and how we have been visited in the past.'

'Wait.' Cassandra held up her hand as if she'd just seen or thought of something. Dash instinctively readied his rifle. 'You watch documentaries?'

Dash lowered his rifle, cocked his head sideways and smiled. The blue glow from the force field complimented Cassandra's eyes. As the light bounced off the silver walls around them, an angelic halo outlined her hair and wrapped around a perfect face. Here, on an alien vessel parked in orbit around the Moon, Dash discovered real, natural beauty. His eyes lingered on her, it didn't take

64

much for Cassandra to abate her nervousness and Dash liked her spirit.

Gazing right at her, he thought maybe he'd been staring a little too long, borderline creepy. 'Only when I can't find the remote,' was the best he could come up with.

He met her eye and she immediately blew out a breath as though embarrassed, as though she'd been holding her breath without realising it.

'We ... we need to stop this,' she said, sounding and looking flushed. 'The force field, I mean.'

'I'm sure it's controlled from the bridge, but maybe one of these rooms belongs to the captain. Perhaps there's an override in there?' said Dash. He pointed to two sets of doors either side of the corridor just before the force field, one intact, one just a hole. 'You check that one.' He indicated the gap. 'I'll have a look in the other.'

Cassandra hesitated. Crap, he thought, she won't want to split up. Before he could speak, she handed him his gun back.

'It gets in the way.' She turned and stepped through into the room behind her.

Dash turned to his room and almost walked into the door. He'd become so used to stepping through holes, he assumed the intact door would open by itself. Nothing for it but to pry the damn thing open.

Dash was still puzzling over where to begin when Cassandra called him in to her room.

'A panel hidden in the wall, stained with black scorch marks so I guess the Greys found it too,' she said when Dash walked in.

She opened the panel, revealing three symbols, a vertical line, three horizontal lines, with the middle one twice the length of the other two and finally another vertical line, topped with a chevron. All in red and next to a small skeletal hand, like that of a child's.

'The icons are similar to the word "queen" in cuneiform,' she said, although it came out more like a question than a statement.

'OK,' said Dash. 'So, I would say the symbol is like the word, "You get your hand cut off if you press me," in English.'

Cassandra smiled. 'Probably by something like that force field.'

'With or without the vaporising part?'

'Um …' Cassandra looked at the small skeletal hand. 'I have a theory, but it's risky.'

'Let's hear it,' said Dash.

'Well, a lot of these consoles are overturned or partly dismantled.'

'Yeah …' said Dash, wondering where this was going.

'I think the Greys can't use the consoles like we can, otherwise there wouldn't be all these blown doors or ripped out guts of computers everywhere.'

'Yeah?'

'We managed to press the symbols and they worked for us. What if these symbols we're pushing are biometric?'

She smiled.

'You mean DNA encoded. A pretty big leap, Cass.'

'Yes, but think about it, should it really be that easy to fly an alien spaceship? Everything in here has responded to us, and by all accounts nothing has worked for the Greys. They must be doing everything manually, which must be taking years for them.'

'It's a good theory.'

Without waiting for permission, Cassandra darted forward and pressed her hand firmly on the red symbol. The shimmering light from the force field outside disappeared.

'Jesus Christ woman!' yelled Dash in surprise. 'That was a stupid thing to do. There's no way I could have protected you from, whatever …'

'At least now we know my theory's sound. I still have my hand.' She held up her hand and wiggled her fingers. Her smile was beaming.

'Perhaps,' said Dash, a bit calmer now. 'But don't do anything like that again. I want us all to get home in one piece.'

'OK, I promise,' she teased.

'You'd better.' Dash returned her smile. 'Now let's open those doors and see if we're right about the bridge being behind them.'

Within a couple of feet, the doors slid open and disappeared into the recess of the wall. Dash raised his weapon and stepped through first. 'Wait here.'

The dim light, which had followed them around the ship since they had come on board, brightened and lit up the bridge as if it were daylight. Dash found himself raising his hands to cover his eyes from the harsh glare. Ahead of him two gently sloping ramps swept downwards in a curve ending on the main floor of the bridge. Different types of consoles lined the walls at five specific stations. An alien, but recognisable layout. Dash knew in an instant that it was the command floor. At the head, three stations stood in front of large windows which were more than twice his height, though he could not remember seeing any such windows on the outside of the ship. Perhaps it was a three-dimensional display rather than real life. Whatever the case, the exterior certainly looked real. As if he needed reminding. He was in space with the dark side of the Moon looming outside.

The floor, walls and ceiling were made from the same black silver-flecked material as the rest of the ship. The consoles glinted silver. Off to one side in the recess of the upper floor were six pods, each about twelve feet in height with more cuneiform symbols over them. They were glass fronted and empty, until Dash came to inspect the last one. 'Hey Cass, you're going to want to see this,' he called.

Cassandra entered the bridge, but the second she stepped over the threshold a blue beam of light enveloped her. A secondary white thin beam shot out and scanned her from top to bottom. Like a deer caught in the headlights of an oncoming car she froze.

At that same instant the pod in front of Dash hissed open.

The Professor rose up from his notes and pressed a sequence of symbols on the console. Nothing happened. He let out a deep, frustrated sigh and turned the pages in his notebook, clicked his fingers and pressed one more symbol. The holographic image, showing the deck Will was on, zoomed out to reveal the entire ship again. The red markers indicating damaged areas of the ship disappeared, to be replaced with to five white dots and three green dots.

'What's that?' asked John

'I think the white dots are us. There's two dots there,

standing outside that room at the bow of this ship.' The Professor pointed to the image. 'I think that's Dash and Cassandra and the one two decks down, must be Will.'

'Could be right. There's also two dots in this room, which must be us.'

'But what are the green dots?' said the Professor. 'One of them is in the same room as Will.'

'Dammit!' said John.

'What, what is it?' The Professor's panicked gaze darted around the room as if something was about to leap out. John's ear piece crackled to life. It was Will. 'This is Trident 2-1. Tango down.'

John checked the holographic image, the green dot in the same room as Will winked out.

'Alex, listen to me very carefully. I'm going to move to that doorway.' John pointed to the door Will had gone through. 'From there I can see up to the door with the blue light, where Dash and Cassandra have gone.'

'What do you want me to do?' said the Professor.

'Keep tabs on these two remaining green dots. You know where they are going.'

'They're going to ... the same place as Dash and ...'

The Professor dropped his note pad, hands sweaty. He stared at John wide eyed and silent.

'Calm down Alex, I won't let anything happen to them.'

John placed his hand on the Professor's shoulder and looked him in the eye. 'I need your help. I'm going to cover Dash's corridor, I can see all the way down from that doorway just over there and there's only one way in or out of his room, but what I need you to do is tell me the moment one of those green dots appear, OK?'

The Professor nodded.

'Good man, you can do it, just focus.'

The Professor swallowed, took a deep breath and handed John his pistol back. 'You might need both?'

John leant against the side of the door with a pistol in each hand. He'd only get one chance at this. He held his throat mic and whispered, 'Trident 2-2 to Trident One, engaging enemy.'

Will had only taken a second puff of his cigar when John's voice came over the comms. 'Trident 2-2 to Trident One, engaging enemy.'

'No rest for the wicked,' he said, leaping up and grabbing his assault rifle.

Dash backed away, weapon raised at whatever was emerging from the tube. 'Don't move Cass.'

'Not planning to,' she said, voice steady but with an undercurrent of worry. The light surrounding her didn't seem to be doing any harm. Dash's ear piece crackled to life. 'Trident 2-2 to Trident One, engaging enemy.'

Other than the obvious, this also told Dash, Trident Two had split up into two different groups, Trident 2-1 and Trident 2-2. Why, was not his biggest concern right now. In his peripheral vision, he saw the bright white beam scanning Cassandra switch off, leaving her bathed just in blue.

'You OK?'

'Seem to be.'

Cold air hit Dash first, then a thin white cloud of gas spewed out of the pod. Could it be a cryo chamber, a life support or hibernation device? A figure emerged from the pod, female, around seven foot tall and humanoid. Jet black hair tied up into one long braid that ended around her waist. Clothes made from some type of glittered silver material, sparkling almost cabaret in appearance. The skirt ended just above her knee high boots, with a split either side reaching up to her hips, the same material covered her chest leaving the abdomen exposed. Her skin however was made of tiny blue-green scales, glinting in the light. Reptilian eyes examined Dash then flickered to Cassandra. She slowly lifted her arms facing the palms of her hands away from her. Dash recognised the gesture. Peace.

'Now!' shouted the Professor as two green dots, blinking in and out of existence moved into the corridor towards the bridge. With lightning reflexes John spun around the doorway, brought one of his pistols to bear and fired two shots at one of the Grey aliens. The projectiles launched from his barrel, through the suppressor with a pifft sound. One missed, but the other caught the alien in the back of the head. It collapsed to the floor. John fired at the next one, but the Grey dove back into the other passageway.

'I think it's turning our way!' called the Professor. 'Take the corridor to your right and cut it off.'

The Professor studied the map, checking the location of the final green dot. Then he noticed another fainter dot that became brighter. It was right behind a white dot, a white dot which represented the Professor himself. The Professor just had to check.

He examined the décor of the newly renovated services, off junction thirty on the M5. The place was more open now, Burger King was still here, but an Indian deli had been added which filled the place with the smell of curry. A smell he loved, it reminded him of his wife who he'd met at Cambridge. She was the first Indian woman he'd met who was an atheist. Until then he'd wrongly assumed all Indians were associated with some sort of religion or belief. Silly, as of course they weren't.

'You'll find all the documents are correct and above board,' said a suited man with a strong New York accent sitting in front of him. He was drinking an espresso. Such a small but potent hit of coffee, the Professor never understood the point of something so harsh. He took a sip of his tea then picked up a fountain pen. The documents in front of him weren't above board. He wasn't stupid. The fact they included two passports, one for him and one for Cassandra proved it. He already had a perfectly valid passport in his sideboard at home. But the agency he was having drinks with were the only ones willing to finance his alien exploration.

'I've got to tell you, getting you into Iraq was not easy,' said the suited man. His tone turned serious. 'You're going to owe us ... a lot.'

'I'm certain I can find evidence, strong irrefutable evidence of Anunnaki involvement on Earth. I believe there is something significant under the temple of Ur,' replied the Professor.

'And I believe you, Professor. Remember, those documents there. All your findings come to Majestic 12 and only Majestic 12. You are not to share your details with anyone but us. Above top secret, you understand. This will not redeem you, Professor.'

The Professor hovered his pen over the part of the page which read, sign here.

'But you will know the truth,' the suited man said.

The Professor signed.

'Your daughter will need to sign too,' said the suited man.

'Yes,' said the Professor and stood up to get a better view of the services, turning his back on the suited man.

'You let him know we're Majestic 12,' said a figure standing behind the suited man.

'If he blabs you can ... sort it out. Besides, we've got bigger problems. It seems the Russians are sending a man to Iraq as well.'

The Professor spied Cassandra walking towards them. He turned back to let the suited man know he'd seen her and spotted the figure behind him. The man was wearing pale trousers and a dark top. He had a pistol in each hand. It was John.

'Alex?' said John.

The Professor took a step back, but John moved forward and grabbed him. 'Alex. Are you OK?'

The Professor leant on the pedestal in the middle of the map room and almost tripped but John caught him. There was a dead Grey behind John.

'John?' said the Professor, then chuckled as adrenaline rebooted his awareness. 'John.'

'That Grey had you caught in its sights.'

'Yes. Not a pleasant experience I can tell you.'

'Trident 2-2, this is Trident 2-1, I'm in the elevator,' said Will over John's comms.

The Professor checked the map. The green dot was heading towards another hangar bay on the starboard half of the ship.

'Trident 2-1, Trident 2-2 in pursuit, head right when you're on this deck, there's another hangar,' said John. He left the Professor and headed out of the room. Ahead of him a hundred or so metres he saw Cassandra standing in a radiant blue light. She was staring at something in the room, but he couldn't stop. To John's right, Will stepped out of the elevator and further behind Will, the Grey shot past, sprinting through a door at the other end.

'Go,' said John and they both ran down to the end of the corridor. 'It's trying for the other hangar.'

Both men ran after it and burst into the hangar bay. Empty, except for a small ship around half the size of the saucers they had come in on. The ship was squat and oval, made from a duller, greyer kind of metal. It too had four small retractable landing gears and a ramp from its belly led into the ship. The Grey had stopped at the end of the ramp, waiting for the men chasing it. As they entered, it let fly a green burst of energy from its hands.

Will dived forward, rolled along the ground and came up standing, then immediately fired at the Grey engaging full auto on his rifle. Walking towards the alien with his trigger finger firmly pressed down, Will was not to be intimidated. Bullets spat like angry hornets around the Grey, one catching it in the arm, black blood splattering against the hull of its ship.

The Grey turned and ran up the ramp which closed seconds after it. A moment later, after Will had emptied a magazine, the ship took off and silently left the hangar. A force field lit up around the fleeing ship as it left, stopping the atmosphere leaving the ship with it. After it had departed the hangar doors closed.

'Almost got it,' said Will. 'Any more of the little Greys on board?'

'No, that was the last of them. Let's go back and pick up Alex. There's something else going on with Dash.'

Cassandra was oblivious to the two Greys in the corridor behind her. One of them slumped to the floor while the other ran off. Her attention focused on the beautiful but strange creature who had emerged from the cryo pod. She could almost have been human apart from the scaled skin and the reptilian eyes. The lizard woman's gaze fixed on Cassandra and she spoke. 'My name isss Ki of the Anunnaki. I mean you no harm. Pleassse tell your bodyguard to lower hisss weapon.'

Dash stood confused. The alien in front of him spoke but he couldn't make anything out. Except for the friendly softness in her tone, it was mere noise.

'Lower your gun, Dash,' said Cassandra.

'You understand her?'

'Yes.'

'How? I can't make out a word.'

'I don't know, but she means us no harm.'

'That's probably what a spider says to the fly just before it eats it,' said Dash. The reptilian woman in front of him laughed.

'She's laughing. I think she can understand you OK,' said Cassandra.

'Oh, you think?' said Dash lowering his weapon, but Cassandra could tell he was still tense.

'I wish to thank you and your servantsss for ressscuing me,' said Ki, her body glinting in the light.

'My servants?' asked Cassandra.

Ki made a sweeping gesture toward Dash.

'Oh,' said Cassandra. 'He's not my servant. In fact he's in command.'

'Really,' said Ki. 'How interesssting.'

Ki beckoned Cassandra out of the blue light. 'If your man wishesss to understand my language, he should ssstep into the light.'

'Well, he's not my man as such.'

'Would you two stop speaking in a language I can't understand,' said Dash.

'Ki said, if you wish to understand then step into the blue light,' said Cassandra and shrugged. A few hours ago, she'd been studying ancient Anunnaki writings in an old temple in Iraq, now she could understand and was fluent in the old tongue. What more could she say, other than to shrug and smile. She was happy to receive a similar shrug back from Dash. Seeing no other choice, he approached the blue light.

'Great,' he mumbled. 'Now I do feel like a fly.'

The same white light shot out and scanned him from top to bottom, then went out.

'I don't feel any different,' he said.

'But you underssstand better,' said Ki.

Dash blinked, stunned. 'I know what you're saying?'

'You are now fluent in all languagesss known by the Anunnaki.'

Will, John and the Professor entered the room but before they even thought about raising their weapons Dash held out his hand and yelled, 'Stand down.'

The Professor ignored him and moved to hug Cassandra. 'Are you all right, dear?'

'Yes, I'm fine. This is Ki of the Anunnaki,' she said, so full of happiness that she was able to see redemption for her father's studies. Here, alive, in front of them all.

The Professor, dumbfounded, walked towards Ki and knelt. 'My lady, this is such an honour.'

Ki touched the Professor's head gently. 'The honour isss mine.'

John had moved to a better firing position should the need arise and Will stood there with his mouth open gawking at the alien in front of him. Dash gave Will a friendly clout over the head. 'Stop staring.'

'Can't help it. She's beautiful,' he whispered back grinning.

'If you want to understand what she's saying, the rest of you will have to step into the blue light,' said Dash. 'If that's OK?' he quickly added. Ki nodded and gestured for the rest of them to enter. After they had all been scanned, Ki activated one of the symbols and the blue light vanished.

CHAPTER 6

Dash introduced everyone to Ki, who in turn thanked them for their help. Which led Dash to ask the obvious question. 'So, Ki, what are you doing here and what happened to you?'

'Long ssstory,' said Ki.

'We're not going anywhere in a hurry,' replied John.

'OK,' said Ki with a gentle nod of her head. 'You might asss well sssit down and I'll exxxplain all I can.'

The group sat in the seats on the lower command floor whilst Ki stood in front of the view screen, silhouetted by the Moon behind her. Darkened in shadow she might pass for a tall human, if it weren't for a few splashes of light bouncing off her scales. She stared out, with her back to the team.

'Where to begin? My people discovered your planet over two billion years ago,' she started.

'Exactly how old are you?' interrupted Dash.

'I'm quite young, about a hundred and fifty thousand of your yearsss.'

Ki turned around, her skirt gently swishing and her scales glittering green and blue sparkles.

'How come you need the cryo chamber then if you live so long?' asked Cassandra.

'I ssstill need to eat to survive ssso the chamber helpsss keep my body sussstained for long periodsss of hibernation,' said Ki.

'Oh, I hadn't thought of that.'

Ki smiled. 'Like I was sssaying, my people found your planet around two billion yearsss ago, back then only microssscopic complex cellsss had evolved, but it wasss enough to enact the Star Protocol.'

'The Star Protocol?' said Will.

'We look for life, very early sssigns life, sssomething we can manipulate at a molecular level. Ssso, when we find a planet like Earth, we guide the microbes to evolve into the intelligence you sssee in yourselves today. This takesss billions of yearsss, but our average life ssspan is around five hundred thousand ssso we can be patient.'

'Why bother at all?' said Dash.

'Why not see what those microbes would evolve into on their own?' added the Professor.

'The ethics alone ...' said Cassandra but was cut short.

'Our ssspecies can't reproduce. We ourselves are hybrid creations of the original Anunnaki, the True Bloodsss. We refer to them now as the Blood Princes. They are the ones who created us. Long ago they shed their material bodies. They're multi-coloured ballsss of light now and a sssight to behold. They rarely venture out from below the citiesss they had us build.'

Ki turned to face the Moon once more, she sounded distant now to Dash, reminiscing rather than telling her history. 'Rumour is they are planning to leave usss.' Ki took a deep breath. John caught the Professor's eye, but the Professor just shrugged.

'Where they would go we do not know, but the talk of it has caused sssome worry within the High Council,' said Ki, then a little more upbeat, 'We sussspect it's the Blood Princes who altered our own DNA so no matter what we try, we can never create children of our own. Every attempt in our eight billion yearsss failed.'

'How awful,' said Cassandra and involuntarily put her hands to her own stomach.

'We don't dwell anymore, but we want to reverssse the effectsss,' said Ki. 'Ssso now we manipulate other life to better understand the secretsss of the Blood Princes.'

'But with the Blood Princes leaving and no way to reproduce, your species will eventually … die,' said John.

'Correct, which is why your planet is so important. Earth is only the twelfth planet in all our years of searching which exceeded our expectationsss. At timesss we had to drastically alter the sssituation. The first time was to extinguish most of what you call dinosaurs. They were too large and their brainsss too sssmall. Later, we had to raise sssea levels which caused floods and the world turned to ice, but eventually your ssspecies started to dominate the planet.'

Ki seemed to sense the indignation from Cassandra.

'Were it not for usss, Cassandra, you would not exist.'

Ki walked over to a console and keyed in a command. The lights dimmed, solar shielding descended over the windows cutting out the view of the stars and Moon. A large hologram of Earth, slowly rotating, appeared in front of them all. Cassandra tried to touch the light and created ripples in the display as if running her hand through water.

'Over the last two hundred and fifty thousand yearsss we came and went, keeping an eye on your progress, increasing brain capacity every fifty thousand years. Then, about ten thousand years ago we initiated the sssecond part of the Star Protocol. We set up permanent embassies on your planet.'

Images popped up across the hologram. They all recognised the Pyramids of Egypt and the Ziggurat in Iraq. 'We started to help. We guided your species, inspired them to build incredible monuments in place of our embassies.'

'How could you guide us without revealing yourselves?' asked the Professor. 'Why do we think you're a myth? I devoted my life to the Cuneiform texts, to much ridicule I might add.'

'There are three branchesss of Anunnaki, three ssseparate genomes of which I am one. The two other genomes are fewer, but their molecular level hasss been enhanced by our Blood Princes. One branch is telepathic.'

Dash and Will gave each other a quick glance, John remained quiet and attentive.

'But the process to become telepathic resultsss in elongated skulls.'

Ki made a gesture with her hand as if stretching her own head up. 'Which is good. You know which ones can read your mind.' She winked at Will who shifted uneasily in his chair. 'Then there are the shape-shiftersss, who can alter their bodiesss to almost any living material they can imagine.'

Dash pointed an accusing finger at John who laughed and said, 'You think I'd shape-shift into this?'

The Professor was impressed, years of research finally gelling to make perfect sense. 'So, you could use your advanced wisdom and be elevated into the upper circles of power,' he concluded.

Ki nodded. 'Yes, some became priests or wise men, some Pharaohs and Queens.'

'What went wrong?' said John.

'The creaturesss you encountered on this vessel attacked

us around two thousand yearsss ago. They were a peaceful race when we first discovered them, too far developed for an effective Star Protocol although we did do some work on them. Eventually they turned on usss in the hope of stealing our gene for long life,' said Ki. 'Because of our manipulation they were able to splice our genes with their own and they did have limited successss, prolonging their lifessspan by a few hundred yearsss. Unfortunately for them they also took the gene which causes infertility. Now they rely on cloning to reproduce, to continue their species.'

Ki accessed the hologram console once more. The Earth disappeared in exchange for three galaxies including the familiar Milky Way. 'When our paths cross, violence is inevitable.'

'Is this what happened here?' said Dash.

'Yesss, we were ssset upon by a superior force. Those who couldn't escape back to our home planet dispersed and hid amongst your world's population. Otherss like me tried to ssstay and fight for as long as we could. My ship was the only one to survive. I managed to shut down most of the ssship including the engines. Our system worksss on DNA touch so the invaders had no choice but to leave my ship here and try to figure a way to extract our knowledge from the on-board computersss without any help from me.'

'What happened to the rest of your crew?' said Will. Ki turned off the holograms, and the solar shutters opened to reveal the Moon still waiting outside. She paused to take in the view. What had happened to the crew was obvious.

'Killed or captured or living on Earth. I locked myself on the bridge, hoping my people would find and rescue me,' said Ki.

Cassandra studied her hand. 'I take it then, a small amount of your DNA is within us, within humanity?' she said.

'Yes, part of the ongoing evolution of your race.'

'So, you meddle with us, on a regular basis?'

'It is necessary to get your speciesss to develop a more complex brain.'

'So even with a small amount of DNA, we were able to access the consoles on this ship and the flying saucer'

Ki nodded. 'Yes.'

'Cool,' said Will, which made Ki smile, though Dash spotted Cassandra shaking her head.

'Before you go back to your planet, would you mind dropping us home,' said Dash.

Ki's vibrant scales dulled slightly. 'I am afraid I cannot do that, I ssstill need your help.'

'What do you mean?' asked Dash.

'For one, I need to get the central computer back on line which will then activate the automatic repair sssystem.'

'That's OK. None of us have a problem with that.'

'But that's not all, is it?' said John. 'There's a war going on, isn't there? One no one knows about.'

Ki turned to John, her eyes narrowed, thoughtful. 'Yesss.'

'Wanna tell the rest of us?' said Will.

'The Anunnaki survivors on Earth are battling the Greys aren't they, both trying to get an advantage over the other,' said John.

'Each alien side is using the resourcesss to hand,' said Ki.

'Our technological advancement in just the last one hundred years has been staggering compared to the last five thousand years,' said the Professor.

'But how do you know what's been going on for the last

few thousand years if you've been stuck in that cryo tube?' said John.

'It's not technically a cryo tube, it sssustains my body, ssso I don't have to eat or drink, but I can still observe what goes on, with the use of a headset linked to probes around your planet, many of which are now lost, captured or destroyed.'

'So why don't you just send a message to your people?' said Cassandra.

'She did,' said John. 'But they didn't come to rescue her.'

'Which means either the message was blocked, or it wasn't received,' finished Dash.

'Either way you'd have to return to report in, find out what was going on and deliver the message personally,' said Will. 'That's what we would do.'

'I can't fly thisss ship alone,' said Ki.

'So, where's your planet and how long will it take to get there?' said Dash.

'My planet is called Nibiru, located in the Andromeda galaxy, once we escape your Sun's gravity well we will be able to jump directly to the edge of the Zaos system, my home solar sssytem,' said Ki.

'I'd like to know how that works,' said the Professor.

'Not right now, Professor. I'm sure Ki can tell you later. Right now we have a decision to make,' said Dash.

'Before you decide, remember, without our help the Greys, as you call them, will take over your planet, it isss inevitable. Ssso few of usss are left here to hold them off,' said Ki. 'If you help me now, I will convince the High Council to return and help the humansss remove the Grey threat.'

Dash nodded and stood up. Being in space was far from

his comfort zone, in fact as of right now he was two hundred and thirty-eight thousand, eight hundred and fifty-four point nine eight miles above his comfort zone. He turned to his team. 'OK, this has to be your own decision, I'm not going to make it for you. If you want to leave, we take the ship we came in and get back home.'

'Would you let us do that?' asked Cassandra.

Ki sighed. 'Yesss, I will not ssstop you.'

Dash turned to Will. 'What do you say?'

'I say we help her. It's what we do, help people in trouble,' said Will.

Ki's scaly skin started to glisten again, hope perhaps.

'Professor?' said Dash.

'Are you kidding? This is an opportunity of a lifetime.'

'Cass?'

'I'm staying with my father.'

'John?'

'I'm in,' he said, looking at the Professor's grinning face. 'Besides who's going to stop the Professor here from getting into trouble.'

'OK, it's unanimous we're all staying,' said Dash. Turning to Ki, focusing into her eyes. 'A few conditions though.'

Ki nodded and beckoned for Dash to continue. 'One, you can tell us what to do on board your ship. I'd only press the wrong button anyway. However, if we get into combat and I've a feeling we might, I take command.'

'Yesss of course,' said Ki.

'Two, once we've helped you, you help us get back home.'

'I accept those termsss. Gladly,' said Ki with a beaming smile.

CHAPTER 7

Ki marched over to one of the consoles and tapped on the symbols. 'Once the main computer core is back online, I'll be able to enhance your physical bodiesss in the sick bay with a healing gene. Minor cuts and bruises will heal automatically, larger wounds will heal a hundred timesss faster. Any traumatic damage to the head will ssstill be fatal though.'

'So, if my arm gets blown off I can grow another one?' said Will. 'Like a lizard?'

'No, but if you sssave the arm I can reattach the appendage with the help of equipment in our sick bay,' replied Ki. 'You will ssstill suffer intense pain, but the healing gene might sssave your life.'

'Right,' said Dash. 'First thing is to get the core online. Cass and the Professor go with Ki and give her a hand. John patrol the ship and Will, we'll get the rest of our gear left on the saucer. Take an inventory of what we have.'

Ki opened a panel near one of the cryo tubes and handed out a metal cylinder to each of them. 'Thisss is the only food here. One pill a day should give you enough ssstrength to sssee you through.'

'Man, ah would kill for a burger,' said Will.

'We have plenty of food on our planet and you will be able to eat what you want, although sssome will be ssstrange to you, but your stomachs should adapt OK.'

'Look forward to it,' said Will with a dubious tone.

'Let's get the core online,' said Dash.

The Professor, Cassandra and Ki headed to the Core Room. The Professor recognised the place as the same one he directed Will to earlier, though when he got there, the small hologram hadn't prepared him for the massive real life counterpart that the room actually was. A huge sphere suspended in mid-air floated between two huge cones, edges scarred with black burn marks. A moat of liquid water surrounded the device, which rippled, caressing the sphere and entire room with gentle refractive light shimmer.

'Amazing,' said Cassandra echoing the Professor's thoughts.

'Behold, the high density jump drive, sssuspended between two powerful electromagnetic field generators,' said Ki and indicated towards the cones.

'What's with the water?' asked the Professor.

'The liquid is super dense water. When the force field surrounding the jump drive isss activated the water inside coversss everything, keeping the jump drive and the generators cool enough to operate. The moleculesss in the water are tightly packed together giving the liquid a higher density than ice.'

'Must generate massive amounts of heat,' said the Professor.

'Yes, but all the heat ventsss out when the jump drive is in operation. The underside of the hull opensss up to allow the heat sinks, made of gold, to dissipate the heat into space.'

'Gold?' said Cassandra.

'It's the best conductor of heat,' said the Professor before Ki could answer. 'How does the actual jump drive work?'

Ki tapped her lips with a scaly finger. There was a long pause.

'Stretch out your arm,' she said. 'Imagine your shoulder is where you currently are in space, the tip of your finger isss your destination. The high density jump drive createsss a massive gravity well, a huge density of mass which brings your finger tip to your shoulder.'

She held the Professor's outstretched hand then encouraged the Professor to bend his elbow and touch his shoulder with his finger.

'So now you only jump from the shoulder, your current position, to the tip of your finger, your destination, without having to travel the length of your arm. Turning off the jump drive ssstops the high density gravity well, you can travel billionsss and billionsss of light years in secondsss,' said Ki.

'So, you bring the destination to you,' said the Professor.

'Yesss exactly, although you have to be in the right place before you can power up the drive. We need to get out of the Solar System otherwise you could, in theory, generate a field big enough to bring something else with you,' said Ki.

'Like another planet?'

'Possibly but we've never tested the theory as it was deemed too hazardousss to even try. But it's what the math suggestsss.'

'What is the sphere made from?' said Cassandra.

'The same as most of the ship's hull and our scout vessels, we call it Thuram, on your periodic table it's element one hundred and fifteen called Moscovium.'

The Professor took a step back. 'I'm not a chemist, but …'

'Radioactive, yesss, highly, but you're sssafe I assure you,' said Ki anticipating the Professor's next question. Cassandra noticed Ki's tongue, visible only when she was talking. It was long and pointed, with three forks. She watched as Ki wandered over to the far wall, stepping over the dead body of the Grey Will had killed. Ki's hand reached out and a panel opened in the centre of the wall. She pressed the symbol behind it and a concealed door slid open. Cassandra stared at the huge glass pillar that was revealed. Intertwining fibres floated inside it, apparently in water. The whole thing was bathed in a green blue light.

'Cassandra, I need your help. Thisss is going to take two of usss.'

'What do you need me to do?'

'There are two consolesss, one here and one at the back of thisss room. To activate the core requiresss two people entering the same combination.' Ki showed Cassandra a five-symbol combination on her console. 'Can you remember?'

Cassandra nodded and went to the other console.

'On my command,' said Ki.

'Ready.'

'Now,' said Ki punching in the combination. Cassandra did the same. The room started to hum and the glass, housing the alien computer, turned blue.

'Greetings Ki,' said a soft, synthetic female voice. 'Assessing damage. Deploying repair bots.' A circular doorway opened up in the jump drive room and a sphere the size of a football descended. Six, two-foot tentacles snaked out of its body and started to repair the damage caused by the Greys.

'Repairsss will take a while, but there is at least one repair bot in each room now. When this one finishes here it will locate to the next most damaged room and help in itsss repairsss.'

'Impressive,' replied the Professor.

'We ssshould return to the bridge and sssee what'sss happening.'

'What about … that?' asked Cassandra and pointed to the body of the dead Grey.

'The repair bot will dispose of the corpse,' said Ki.

'What about their weapon, the metal thing on its hand? Will talked about a green laser ball.' said the Professor.

'Leave it,' said Ki. 'The metal sparksss react to their DNA. I could sssplice Grey DNA into you, so you could probably use the weapon, but I wouldn't recommend it.'

'No, quite,' said the Professor.

Leaving the repair bot to its work they made their way back to the bridge.

John set out a patrol route and started for the bottom deck below, taking the glass lift. A good place to start, he thought, as this far down the ship had yet to be explored. On his own, with the sound of his own footsteps clinking on the metal floor, he began to piece together the events leading him to this alien place. A successful mission. The Russian agent, eliminated. Another kill on his conscience not that it mattered. John lost count of the number of people killed by his hands many years ago, but he always remembered his first for MI6. The Caribbean Sea, off the coast of the Dominican Republic, near Santo Domingo.

His target, an American business man suspected of supplying terrorist organisations with weapons-grade nerve agents. MI6 had tracked him down and sent John on a kill order. He remembered pulling up in his speedboat alongside the businessman's yacht. It was night, but the Moon was full and drenched the area with a cold blue ambience. And it was silent save for the lapping of gentle waves against the vessel. John stood on the lower deck at the stern. 'I've boarded the Great Pretender. Looks like they had a party here last night. This might be easier than we thought.'

In front of him, sprawled out on the deck were a couple of partygoers, sleeping under the stars with a few empty bottles of beer and wine around them.

'Roger, proceed with caution,' crackled John's ear piece.

He stepped over a chap in Bermuda shorts and made his way into the yacht, checking the picture of his target on his digital watch, which highlighted eye colour, hair colour and even the distance from ear to ear. He'd memorised the layout of the vessel. The lower deck, the easiest way to board, contained the bedrooms – the best place to start. Unfortunately his target was not there, just more revellers, asleep or passed out. 'Wish I'd been here earlier today,' whispered John to his handler.

'Have you found the target?' was the clinical reply. He rolled his eyes and continued his search. On the upper deck, crashed out on a cream leather sofa, was the businessman, alone, fully dressed and snoring, a half-drunk bottle of Old Fitzgerald on the floor next to him. John set a timer on his watch then took out a pill which he slipped into the guy's mouth. A gentle motion to force the man's chin up, and the pill was down his gullet without him waking.

He checked his watch, as it counted down from five minutes. He had time. He found clean whisky glasses in a cupboard, took one and poured himself a small glass. This was one of the world's most expensive bourbons. He wasn't about to waste the opportunity. A lingering sniff to savour the rich aroma, then he sipped it down.

The businessman stirred. John's watch showed three minutes. 'Right, let's get you outside.'

It was not easy to drag his target through a door and towards the bow of the ship. The process was without finesse or ceremony, but the man showed no signs of waking. That's what half a bottle of four-thousand-pound bourbon will do to you, he thought.

Reaching the safety rail, he pushed the man upright, checked his watch again … three … two … one …

John grabbed hold and lifted the man up and over the rail …

'Abort, abort, abort,' yelled the voice in his ear. 'Do you read? Abort. Intel is wrong. Over.'

The man's eyes snapped open, sheer panic written in them.

John clutched at the man's shirt and desperately tried to haul him up. His grip was slipping. The man couldn't help himself, paralysed by the pill which was now kicking in. Buttons popped, material ripped, and the weight was gone from John's arms.

Just a splash from the ocean below and the brief image of a face, soon swallowed into the black water.

It was a face that would haunt John. His first kill had been an innocent.

He did not like MI6.

Suppressing any feelings which might compromise him, he went on to excel in the assassination of hard targets, sometimes going into deep cover for months to get close to the enemy. Two years ago MJ12 had approached him. Majestic 12, an organisation which worked outside government borders, answered to no nation and whose goal was purely the betterment of mankind. Yeah. Right. Of course, if the betterment of mankind didn't float your boat, they also paid. A lot. That had been an interesting conversation.

John loosened the strap on one of his shoulder holsters. He couldn't remember what his kill count was. Perhaps that was a bad thing. Maybe it was time to retire if Queen and Country would let him.

Alone on this alien vessel, parked outside the Moon, John had turned a page on it all. He was on a new chapter in his life now and at least he was operating in a group again. It had been a long time since teamwork was needed and it felt good. The two Delta soldiers seemed to know what they were doing, and they got along with each other well. Cassandra was nice enough though he'd lost the ability to really care for people like her, civvies, it was a weakness in his line of work. The only exception was the Professor who reminded him of his late father. They had hit it off at once, both liked getting into trouble and both had the same sense of humour.

John stumbled over some loose wiring. The light was dim in this part the ship. That's why he'd hit it off with the Professor. They shared an interest in alien spaceships.

Ki was unexpected and an unknown. That bothered him. He hadn't expected to bump into two alien species today. She seemed on the level, but he'd been caught out like that before. He resolved to keep a watchful eye on her until she proved herself to him.

Power graced the ship again. John heard the thrum of it moments before the lights came on. Bathed in white he stepped into the Injection Core. That was what Ki called it. To him it was the engine room, albeit one that could propel the ship to faster than light speeds. Ki explained the FTL Injector was used when in solar systems to get from planet to planet quickly. The engine room appeared exactly like he'd have pictured one, massive alloy pipes and holographic gauges attached to consoles. Walkways and gantries lined the walls with more computerised consoles attached to them. He wandered around and eventually found another door, stepped through it and down another corridor. He came to an undamaged, sealed door at the end, and reached for the panel at its side. The door slid open. Slowly a smile crossed his face.

Dash and Will entered the flying saucer which had brought them here and grabbed their backpacks and the sniper rifle left there.

'Let's see what we've got then,' said Dash.

Both men emptied the contents of the packs on the floor and started to sort it out. Dash piled the weapons together. 'Three HK416 assault rifles with nine spare mags, three Colt M119a1 pistols with four spare mags, one M2010 sniper rifle with two spare mags, five sticks of C4 with one remote detonator, six frag grenades, some medical supplies and not much else.'

'Not enough for a sustained gun fight,' said Will.

'You still got a knife?' said Dash.

'Yeah, why where's yours?'

'I threw it at a force field … which destroyed it.'

'Dumb ass.'

'Yeah that's what Cassandra said,' laughed Dash.

'Ah reckon you like her, don't ya?'

'What do you mean?'

'Y'know what I mean. It's been a long time since you were *that* protective of the fairer sex.'

'Haven't got time for that.' Dash felt his tone was a bit too defensive. Will was bound to pick up on it.

'Got your feathers all ruffled there, did I?'

'OK, OK, I like her. We've only just met, but there's this spark,' said Dash.

'Ah don't see it,' said Will with a massive grin on his face.

'Screw you.' Dash returned his grin. 'And besides who's got the hots for an alien lizard?'

'Yeah, is that wrong?' winked Will.

Dash smiled and shook his head. 'So wrong,' he muttered and gathered up their gear.

* * *

Dash and Will met Ki, Cassandra and the Professor on the bridge.

'How'd you get on?' said Dash looking at Ki.

'We have restored the central computer, and my repair botsss are restoring the ssship.'

'Good start,' said Will, winking at Ki.

Dash caught the wink and rolled his eyes. 'So, what's next?'

'I ssshould be able to get internal communicationsss up, so no matter where you are in the ssship you just have to activate the computer and talk to whomever you want.'

'And then what?' said Will.

'We have to wait until the botsss have finished or get to a sssafe repair ssstate and then we can bring the enginesss online to move out of thisss system,' said Ki.

'Oh good. Down time,' said Will.

'Yes, it would do everyone good to take a break and rest up. That includes you, Ki,' said Dash.

Ki nodded. 'I've been in hibernation for two thousand yearsss, but if you insist.'

A sense of humour from the lizard alien, a good sign, thought Dash.

'Where's John?' asked the Professor.

'Dunno, ah guess we go look for him,' said Will.

Ki spoke out loud. 'Nilah, where isss John located?'

'Nilah is the name for the central computer,' whispered Cassandra to Dash's puzzled expression. A soft, silky voice resonated from everywhere in the room. 'John is located in the baths.'

Cassandra mouthed the word 'Baths' to Dash, in wide-eyed surprise.

'The computer knows our names,' said the Professor.

'My name is Nilah. Please use this as I find "computer" to be a cold title.'

'I … I'm ever so sorry, Nilah, I didn't mean to offend you,' said the Professor.

'Your apology is accepted, Alexander, and to answer your question, when I scanned your body I also accessed your recent memories and filed them away. Until now I didn't know if you were hostile,' said Nilah.

'Ah OK,' said the Professor, clearly not sure what else to say.

'So, I'm wondering when John was going to tell us about the baths,' said Cassandra. It hadn't been so long ago they were in a sweltering desert and she now realised how grubby and dirty she was feeling.

John was enjoying a hot, steaming bath. A hot, large bath, about half the size of a regular swimming pool. He leant back. The rippling water soothed his mind as he remembered the times he had come home from operations and felt all his muscles relax as warm water soaked away his tiredness. It was a great feeling and he would tell the others about it soon. But just a little longer in the tub first. He closed his eyes and then … heard a cough.

He wanted to ignore it, but his eyes flickered open, knowing what he would see. His companions lined up at the opposite end of the pool, arms folded across their chests, all staring at him.

'What?' he said. 'I was going to tell you … eventually.'

CHAPTER 8

After a few days familiarising themselves with the ship and its controls, Nilah told Dash the ship was spaceworthy, though repairs would be on going.

'Before we leave,' said Dash. 'I want to contact my base command and apprise them of the situation.'

As the others took their seats on the lower command deck of the bridge, Ki turned to Dash. 'I'm afraid we can't. Your people are ssstill not ready and if we made our presence known so too would the Greysss. A hidden war would become open war, with your speciesss trapped between two powerful forcesss.'

'My Commanding Officer knows what he's doing.'

Ki touched Dash's arm. An excuse was coming. 'I know Dash, but this isn't a warship. With no means of encrypting our communicationsss, anything we sssay would be picked up by the Greys. Worse, they would know our position.'

Better to play this out then. He would need to find another way to contact Earth, in his own time.

'Are we ready to go?' said the Professor.

'A bit eager, aren't you?' said John.

'Oh yes, I can't wait. Think of all the wonders we're going to witness, sights no other human has ever laid eyes on.'

John sighed. 'We're ready.'

'Nilah,' said Ki.

'Yes Ki?'

'Take usss to a safe jump position and lay in a course for the Zaos sssystem.'

'Course plotted, engaging sub light engines, estimated time to jump, two hours,' said Nilah.

Dash gripped his seat, in fact he realised everyone but John was grabbing hold of their seats. All expecting the ship to leap forward at an accelerated speed but instead it gently sailed away, and the Moon disappeared from the view screen. Will and the two archaeologists relaxed. The ship, silent in the cold vacuum of space, broke its orbit, on course for the jump point.

'The repair botsss are still working on some damaged systemsss, ssso we can't risk FTL injection to reach faster than light ssspeeds,' said Ki smiling. 'But we can get close.'

'So, Ki?' said the Professor. 'If your people can't give birth how do you reproduce?'

'Dad!' exclaimed Cassandra.

'What? I'm sorry, it's just, I just … I … I've been digging up scraps of details of Anunnaki all my life. I've never come across this, and … well, and I have Ki in front of me.'

'But you can't just blurt out questions like that.'

'It'sss fine. Knowledge is power and besidesss, a long journey awaits usss. The Blood Princes create us. On our world, we …' Ki struggled for a word then said. 'We have hatcheries, places where eggs are delivered up to usss from the realm of the Blood Princes. When our population startsss to dwindle, more of these eggsss appear and we hatch from them.'

'So, you're clones?' said Cassandra.

'No, a clone is a replica of sssomething else. We are all individual, like you.'

Cassandra opened her mouth to ask another question, when Nilah spoke. 'Life signs detected on Mars.'

'What, how is that possible?' said the Professor.

'Our outpost on the red planet, built many, many yearsss ago,' said Ki. 'I assumed the installation was destroyed by the Greysss.'

'How many life signs?' said Dash.

'Thirty,' said Nilah.

'Either your outpost is still operational, or something else is in control now.'

'How many of them are Anunnaki?' asked Ki.

'Six detected, one of which is faint. Vital signs are critical,' said Nilah.

'Damn,' said Dash.

'The other life signs?' asked John, although knowing very well what the answer was going to be.

'The twenty-four other life forms are the ones you designate Greys.'

'We must rescue them. We must rescue my people. If there isss a possibility, any hope they are ssstill alive we need to try.'

'Calm down,' said Dash. 'Have they detected us, Nilah?'

'No, and I have reduced our heat signature further still.'

'Good, the advantage is ours.'

'Why not fire at them from space, then go down?' said Will.

'Thisss ship is built for research. We have a few defence lasersss but nothing big.'

'No Phasers? What kinda space ship is this!' said Will.

'A class two, X51 deep space research vessel,' intoned Nilah.

'Great, reckon we'll be doing this the hard way,' said Will. Dash nodded in agreement.

'OK, you said this is one of your outposts,' said Dash focused on Ki, forming a plan. 'Can you can get us in?'

'The saucer can take you down and Nilah will communicate with the station to open the hangar doors.' Ki told him.

'John, Will, kit up and meet me in the hangar bay.'

'What about us?' asked Cassandra.

'You, the Professor and Ki will stay on board, if something goes wrong and we don't come back, you must carry on with the mission,' said Dash.

'But I ssshould go with you, in case you need my help.'

'No, if you die then we can't get you home to warn your people about Earth and the Greys,' said Dash.

Cassandra was about to say something when the Professor put a hand on her shoulder. 'He's right, darling, we would only get in the way.'

'Bring them back,' said Ki.

'It's what we're good at,' said Dash and turned to leave the bridge.

'Good luck,' said Cassandra, then walked to Ki and gave her a big, reassuring, human, hug.

Dash turned his head, and before he left he winked at Cassandra. If she was the last woman he was going to see before he died, it wasn't all bad.

Dash met Will in the hangar bay where he stood next to the saucer. John strolled down the ramp. 'This ship is not designed to take nine people,' he said.

'So, it'll be a bit cosy for a while,' said Dash.

Dash clambered up the ramp and took his place upfront.

John joined him with Will on one of the console stations in the back room. 'Ready?' asked John, Dash gestured for John to go right ahead, so John hit the launch button and the ramp retracted, the engine started up, the saucer hovered then headed out of the hangar.

'I have plotted a course for you,' said Nilah. All three men jumped hearing her voice. 'Thank you Nilah,' said Dash. 'I didn't expect to hear you.'

'Me neither,' said John.

'I have a communication link with all external X50 scout research vessels. For long range missions I can embed my AI matrix into many systems,' said Nilah.

'Can you bring up a schematic of the outpost, show us where the Anunnaki are being held?'

'Yes, Will.' A holographic image of the outpost replaced a spinning representation of Mars on the central table. A smaller version appeared on the dashboard in the cockpit. Within the new image, six white dots blinked, five were located on sub level two and the sixth on sub level three. 'I can guide you to their location if you give me permission to use your communication devices,' said Nilah.

'Granted,' said Dash.

'We'll need a diversion, once we have the precious cargo,' said Will, referring to the Anunnaki prisoners.

'Do you have any spare C4 in that backpack of yours, Will?' asked John.

'Yeah. Why, what ya got planned?'

'Dunno. I'll think of something when I get there.'

'Knew he was going to say that,' muttered Will.

'I can hear you, Will,' said John.

Will rolled his eyes. 'Spooks.'

Dash grinned. He couldn't have a better team with him. 'Will, you get the five grouped together. Is that a cell complex?'

'Would appear to be,' replied Will.

'Funny kind of "outpost",' John thought out loud.

Dash nodded but chose to continue with the current plan. 'Let's not get side-tracked. I'll rescue the Anunnaki on level three.'

'Roger that,' said Will.

'Two minutes to target,' said Nilah's soft, soothing voice.

'Hey, you're picking up the lingo.' Will smiled.

'Thank you, Will.'

'Let's get ready,' said Dash. 'Nilah, can you land this saucer for us and deploy the ramp?'

'Yes Dash, I'll keep the ship safe until your return. No one will get on board.'

Dash marvelled at the surface of Mars racing up to him. They were going to be the first humans on the planet. A dry barren wasteland littered with extinct volcanoes and impact craters. A dry barren wasteland every astronaut on Earth would give their right arm to step on to and yet, it was two Delta Force commandos and one British spy who would take the next giant leap for mankind and no one would know about it. Now was the time to focus on the mission, a rescue mission, the kind he'd done many times before. He squeezed his fists together so tight the knuckles whitened, closed his eyes and took a deep breath. The iron oxide dust giving the planet its characteristic red hue kicked up as the saucer came in low. At the base of a long dead volcano, Nilah spoke. 'Activating hangar doors.'

The ground opened, massive doors just under the surface started to move apart. Martian soil shook and fell away as a gaping hole in the ground appeared. Their ship hovered over the hole and then descended into darkness. Two hundred feet down they found themselves in a hangar much like the one aboard the X51 mother ship. Nilah landed the X50 saucer. 'We have been detected,' she said.

'OK let's go,' said Dash. Nilah lowered the ramp and the three-man Special Forces team disembarked, weapons up and at the ready. On the guidance of Nilah, who was now speaking to them through their ear pieces, they each took a different door.

The door in front of John slid open. When it did he let out a small, disheartened huff. 'Another dimly lit corridor. What a surprise.'

'Your target should be the power generators and the life support system located on this level,' said Nilah. John nodded in acknowledgement. 'Distance to target?'

'Two hundred metres from your current position, taking the most direct route.'

'Copy that,' said John and tightened the backpack, with the borrowed C4, then pulled out both his pistols before continuing deeper into the base.

'There are five enemy targets behind the door you are approaching John,' said Nilah.

'Copy,' said John and did a quick memory test for how many bullets he had left. The pistol's capacity was eight in each and he was pretty sure he'd only fired five times since this mission had started so that meant he had eleven left. *That's enough*, he thought.

He approached the door with both his guns stretched out at arm's length in front of him. He got within a metre and the door opened. Five Greys were waiting for him. They stood in a semi-circle, their long spindly arms dangled by their side. The middle Grey locked enormous, gloss black eyes on him.

John could hear the squawk of seagulls through thin metal walls. It meant they were near land which cheered him up as he'd been at sea on this container ship for over two months now. In front of him, hanging with both arms chained above its head a badly beaten Grey stared at him. He could feel the Grey trying to bore a way into his mind. A bead of sweat rolled down its face. John fired a shot and the middle Grey dropped to the floor. He continued to stride into the outpost room. The other four Greys froze for a moment too long, surprise or shock plastered their otherwise emotionless faces. Using both pistols at the same time, he finished them off; two with the left gun, two with the right. Six bullets left.

He holstered one of his guns and stood over the first Grey he had killed. 'Mind tricks don't work on me, sunshine,' he said, then continued on to the next dim lit corridor.

Will entered the passageway, weapon up and at the ready. 'Next right,' said Nilah through his ear piece.

He stepped into a long corridor and Nilah spoke again. 'Two Greys have entered the cell area.'

Aware the Grey's knew of their infiltration, Will broke into a run as time could be of the essence. If they started killing the prisoners ... A set of stairs, a minor obstacle. Leaping down three at a time he launched himself into the corridor below. 'One of the prisoner's cell doors have been opened,' said Nilah.

'Damn,' said Will. 'How far?'

'At this pace one minute,' said Nilah.

'They don't have a minute; can you override the cell doors? Open all of them,' said Will.

'Confirmed. Cell doors open.'

'Status?'

'They are too weak, Will. Some are moving but not fast enough.'

'Time on target?' Will crashed through a room, not caring if anything was in there.

'Forty seconds. Turn left down the stairs.'

Every muscle strained as he turned left then vaulted down the stairs.

'Time?'

'Twenty seconds. We're going to be too late, Will. The door at the end of this passageway leads to the cells.'

Will dived to the floor, letting the inertia slide him closer. Lying prone, his assault rifle up, he focused down the scope. 'Open the door! Open the door!' he shouted. To hell with stealth.

The door slid open and he regretted his earlier decision to let the prisoners out, for though they were free from their cages they were still stuck in that room with the Grey. And one of the first things Will saw was an Anunnaki pinned up against the left-hand side with strips of twisted metal torn from the very wall, wrapped around his neck and arms. A python grip, squeezing the life out of him, scales dull with great patches of charred lizard skin hanging off him. Will scanned, searching for the Grey that was using its telekinesis to hang that poor wretch, like another had tried to do to Will before. It was manipulating its surroundings to deadly effect, more effectively than the one Will had shot, or perhaps this Anunnaki was too weak to fight it off. Will took aim and fired. The Grey took the bullet in the head.

Another Grey was looking directly at two other Anunnaki with an evil grin across its face, delving into the minds of its victims literally scaring them to death, but not on Will's watch. The Grey turned to face Will, but a bullet was already on its way, hitting the small alien in the side of the head, battling its way through its brain and exploding out through the skull and flesh on the other side.

'You did it, Will,' said Nilah. 'You saved them.'

'Don't count your chickens yet.' Will stood up and helped the Anunnaki down, cutting his hand as he untwisted the sharp scraps of metal.

'Hi y'all,' he said to the three lizard-like people, who in return, gaped at him. Will was sure they could understand him because of the beam he'd been hit with on first meeting Ki. They didn't say anything though, then Will realised why; in another cell, a female Anunnaki cradled a male. He had been too late to save them all. Anguish spread through him and he screamed his despair, furious with himself. Alien or not, he never wanted to see hostages down. The other Anunnaki flinched from him. He took in the situation and calmed down, a soldier again. He held his hand out to the female. 'Can ya walk?'

She nodded in surprise. Seeing a human saviour this far from Earth must have been the last thing she'd expected.

'Good.' He turned to the group. 'Let's go then.'

Grabbing Will's arm, she forced herself up and out of the cell. Her face was wet with tears. He took a quick, mental sit-rep of the group. They were all in a bad shape, but he picked out the strongest two. 'You two, pick up that body.' He pointed to the dead Anunnaki. They nodded and bent down to retrieve the body.

'That will only slow you down, Will,' said Nilah.

'Leave no one behind,' said Will. 'Follow me and stay close,' he told the group. 'I'm going to get y'all out of here.'

Hope for the first time in a long time shone in their eyes.

'Behind you!' screamed the female Anunnaki.

Will spun round. A Grey had followed him. A green bolt of energy flew at him. He couldn't dodge or it would hit the group behind, so he stood his ground and raised his weapon.

His burst of gunfire leapt from the rifle as the fiery bolt hit his shoulder. Pain gritted his teeth, the stench of burning flesh blossomed. The blast spun him around.

'Ha! I'm still alive,' he cried, mocking the enemy.

The pain exploded through him, but adrenalin flooded his body. He wasn't about to pass out. Holding his assault rifle one-handed he scanned the corridor. The Grey was trying to crawl away, blood bubbling from its mouth.

Wincing with every step, Will forced himself towards it. The Grey redoubled its efforts to scramble away, but was too badly injured. He stood over it and watched it bleed out, peering into its dying eyes. At that moment it wasn't malevolent, it wasn't evil. It was just another soldier and didn't deserve a slow death. He shot it in the head. 'Nilah, inform the others. Precious cargo, on route.'

'Message sent, Will.' Did he detect a tone of satisfaction?

He beckoned the Anunnaki to follow him and took point.

Dash had made it to sub level three using an elevator Nilah pointed him towards. It felt empty, devoid of life. Too easy he thought. But he plunged on deeper into the complex.

'Second corridor on the left, third door on the right,' said Nilah into his ear piece. 'Anunnaki. Life signs critical. Two Grey contacts still in the same room and something else has entered.'

'Another Grey?'

'No, something else. Unknown.'

Dash approached the door. 'Ready, Nilah?'

'Ready, Dash.'

'On my command.' Dash readied his weapon.

'Confirmed.'

'Now.'

The door opened. Dash saw what appeared to be a medical operating table with various attachments at one end. A thin lizard-like humanoid lay on the bed. Its head reminded him of a gecko, but flatter. This was a different type of Anunnaki. The body was soft skinned covered in tiny red scales. Its whip-like tail hung limp. Its arms and legs were tied, but its pupils, dark black slits in its golden yellow eyes moved but a fraction, spying Dash at the doorway. Cuts and incisions over the lizard's body were testament the Greys had operated without thought for its life. Dash couldn't see any other life form.

Two Greys stood talking, a hologram of another Anunnaki between them, a gecko again with a black streak across its eyes almost like a mask.

The hologram pointed to the door then its signal cut out.

The two Greys spun to face Dash. He shot them both, once in the chest and once in the head. Then he approached the lizard.

'Don't worry buddy, I'll soon get you out of here.'

The lizard man struggled and managed to shake his head. Dash saw the dark, unmistakable gaze of fear in the man's eyes. He checked his assault rifle, moved his finger to the trigger and turned around. Slowly. Two green eyes regarded him with a voracious appetite. Dash stared and locked eyes with a creature that resembled a black panther. A cloak of short hair glistened as huge muscles rippled with power. It stalked its fresh prey. Then six tentacles, slimy and covered in suckers, emerged from its back. They were thin – each one at least six feet long – and curled and whipped about the creature's body. As a commando, Dash wasn't easily shocked, but this was one of those rare moments.

The creature pulled back its lips and snarled, exposing long, pointed teeth, dripping with saliva. It darted forward so quickly Dash didn't have time to fire.

He managed to dive, barely avoiding a tentacle that whipped past his face.

The panther-squid monster skidded to halt, then turned and leapt at Dash again. Sharp razor claws sprang from its massive paws. Its fur rippled a red wave of colour down its back, putting Dash off his aim, though he let off a burst of rounds.

One caught the creature in mid-flight. Just enough to knock it off balance.

As it landed, an explosion of bright green spread up its legs and body before returning to black. It snarled as a tentacle snaked out and wrapped around Dash's legs

He was pulled to the floor, watching helpless as his assault rifle clattered away. He fought as he was dragged closer to the beast's open mouth. If only he still had his knife.

With a desperate lunge he grabbed a table leg, braced and kicked hard, yanking his legs free.

The monster howled and sprang again.

Dash threw himself into a sideways roll. As the creature landed he punched it with his solidest right hook. The beast roared in pain. Its paw lashed out. Dash felt the sting of sharp claws as he was hurled across the room banging up against the solid metal wall.

Something warm trickled across his chest. The Kevlar body armour had saved him, but the panther-squid's attack had ripped it through to his flesh.

Dash braced. The panther was relentless, already coming at him again, snarling, snapping its teeth while tentacles whipped out in front of it.

He had two options, finish this or bleed out. He pulled out his sidearm.

The creature feigned a leap. Two shots fired in haste whistled through empty air. Sensing victory, the beast launched four of its tentacles towards Dash. He twisted away from three of them, but one snaked around his left leg, and this time sharp claws dug into him out of the hundreds of tiny suckers on the tentacle's arm.

He cried out in agony. The beast pounced. Paws

outstretched, claws extended, its mouth open with a roar of triumph, a wave of colours washing over it.

At the last moment, Dash brought the pistol to bear, unloading the magazine into the gaping mouth.

The panther-squid monstrosity crashed into him as it fell. Dash gasped, winded, as its weight landed on him.

After a second, he heaved the creature off and carefully stood up. He was a mess and he knew it. He looked to the lizard man. 'Let's see if we can't rescue each other,' he said with a painful grin.

Dash cut the lizard man free and hobbled over to his fallen assault rifle. The Anunnaki slumped off the table, his injuries worse than Dash had realised. Far too serious for him to walk, so Dash limped over, picked him up on his strongest side and they helped each other out of the room.

Cassandra viewed another green dot on the holographic image wink out. John was now in the power plant room but hadn't moved for a couple of minutes and she surmised he must be setting the charges. Will had succeeded in reaching the cells and was now leading four of the Anunnaki back to the hangar. One of the white dots, representing Anunnaki biology, had faded before Will had managed to get there and Cassandra had seen Ki wipe a tear from her face. Dash had rescued the other Anunnaki from the lower level but was now moving painfully slowly back to their ship.

Green dots were converging on the saucer, five of them. The other green dots, the other Greys, were too far inside the base to make a difference unless the five near the saucer held Dash and the team up.

John's white dot began moving back towards the saucer at a quick pace.

'Get the med bay ready,' Cassandra whispered. 'I think we're going to need it.'

Ki nodded. 'Professor come with me.'

They both left the star map room and headed for the med bay.

John ran quicker than he had in a long time, leaping over obstacles, sliding across tables and sprinting down corridors, every muscle burning. Nilah had warned him of the approaching Greys. He had to get to the saucer before they did.

'Nilah,' he panted.

'Yes John.'

'I need to know priority targets. Which Grey is closest to the hangar?'

'At current speed, the east entrance is most likely.'

John burst into the hangar bay. 'Awesome, thanks Nilah.'

'The east entrance …'

'Is on the left, I know. You call the targets. I'll kill them.'

'Confirmed.' Did he imagine a hint of vengeance in Nilah's voice.

'Contact rear,' said Nilah into Will's ear piece.

'Down!' yelled Will, as a green bolt shot past, warming the air above their heads. 'Go,' he commanded.

They were only a few yards from the hangar bay and damned if he'd let any more of the Anunnaki die. He knelt, pain racing through his chest, adrenaline pumping his heart, assault rifle, ready. As the Anunnaki raced past him he fired a suppressing burst of rounds down the corridor, forcing the Grey to dive for cover. Will took the moment and chased after the Anunnaki.

They all raced into the hangar bay and headed to the lowered ramp of the saucer. Will turned and let loose another burst to keep the Grey's head down. He saw the Anunnaki climb into the ship. He ran to the ramp, crouched in front, brought up his rifle and realised he was out of ammo. Then, the Grey stepped into the hangar.

The Grey inched forward past the edge of the doorway, a black shadow masking its dark skin. It had a perfect shot on Will and generated a large ball of green energy between its hands. Nothing could stop the alien from finishing off this irritating human.

Almost nothing …

'Hello, old bean,' said John. He'd been hiding behind the entrance and now stood right next to the Grey, his pistol point blank range.

It fell dead. Five bullets left.

'North entrance,' said Nilah.

Two Greys burst into the hangar room. He thought he had a good shot from where he was, but missed the first, cursing himself for dropping his aim at the last second. It was enough to stall the aliens, because they'd been focused on Will. The next two shots were easier and the Greys fell.

Dash was the last to limp into the hangar room. He came in through the west entrance. Will ran over to help.

'Jesus what happened to you,' said Will.

'Could say the same to you.'

'West,' said Nilah to John.

John walked at pace towards his fellow soldiers, and held his breath. A Grey had sneaked up on Dash and Will, who were busy helping the gecko limp back to the saucer. John caught the glint of a surgical knife in the Grey's hand. Aim. And breathe. John's bullet passed both Dash and Will within millimetres then took the Grey in the right eye. John hadn't broken his stride. One bullet left.

'Holy crap,' said Will.

'Remind me not to annoy him,' said Dash knowing a highly trained marksman when he saw one.

'Come on, let's get the hell outta here,' said Will.

They scrambled into the saucer. As soon as they were on board, Nilah engaged the autopilot and the ship took off. A Grey ran into the hangar room and raked the hull with green fire. Nilah shot out a tractor beam and grabbed it, taking off with the Grey in tow. John reached into his backpack and produced a detonating switch. He looked over to an exhausted Dash for an order.

'Do it.'

John flicked open the protective cover and pressed the button. On Mars, next to an extinct volcano, the ground heaved and bowed upwards as four sticks of C4 destroyed the power generators. When the explosion was done, all that remained was another huge crater.

As they shot out of Mars orbit, Nilah released the tractor beam and the Grey floated off into space. Deprived of vital air it died, just before its blood boiled.

CHAPTER 9

Dash put a hand over his bandaged stomach. John had done a good job using the few medicals supplies they had with them, but it still stung like hell. He lifted his palm. It was as red as the bandage. Don't close your eyes, he told himself.

The landing ramp descended. God, he wasn't even aware they had landed. Nilah was a better pilot than any of them. Very smooth. He chuckled, which was a mistake.

'You trying to ruin my bandages?' said John, looking down at the spreading red stain.

Dash glanced across at Will who hadn't seemed in much better shape, but who had now risen to his feet to help the Anunnaki disembark.

He sat, unable to move until John eased him upright and helped him out.

The X50 hangar bay was lit up, bright as day. Cassandra and the Professor were already there helping the Anunnaki survivors. Dash saw horror spread across Cassandra's face as John helped him limp down. His bandage hung loose, his chest ripped open, leg torn to shreds. Blood dripped from a hundred different cuts and splashed on to the floor.

'Oh my God,' said Cassandra.

'Get the Anunnaki to the sick bay,' commanded Dash. 'I'm fine.'

She nodded uneasily but he could she was well out of her comfort zone. With the Professor's help she guided the Anunnaki to the med bay.

'Liar,' said Will, coming out from behind Dash.

'I'll live.'

'Only just,' said John, watching the Anunnaki leave with Cassandra and the Professor. 'We best follow them before you do actually die.'

'Yeah but slowly, eh,' said Will.

'Thanks John, you saved us both back there. That was some shooting,' said Dash. Will nodded in agreement.

'We're a team, I wasn't going to leave you. Besides, couldn't let you have all the fun.' John grinned.

'Yes, we're a good team. That includes you, Nilah,' said Dash.

'Thank you, Dash. I've never been part of a team before.'

'Well, you are now.'

In the computer core a blue light surrounding the central processor, Nilah's brain, glowed a little brighter.

'I hope we don't need to do that again,' said Dash.

'Who dares wins,' winked John.

Dash nodded. 'Come on. Let's get patched up.'

'Spook never even got a scratch,' muttered Will to himself. John smiled.

John helped both men get to the sick bay. All three of them entered together and were met with organised chaos. More beds had risen from the floor to contend with the influx of patients. Thin robotic arms were doing the nurse jobs. Metallic arms seemed magically to appear out of the ceiling and floor; the more seriously wounded having more around them. Ki pointed towards two empty beds. Dash lay down and let out a deep sigh of exhaustion. 'Can't remember the last time I had a kip.'

'That creature you lied about, knocked you on your ass. You had a couple seconds rest then. What you moaning about?' laughed Will on the next bed.

Dash glanced at Will, seeing him clutch his arm as pain hit him. Shouldn't have laughed, he thought. 'Oh yeah and you're at the peak of your fitness,' he retorted, laughing back at him, then wincing in pain.

'Will you two stop trying to hurt yourselves,' said Cassandra.

'Yes ma'am,' said Will.

'Who are you most scared of?' whispered Dash. 'The Greys or Cassandra?'

Will's gaze resting for a moment on Cassandra helping Ki with one of the injured Anunnaki. 'That's easy bro, Cassandra all the way.'

Both men laughed, then groaned again in pain. Cassandra spun round with an angry glare.

'I'll be on the bridge with the Professor if you need me.' John grinned.

Dash grabbed John's arm as he was leaving. 'Thanks again, John.'

'Any time guys, any time.'

John was at the sick bay door when Will shouted after him. 'What's your second name?'

He flashed him his best grin. 'Black,' he said and left.

'Spooks never take anything seriously,' said Will.

'I don't know about that, but I'm glad he's on our side,' said Dash.

'Yeah me too, but I'm not going to admit it to his face,' said Will.

Dash chuckled and then sighed as his chest started to throb with pain.

Ki made a pushing motion with her hands. The bed holding the gecko-like Anunnaki glided to the far wall and lined up with the other beds. She turned to Dash and Will. 'OK who wantsss to go first?'

'Will,' said Dash.

'Dash,' said Will.

Neither man was looking at Ki. Instead their stares were fixed on the medical instruments behind her. Strange, snake-like probes. Ki followed their gaze and a second later rolled her eyes, hands on hips. 'Ssso, let me get thisss ssstraight. There's no problem putting yourselvesss in harm's way rescuing people you don't even know, yet you see some medical equipment, operated by *me* and you're having sssecond thoughtsss?'

'No, no it's not that, it's …' Dash trailed off and turned to Will. 'You can help out any time here.'

'Hell no, I'm enjoying this.' Will grinned.

'Children!' said an exasperated Cassandra. 'I've never seen so much blood in my life, Dash, and you're acting like this is a game.'

Ki put one hand on Cassandra's shoulder and made another gesture which wafted Dash's bed over to the examination area. 'I've seen soldiers on your planet for thousandsss of yearsss Cassandra and they're all the sssame. Soldiers die. You're frightened, I know. Working in a med bay with all this blood is not what your doctorate isss for, but if a soldier takesss life too seriously, if a soldier cannot laugh in the face of death, that'sss when they become frightened. That'sss when they die.'

'You're wrong Ki. We're afraid of our friends dying before us,' said Dash. Will glanced over to him and then dropped his gaze to the floor.

'And that is why I will never fight. I will always be afraid in the face of death,' said Cassandra.

'You may yet sssurprise yoursssself, Cassandra.'

Dash's bed locked into place. He suffered involuntary eye blinks as probes and dancing silver cables came close to his face. Stick him in a war zone anytime. But this! One of the needles stuck into him without warning.

'Local anaesthetic, tough guy,' said Ki with a hint of frustration.

She cut away what was left of his combat jacket, and then peeled off the old bandages which were now caked in dried blood. Underneath, four great gouge marks ran from one end of his chest to the other. Cassandra gasped. Blood started to well up again as the marks split apart.

'What did thisss to you?'

'The best way to describe it, a big black panther crossed with the tentacles of a squid,' said Dash.

'A genetic experiment, either one of theirsss or possibly one of oursss the Greys have adopted.'

Cassandra held Dash's hand and spoke to Ki. 'You experiment on animals. By mixing them up?'

'Yesss, we've been doing it for a millennium,' said Ki, in a matter of fact tone. 'Where do you think your mythsss of Mermaidsss, Centaursss and the like come from?'

'I just thought they were stories,' said Cassandra.

'Not all of them. Sssome of the ssstories, depicted in old carvingsss around your world are what people witnessed. Some were our experimentsss and othersss were like him.'

Ki pointed to the gecko Anunnaki on one of the beds. 'Shape-shifterssss.'

The gecko-like humanoid held up his hand and Cassandra stared in fascination as a scaly finger slowly turned into a red rose complete with petals and thorny stem.

'Ssstop that,' said Ki. 'You're ssstill not fully healed.'

'That's … amazing,' said Cassandra.

Ki turned her attention back to Dash and deftly manipulated some of the symbols on the console next to her. One of the spindly metal arms moved down towards Dash's chest and from its point a red light beamed out along one of the slash marks, knitting the wound together. It repeated the process three more times healing Dash's chest wound within minutes, though he would forever be left with the four scars. Next, Ki cut open Dash's trouser leg exposing the skin where the tentacle had gripped him. He couldn't help but watch as four of the spindly arms created a webbed laser mesh above the multiple wounds. When the laser web had finished constructing, it drifted down, on to his leg, healing him. Cassandra stood in awe as the small cuts vanished.

'OK, you're done,' said Ki. 'You need to rest, but before you do, now would be a good time to ask if you ssstill want me to inject you with the rapid healing gene.'

'Will I be able to heal like this on the battlefield?' Dash ran his fingers across his newly formed scars.

'Yesss, but no one has tried to inject a human before.'

'Do it,' said Dash.

'You didn't even think that through,' said Cassandra.

'Didn't need to. If we're going up against the Greys and their experiments, I want all the advantage I can get.'

'OK, thisss won't hurt but you might feel ssstrange as the genesss attach themselves and your body adaptsss.' Dash nodded and Ki, with the help of a metallic snake arm, injected him. 'This won't help if you get ssshot in the head. Remember that. Thisss won't make you invincible.'

Dash nodded, or at least tried to as every muscle began to tense. Then came the pressure, like his body was in a hydraulic press, deadening every sense. More anaesthetic. A lot more, he wanted to say.

Ki made a push gesture and Dash's bed moved away. Turning to Will, she said, 'You're next.'

'Hi Alex.'

At the sound of the voice, the Professor turned to see John strolling on to the bridge. 'John, how did it go? And how are Dash and Will?'

'It went OK, and they're getting patched up.'

'Right. Understatement of the year, I'm sure.'

John smiled. 'Seen worse. What are you up to?'

'Yes, I don't doubt it. I'm reading their history, thanks to Nilah.'

'Oh?' John sounded interested.

'Yes, Nilah translates what I can't.'

'So, tell me.'

'Well I'll skip to the highlights. It seems these Blood Princes created the Anunnaki. Three distinct types, the normal ones ... well, the ones like Ki, I mean. They appear pretty much human, except for their eyes and skin which are more reptilian.'

'And pointed tongues,' John put in.

'Yes. You need to look pretty close to see their scales though, if you notice?'

'From a distance Ki could be a human, yeah. A blue, green pearlescent human, but a human.' John smiled.

'Quite. Our gecko friend in the sick bay is a shape-shifter. And from these files, I believe he is currently in his natural form. They closely resemble lizards, more than the other branches of Anunnaki, although they also walk on two legs.'

He worked his way round the computer and brought up another set of images to show John. 'Then there are these, the telepathic ones. If you can see there, they stand about nine-feet tall and here you can see the elongated head Ki told us about before we ended up over Mars.'

'Interesting,' said John, moving to take control of the computer.

The Professor watched him, impressed with how adept he was … almost as though this wasn't the first time he'd used alien technology. John flicked through reams of information, ending on an image of a hatchery.

'The Blood Princes control their population and when their race is running low, so to speak,' the Professor explained. 'They somehow make new eggs which hatch into one of the three types of Anunnaki. They are babies at first, but grow to adulthood quickly, normally within the first six years.'

'That's some population control,' said John.

'That's not all. These Blood Princes rarely speak to their creations. The Anunnaki have no idea where these Princes came from, or what their long-term goals are.'

'A tad mysterious.'

'Yes.' He beamed at John. 'Isn't it wonderful!''

'Talking about mysterious, how come you and Cassandra were even allowed into Iraq, let alone study one of their ancient temples?'

'Oh, nothing shady there, my dear fellow. I was visited by a man who works for a corporation who wanted to back my expedition.'

'Nothing shady? If a corporation can influence a government, a government in a country as hostile as Iraq and then get you into their national monument? Something about that corporation is definitely shady.'

'Yes, well, they were happy to fund it all, so I wasn't about to peer too deeply into their motives, especially after everyone else had turned me down.'

'I not judging you, Alex, but take it from someone with experience in shady organisations … be careful.'

He nodded and tried a bit of a smile, sure that John didn't really understand. One shot at fulfilling his life's work, of course he'd jumped at it. John would have, too.

'Discovered anything else?' John was continuing to flick through the holographic data, apparently happy to let the subject drop.

'Yes,' he told him, and reached out to bring up the information he'd been studying earlier. 'You're not going to like it, John. There's a third part to the Star Protocol that Ki failed to mention.'

Will held up his arm, twisted it and clenched his fist as though trying it out for the first time. 'Thanks Doc,' he said smiling at Ki.

'My pleasure. Do you want the sssame healing gene asss Dash?'

'Don't want to give him the advantage.'

'Men!' Cassandra rolled her eyes and tutted. Ki smiled back at Will and injected him the way she had injected Dash.

As Will drifted into a sleep, she spoke to Cassandra. 'We'll make sssure they are OK before we give the rest of you the sssame gene.'

'How are the others?' Cassandra said glancing towards the rescued Anunnaki on thir beds.

'They'll be OK in about an hour. Once they are up and about I'll ssset them to work around the ssship.' Ki cocked her head and gazed at Will sleeping. 'Doesss thisss one have a mate?'

Cassandra almost fell over with such a direct question. 'Ah … no, I don't think so. I'm not entirely sure. Wouldn't know actually.'

'Guess I'll have to find out sssomehow,' she said smiling.

'I thought you couldn't reproduce.'

'We can still fall in love.'

'Oh …' Cassandra tried to avoid eye contact in an awkward silence.

'I take it you want Dash asss your mate,' Ki said, in a matter of fact tone.

'I … I don't know yet.' Cassandra blushed. She'd preferred the silence but realised it was only awkward for her.

Ki laughed a rich warm chuckle. 'Yesss, you do, even if you don't know it yourself. I can sssense heightened levelsss of estrogen and increased blood flow whenever Dash is near.'

Cassandra gave an involuntary, nervous laugh. 'I think we're needed on the bridge,' was all she could say.

Cassandra and Ki entered the bridge arm in arm. 'What are you two whispering about?' asked the Professor.

'Oh, nothing much, woman stuff.' Cassandra looked relaxed.

'Ki,' said John. 'When were you going to tell us about the third part of the Star Protocol?'

'I wasss not going to. There isss no point now.'

'At least she's honest,' said the Professor.

'What's going on?' asked Cassandra.

'We were preparing to destroy all but a few humansss and ssstart again.'

Cassandra's jaw dropped. 'You can't do that!'

'Jesus!' A part of John had hoped the Professor was wrong.

'We were overdue though,' said the Professor.

'What do you mean?' asked Cassandra.

'There were clues if one recognised them, such as the Mayan calendar. The Mayan people said at the end of their calendar the Star People would come back and there would be a great Armageddon. The battle of the gods and ultimately the destruction of our world. The Mayan calendar ran out December twelfth, twenty twelve. And there are other ancient cultures all of whom prophesise a similar doomsday.'

'Are you telling me, if it wasn't for the Greys attacking Ki and her people …?'

'We'd all be dead,' finished the Professor.

'How could you …?' Cassandra stared at Ki.

'The Blood Princes have existed sssince the beginning, and in all that time they have encountered only one other alien race with a capacity for violence asss great asss the human race. Do you know what the first human who picked up a branch did with it?'

No one offered an answer.

'She weaponised it. That isss the human race. We gave you axesss to chop down treesss and you crushed skullsss; we gave you arrowsss to hunt food and you pierced the heartsss of your enemiesss.'

'Ki,' said Cassandra. 'Do you truly believe that?'

'Ordersss for "planetary advancement" come from the High Council. And they take their ordersss direct from the Blood Princes. What I believe, hasss no relevance. The truth isss, the Anunnaki fear what humanity will become.'

'And that is why I don't think your orders did come from the Blood Princes,' said the Professor. Ki offered a curious glance. The Professor continued. 'Throughout your history, which is vast by the way, your culture has seen these Blood Princes only a handful of times.'

'Yesss, they communicate their wishesss through our telepaths.'

'Which ones?' asked the Professor.

'Only the High Priestess of the High Council hasss that honour.'

'I think you've been told a lie.'

Ki sat down, though she showed no surprise. 'You are not the only one to think that, Professor. There are sssome amongst my kind who would agree with you.'

'Oh, how so?' said John.

'Millionsss of years ago, during the timesss of strife

when the Blood Princes were said to have looked like us, they wanted to unlock the secretsss of black holesss to explore distant galaxies and the entire universe. They created a vast armada of shipsss capable of bending space time to their will. And ssso, they went out into deep space, exploring. They met other racesss, but none held the knowledge they were after. Then, so sssome stories go, at the edge of one of those galaxies they came across an alien race even older than themselvesss. A great war ensued but peace prevailed, and a bargain was struck, what bargain we do not know, it has never been ssspoken of, however it was then the Blood Princes were able to shed their physical formsss. They learned of the eleven universes and the story endsss.'

'Eleven?' The Professor sounded awed.

'So, is it a story or real?' asked Cassandra.

Ki nodded. 'The implicationsss are enormousss. But if true, they no longer needed shipsss to travel through ssspace. Our universe is vast with billions of galaxiesss, and trillions of starsss to explore so they created us to help them.'

'To what end? Why would supreme beings need help?' said the Professor.

'They were searching for something, though they did not tell us what. They just insisted we take a telepath with usss alwaysss. As time went on we realised our own existence was at the whim of the Blood Princes. We could not reproduce. Ssso, we decided to experiment, and to do it on a galactic scale. To find a cure for our reproductive curse we came up with the Star Protocol. By manipulating life, we hoped to discover how to create life.'

'How many times has the Star Protocol worked?' said

John. He folded his arms and casually leant on to the wall behind him.

'In all this time, never,' said Ki.

'And the Greys where do they fit in?' asked Cassandra.

'They were a race we helped in the beginning. Although they were already a ssspace-faring civilisation when we discovered them, they learned of our long life and were corrupted by its appeal. We refused to give them the gene sssequence as they were not Anunnaki, ssso they waged war and from our dead they had limited success. They managed to extend their livesss to around five hundred yearsss. However they also contracted our curse and ssstopped having children. Over thousands of yearsss they became sexless and turned to genetic breeding and cloning to keep their race alive. Now, the Greysss are convinced their sssalvation lies within our genetic makeup and ssso instigated a policy of covert invasion of worldsss touched by the Anunnaki, in the hope of gaining the knowledge to reproduce.'

'They don't know about the Blood Princes, do they?' said the Professor.

'No. Our curse is now theirsss.'

'That doesn't explain why the Princes have stopped talking to you,' said Cassandra.

'Yes, it does,' said John. 'They've found what they were looking for.'

Ki nodded. 'I think it wasss the planet on the edge of the galaxy, where the Blood Princes gained the knowledge for their transcendence from the physical form.'

'I thought you knew where that was?' said Cassandra.

'Some of us think the Blood Princes were tricked, but for whatever reason, they left the planet in their new formsss.

Explorersss have searched, but the planet is no longer there.'

'Destroyed!'

'Lost.'

'How do you lose a planet?'

'We don't know if these ancient alienssss cloaked their planet somehow, or it sssimply vanished.'

'When was the last time any of the Anunnaki were created by the Blood Princes?' asked John.

'There has been none sssince the last batch. I wasss in the last batch, one hundred and fifty thousand yearsss ago.'

'So, your race is dying, albeit slower than most, but still dying,' said the Professor.

'There is normally a batch of eggsss every ten to fifty thousand yearsss, and there used to be millions of eggsss. I wasss in a batch of less than a thousand.'

'If your race dies out, that guarantees the Greys dying out,' said John.

Ki nodded. 'Unless they find a sssolution before we do.'

'Jesus, what a mess,' said Cassandra.

'Yes, these Blood Princes have a lot to answer for,' said the Professor.

John looked up. 'Heard enough?'

Everyone turned to see Dash and Will at the doorway in to the bridge. 'Yes, and it seems our world is caught in the middle of it,' said Dash.

'That isss not the worst of it. The High Council will not be able to fabricate thisss lie for much longer. People doubt the High Priestess. There wasss already talk of the Blood Princes leaving as I ssset out for your world. There are those who remain loyal to the Princes, thinking they would never leave usss and there are those who would ssstart their own course.'

'Open rebellion often leads to civil war,' said Will.

'If the Greys get wind of this they will pick a side, and demand payment in return. The genetic code,' said John.

'The Greys hate usss. They would never pick a side,' said Ki.

'They already have Ki,' said Dash.

'You are wrong, Dash. The Greys would never ally themselvesss with any faction of Anunnaki.'

'Why not?'

'Why not, Ki?' Cassandra repeated.

Ki met Cassandra's eyes. 'The Greys were not alwaysss a hive mind speciesss. They were free thinking, as free as you or I, but we introduced telepathy into their genome. We thought their large brainsss would cope. Unfortunately, only three hundred Greysss could contain their new powersss, the billionsss left were under the influence of the few. They became dronesss, ssslaves. Controlling so many mindsss corrupted the three hundred. Imagine a million people doing exactly as you command, more than that though, the million people were an extension of your own thoughtsss.'

Cassandra shook her head and sat down.

'I'm telling you, Ki, the Greys have picked a side. Before I was attacked by that creature, I saw two Greys in conversion with an Anunnaki via hologram,' said Dash.

'Are you sssure?'

'The Anunnaki gave away my position. He helped them. He was a gecko-shaped one, with a black streak covering his eyes.'

'That soundsss like it could be General Kraktus of the

Order of Eagles. The largest anti-Blood Prince movement in the capital. But it doesn't make sssense. We can't cure the Greys.' Ki too shook her head and sat down.

'Either way we're going to be sailing into a storm,' said John.

'I underssstand if you do not wish to help me anymore.'

'You said you'd help us if we helped you,' said Dash.

'Yesss, but I can't speak for the High Council.'

'But you'll still help us?'

'I will … regardless of the outcome,' said Ki.

'Then nothing has changed,' said Dash.

'It's the Anunnaki, not the Greys who want to wipe us out, Dash,' said John.

'All the more reason to see them, John, to show them they are wrong about humanity.'

'Are they?' asked John, bluntly.

'All I know is, when I first met a Grey, it greeted me with contempt. There was nothing but malice. The Anunnaki … the Anunnaki just need educating. So start up the engines, let's get to your star system, Ki.'

Ki stood amazed. 'After all you've been told and the dangersss ahead, you ssstill want to help?'

'Have you learnt nothing from these humans?' came Nilah's soft voice. 'We're a team.'

Will winked at Ki. 'She's right.'

CHAPTER 10

The X51 Deep Space Research Vessel cleared the last planet in the Solar System and headed for deep space. The Anunnaki survivors had taken positions around the ship, maintaining the consoles and helping Nilah with the ongoing repairs.

'Time to high density jump, ten minutes,' echoed Nilah, across all decks.

Dash shifted in his chair, stood up, stretched his back muscles and sat down again. Everyone heard him huff, although he'd deny he did. Ki had found him and the others clean clothes, made of the same loose, silver metal silk Ki wore; light but incredibly strong with a thin lattice of wire hexagon mesh throughout. The boots and trousers were comfortable sure, but the top, not so much. It was looser than Dash liked, and he felt himself itching which irritated him. He'd been so impressed with the material itself, he'd asked Ki if she could reproduce his combat fatigues from the same stuff; a task taken up by Citalicue, the other female Anunnaki on board, as a thank you for rescuing her. It occurred to him that all the Anunnaki survivors seemed like they were thanking him or one of his team every chance they got; going out of their way to make them as comfortable as possible. Which was ironic as he was far from comfortable now.

'You nervous?' asked Will, next to him on the lower command deck.

'No, why?'

'You fidget any more, and you'll put a hole in that chair.' Will grinned.

Dash ignored Will but couldn't help gazing over his shoulder towards Cassandra. The not-so-long-ago scrubby archaeologist had cleaned up and was wearing an outfit, a similar design to Ki's. Cassandra met Dash's gaze. So now he had to say something.

'You OK?' Smooth, he thought to himself.

Cassandra nodded, then chuckled. 'I'm actually looking forward to this.' Dash let his eyes linger on her for a moment longer as she turned back to her console.

'Time to high density jump, five minutes,' echoed Nilah again.

Dash braced. He couldn't help it. He closed his eyes for a moment whilst letting out a controlled breath.

'We've got the best seats in the house,' said the Professor looking out of the massive digital windows.

'Feels like we're on top of a great big roller coaster,' said John.

'Time to jump, ten seconds,' said Nilah.

'Here we go,' said Will.

Ki smiled to herself.

A green, blue swirl appeared outside the window and slowly grew, becoming a maelstrom of spinning hues. The ship lurched forward and the maelstrom vanished. They were now in the Space between Space. Dash held out his hand. Eyes swelled up with water, like he had yawned twenty times in a row. Different versions of his own hand spread out in front of him; first a red one glided to the right, then every colour of the rainbow; orange ... yellow ... green ... blue ... indigo ... violet and the all the variations between. Could each hand only bounce back photons of one colour? Had he passed through a prism? He faced Ki for answers. Her head was difficult to make out, a blur of colour. She mouthed the words, 'Quantum effect.'

Then Dash saw himself, in multi-coloured versions, one of which stood right in front. 'What the hell?'

Another coloured self raised its hand, pointed to where he was sitting and looked towards Ki. She didn't react. He pulled himself up and moved to stand where his other self was. When he turned, he saw himself still sitting there.

'What's going on?'

'It's the quantum effect,' Ki said, although Dash couldn't see her lips move. In a flash, the colours of his and everyone else's other selves converged. Dash was in his seat.

'High density jump complete. Time to Zaos System, thirty minutes,' said Nilah.

'What the ...?'

'We call it the quantum effect,' said Ki to the blank faces of John, Dash and Will. 'Light can't break its own ssspeed limit, so it getsss confused. To compensate it isss in both places at once. In fact, it isss in *all* the placesss at once. This effect happensss all the time, but in real space no one can sssee it. You can only ever see one outcome.'

'I stood up, I remember standing ... but we came out of the jump and I'm sitting here,' said Dash.

'You witnessed one possible outcome. When we finished the jump, the reality you chose was one where you didn't vacate your sssseat.'

'I have no idea what you're talking about,' said Dash.

'Like the cat in the box,' chuckled the Professor.

'The what?'

'You put a cat in box with a flask of poison, which has a random chance of killing the cat. When the box is closed that cat is both alive and dead until the box is opened, and the universe can see it,' said the Professor.

Cassandra nodded. 'Schrödinger's cat,' she said.

'I think he actually came up with the theory to discount quantum mathematics. Reductio ad absurdum, reduction to absurdity. And until now, I would have agreed with him.'

'I for one am glad it was over quickly,' said Cassandra.

'I thought it was fascinating.'

'A great weapon if used right,' murmured John.

'What?' said the Professor.

'Nothing, just thinking out loud.'

'Kind of proving Ki's earlier point there, John,' said Cassandra.

'Nilah, why are we ssslowing down?'

'Long range detection scans indicate our home world, Nibiru, has planetary defence shields active. And the planet Shalor has been invaded by the Greys.'

'Let usss go to the Star Room,' said Ki immediately.

They stood around the centre console, a 3D holographic image of the Zaos System displayed above the plinth. Zaos, a bright yellow star hovered at the heart of the system, with five of the thirteen planets shown in orbit, their trajectories clearly marked. The closest, Igress, the size of

Mars, was listed as a dry desolate wasteland. Next, the home world, Nibiru, a blue marble, that could have been Earth from this distance with its land masses surrounded by water.

The third planet was Shalor. John's gaze rested on it, a jungle world half the size of Nibiru, now controlled by the Greys according to Nilah. He took note of the trajectories. Shalor and Nibiru orbited each other, coming closest every six months; perfect for an assault on the home world.

Apsu, the fourth planet, twice Earth's size, was covered in ice. The fifth and final one, labelled Ion, was little more than a big rock, more Moon-like than anything else, though about Nibiru's size and with rings around it; not majestic beauties like Saturn's, but angry boiling clouds dancing between red and blue.

'Have we been detected?' asked John.

'No, I have lowered our sig. We are coming in silent,' said Nilah. John smiled at the term 'sig.' She was behaving more like the humans than her Anunnaki creators.

'How do you want to play this?' John looked straight through the holographic image at Dash.

'We can't stay here. We might not have been detected yet but I'm sure we will. We need a place where we can think.'

'If we can remain undetected until we get there, we can hide in the Storms of Ion,' said Ki, pointing to the rings around the fifth planet.

'Is that safe?' said Cassandra.

'For this ssship yesss. For the scout shipsss not really, although they could survive a ssshort flight.'

'OK Nilah, set course for the Storms of Ion, maximum stealth mode,' said Dash.

'Confirm. Time to destination forty minutes,' said Nilah.

'I'm going back to the bridge. There's something I want to look up,' said the Professor.

'Can Dash, Will and John report to the Science Bay? Citalicue wants to see you,' said Nilah.

Dash entered the science bay on deck two, seeing the lizard-like shape-shifter still recuperating on one of the beds. 'How's he doing?'

'Kuan Ti is fine,' Citalicue said. 'He had extensive internal damage, so I've told him to rest awhile longer.'

Citalicue didn't carry her esses the way Ki did, which Dash initially assumed was because of her forked tongue, but had discovered was to do with regional accents.

'What did you want to see us about?' he asked.

Citalicue held up a light matte silver version of the men's combat fatigues. 'Your clothes, as requested. They look the same as your original gear but made from our material. It will stop blades and claws but not energy or sharp projectiles.'

Will scratched the back of his head. 'No offence, but that colour, silver, it's about as useful as a chocolate fireguard.'

'I have fitted these combat uniforms with an adaptive camouflage option,' she said.

'Adaptive?' inquired Dash.

'Arc Ides, our chief of science was working on the technology before the Grey took us. There is a symbol on the sleeve of this jacket, here.' Citalicue held up the arm of one of the jackets, showing a symbol embedded in the sleeve. 'Press it and you can cycle through camouflage presets such as jungle, desert, digital ... Choose one to blend with your surroundings.'

When Citalicue activated the suits, the colour pigments creating the matte silver slid across the fabric changing to different shades of green.

'This is your army's standard green camo,' she said, then pressed the button again causing the dye to move to shades of yellow and brown. 'And this was how your clothes looked when you provided them to me.'

'Arc Ides, where is he?' said Will. Citalicue stood motionless for a moment, a third inner eyelid blinked from the edge of her eye towards her nose wiping away a build-up of water. 'Oh, he was in the cage. The one who didn't make it.'

Citalicue nodded. She was the head of science now. 'The material is a prototype,' she said. 'So be careful with it.'

'Thanks for this.' Dash held one of the combat suits.

'I have also taken the liberty of modifying your projectiles,' Citalicue went on. 'I had some spare time.' Her tone had a hint of smugness.

'Our what?' said Will.

'Ammo, dumb ass,' said Dash.

'That is correct. Your bullets, as you would say.'

'OK, let's have a look,' said Dash.

'I have used our metals, instead of yours.' She held up a silver bullet. It looked expensive.

'Flight dynamic is the same, but penetration is far greater. I could have made it travel faster and longer but would have to modify your weapons, and it appears we don't have the time for that.'

'How many of these do we have?' asked Dash.

'The first batch for each of your different weapon types is two thousand but I am currently in the process of making another thousand,' said Citalicue.

John took a box for his guns.

'Amazing, we're living in high cotton now,' said Will holding up one of the bullets, examining it. 'But do you have any laser weapons?'

'No, this is a research vessel. There were some personal weapons on board which the Greys took when we were captured.'

'What you've done for us is amazing Doc, thanks,' said Dash.

'It is a small price for the service you did for me and my kind. And what you are about to do,' said Citalicue. 'Which brings me to you John, would you like to sit in that chair?'

'What for, I'm not injured.'

'I'm going to inject you with the rapid healing gene. These two don't seem to have had any side effects and I have a feeling you might need it soon.'

John looked at Will and Dash.

'She's right,' said Will.

Dash just shrugged. 'Your call.'

John nodded. 'OK, sounds like a good idea. Always did want to be Superman when I was a kid.'

'Superman was bullet *proof*, though wasn't he?' said Will.

'Pretty sure this injection won't give you the ability to fly either,' said Dash.

John sat in the chair.

The Professor entered the bridge. 'Nilah could you call up the last known position of the Blood Princes' abandoned fleet.'

'Yes Professor. However the last known position was in a system with a black hole. It is assumed the Blood Princes destroyed the fleet so their technology wouldn't fall into someone else's hands.'

'That's understandable,' said the Professor. 'But at the time, could they have been sure their search was over? If so, why would they still be here …? Some Blood Princes must remain even if they don't make contact anymore. A few did create the last batch of eggs?'

'I do not have that information.'

'No. I know. I'm going over it in my head.'

'I see. The records are at your disposal Professor.'

'Thank you Nilah.'

Ki and Cassandra studied the hologram of the Zaos system.

'If my people have activated the planetary defence ssshield it meansss they have already come under attack from the Greys.'

'Are they safe under the shield?' said Cassandra.

'They are unless, however unlikely, the Greys find a way to de-activate it or drain enough of the ssshield ssso it collapsesss. Although that would take a great amount of energy.'

'What was on that planet?' Cassandra pointed to the jungle world, Shalor, the one occupied by the Greys.

'We had a small research colony there. A hostile world

really. Although when we first landed on it our explorersss found cavesss which had been dug into the sssmall mountainsss covering the planet, but there were no signsss of what we would call intelligent life.'

'What would *you* call intelligent life?'

'I must appear rude sometimesss,' said Ki, avoiding the question.

'No, it's OK. I'm still getting used to your Star Protocol.'

Ki put a reassuring hand on Cassandra's shoulder. 'That would have been our mistake,' she said. 'You humansss have ssshown a massive potential. You may even outshine the Blood Princes one day. I'm glad we didn't wipe you out.'

Was that humour coming from the Anunnaki, Cassandra wondered.

'Can we communicate with your people from here?' she asked.

'I have been trying. It seemsss my communicationsss are being blocked but I cannot tell from where, which explainsss why my distress signal didn't reach Nibiru.'

'So how are we going to get a message through?'

'We are not. We are going to have to find another way,' said Ki.

'Your people must be preparing for war. Surely they will attack Shalor soon.' Cassandra had noticed Shalor's current orbit brought it very close to Nibiru.

'We are not a warlike race. We have few warship fleetsss. I believe the High Council will wait it out. If thingsss become desperate they will assume the Blood Princes will help.'

'But if we're right and the Blood Princes have left …' said Cassandra, worry spreading across her face.

'Yesss, it does not look good.'

'The Professor would like everyone on the bridge,' said Nilah.

'What have you got?' said Dash, the first to enter the bridge.

The Professor waited until everyone was in before he began. 'As you know when the Blood Princes arrived at the mystery planet, which has now strangely vanished, they came in a fleet of vessels. Now to my knowledge it was believed after their visit to this planet they unlocked the secrets to the black hole problem they were having and for whatever reason destroyed their fleet soon after. The theory, I believe, is they no longer needed vessels, and so self-destructed, or even set their ships on course into the singularity, to stop anyone else from stealing that information.'

'That's the kind of thing we would do,' said Will.

'Send your aircraft carriers into a black hole?' said John.

'Ah, I wondered when we'd hear the famous British sarcasm. Got to say I thought it'd be sooner than now,' replied Will. John rewarded him with a friendly smirk.

'If I may,' said the Professor, politely shutting up the two men. 'I think they saved a few ships and scattered them around the universe in case they were ever needed again. Of course, they never were. After time I think the Blood Princes forgot about them and just left them.'

'That's great, Professor,' said Dash. 'But it doesn't really help us now.'

'What if I told you I think I may have found a hiding place for one of these ships?'

'You have our full attention, Alex,' said John.

'It says in the records, when the Blood Princes returned to the alien planet, it had gone … vanished. It was then said the fleet left, to be destroyed, and that the Blood Princes would continue with whatever their agenda was. There is however a footnote and in a roundabout way it says they left a ship at the star system on a vigil. It was to monitor the system should the planet ever return. To this day the ship is probably still carrying out its last command waiting for the planet to return.'

'The Anunnaki must know about it. If you can find it, so must they,' said Dash.

'I doubt they have read these recordsss for thousandsss of yearsss. They have probably forgotten about it. Not only that, we would not disturb anything the Blood Princes left behind.'

'Let's say there is a ship there, Nilah. Would you be able to interface with it?' asked John.

'Unknown, John, but I could try.'

'If we could retrieve that ship it would help us here,' said the Professor.

'I don't know, we're talking a lot of ifs and buts,' said Dash.

'Do we have a choice?' The Professor seemed close to begging. 'We need any tactical advantage we can get our hands on and if that means going after a bigger ship I say we give it a try.'

'Talking like a soldier now, huh Professor? We can't just leave Nibiru in the hope the Greys don't mount an attack in the time we're gone,' said Dash. 'We've all seen how close the two planets are aligned, which means if they are going to attack, it's going to be very soon.'

'Then we split up,' said John, taking the Professor's side. 'We jump to this other system. I'll take Alex and one of the Anunnaki survivors we have here, and we hunt for this ship whilst you delay the Grey attack ... somehow.'

'Can it be done?' said Dash.

'With my help, Citalicue could retro fit a jump drive to an X50 saucer,' said Nilah. 'But it would likely burn out after the first jump. You would be stuck unless you found another way back.'

'I don't like it,' said Dash.

'I don't either, but Alex is right, it's worth the risk,' said John.

'The X50 can sustain us for years if necessary,' said the Professor.

'Can it?' questioned Cassandra.

'It can,' said Ki. 'Assuming nothing happensss to usss, we would be able to retrieve them later.'

'I'll go with you,' said a deep voice at the edge of the doorway. Everyone looked round to see Kuan Ti, the shape-shifter, enter the bridge.

'You are all better, I sssee,' said Ki.

'Yes, thank you, and I am ready to serve. If you need my help, John, I am with you.'

'Thanks, Kuan Ti,' said John.

'Call me Ti.'

John nodded. 'That should be enough; me, Ti, Alex and Nilah. Keeps the team small and stealthy.'

'I can download on to the X50 *and* remain here with Dash,' said Nilah.

'Impressive,' John acknowledged.

Dash sighed. 'I can't think of a good enough reason to stop you, and if it pays off, it could swing it our way. OK, take what you need. Nilah, how soon can we fit a jump drive to the X50?'

'I estimate twelve hours, Dash.'

CHAPTER 11

The hangar bay doors opened and a thunderous clap of electromagnetic lightning engulfed the ship for a brief second. The Storms of Ion, angry red clouds, warned the crew of the X51 Research Vessel not to outstay their welcome. John, the Professor and Kuan Ti were ready to board the small X50 scout saucer. Citalicue had finished her modifications and the ship now had a large ugly, black box-like section protruding out the back, ruining the sleek lines of the original disk shape.

'It'll get you there,' Citalicue had said when she'd caught the Professor's worried look at the makeshift engineering job.

'Good luck, John,' said Dash and shook his hand.

'We'll be fine,' John replied. 'We're off on another adventure. You're the ones with the hard part.'

'Take care, Dad, and follow John's lead.' Cassandra gave the Professor a big hug.

'I'll be fine. It's you I'm worried about.'

'Look after both of them, Ti,' said Ki.

'I will,' came Kuan Ti's gruff tone. 'You do the same.'

The three men boarded the ship. Kuan Ti took the pilot's seat. John threw the box of ammo he'd had from Citalacue on to the table in the main room. He only had one bullet left in his pistols. Plenty of time. He would reload them later.

'Nilah?' asked Kuan Ti.

'My AI subsystem is installed and ready, Ti. We can leave any time.'

John joined Kuan Ti in the cockpit and settled into the seat next to him. Outside, through the window were the dark, foreboding clouds of gas. 'We going to be OK in that?'

'As long as we're not it in for long.'

Dash, Will and the others took a safe step back as the saucer took off and sped out of the hangar. Within moments it had disappeared into the swirling reds and blues, chased by brilliant white flashes of lightning. After what felt like an age, Nilah spoke up. 'They are safely away.' Cassandra realised she had been holding her breath, and gave a big sigh of relief.

'We need to find out what's going on with the Greys and the only way to do that is to take the last scout ship down to Shalor,' said Dash.

'Let's get kitted up in our new gear then,' said Will.

'What do you want us to do?' said Cassandra.

'Work on a way of getting communications through Nibiru's shields or whatever it is blocking our signal,' said Dash.

'I thought that was impossible?' said Cassandra.

'Thisss isss a research vessel. We will find a way,' said Ki.

'Good.' Dash nodded. 'Me and Will'll head to Shalor … get a scope of what's going on.'

'Do we have any drones on board? The ones you used to keep an eye on Earth?' said Will.

'Unfortunately, no,' said Ki. 'They were either taken or destroyed. The few I had left on Earth are ssstill there.'

'Pity. Hard way it is then,' said Will.

Citalicue entered the hangar.

'Come to see us off?'

'No. I've come to give you these.' She handed over two slim belts made from the same material as their new fatigues. Along one surface were symbols. 'These will keep the gravity of a planet at equilibrium to that of your own Earth's gravity. So, you won't float away or get crushed.'

'Thanks,' said Dash. He hadn't even thought about gravity.

'The rest of your gear is already on board the X50, so you can kit up on your way down.'

'This is it,' said Dash turning to Cassandra. 'Keep an eye on Ki.' He winked.

'We all ready Nilah?' said Dash on entering the saucer ship.

'Yes. A course for Shalor is set. I can keep our heat signature low and off their scanners, but there is a chance we will be visually spotted.'

'Do your best, Nilah. Once we land I want you to dust off as soon as we're clear and find a hiding spot.'

'Confirmed.'

The soldiers started to kit up in their new gear. 'I'll take that,' said Will and grabbed his favourite high-powered sniper rifle.

'OK let's go,' said Dash, picking up some black and green face paint.

'You're wearing silver,' whispered Will.

'Habit,' shrugged Dash and continued to paint his face. Will couldn't resist and took the paint, too. Nilah fired up the engines, opened the hangar bay doors and they shot out towards their destination.

The X50 saucer ship cut a path through the Storm Rings leaving a wake of parting purple clouds as if it were a ship through water. All the while, lightning was drawn to the hull.

'They will be OK,' said Ki, trying to convince herself as well as Cassandra.

'I still can't help but worry,' replied Cassandra.

'Nilah.'

'Yes Ki.'

'We need to find a way of communicating through the planetary shieldsss.'

'I will start to work on the problem immediately.'

Ki and Cassandra left the empty hangar.

'Why can't we communicate through the shields?' asked Cassandra. 'How are they blocking us?'

'That isss the big question. It must be a blanket jamming sssignal as I doubt anyone knowsss we are here.'

'Are ships equipped with shields then?'

'Only a few of the bigger shipsss, onesss which house power plantsss big enough to generate external ssshields around the hull. Internal force fieldsss are different. They only stop matter from passing through and require less power.'

'So external shields are used as a last resort then?'

'Dependsss on the captain. Our hulls are designed to withstand a battering. External shieldsss require a lot of power, but it would allow you get away from a hostile sssituation, if the hull was failing. Unless the enemy possesses enough fire power to overload the shield generatorsss as well.'

'And with planetary shields?' asked Cassandra.

'Then it isss a waiting game. We live for a long time. We have not met a longer lasting race, ssso most speciesss would give up. As for overloading a planetary ssshield generator, it would be a massive undertaking,' said Ki. 'If it could be done at all.'

'Maybe we're going about this the wrong way,' said Cassandra.

'How ssso?'

'How high do the planetary shields extend around the planet?'

'About half a mile above the outer atmosphere.'

'I take it they can tell what goes on above the shields.'

'Yes, observation craft near the limit of the shieldsss will be on patrol.'

'We need to draw their attention and get them to lower the shields for us,' said Cassandra.

'You mean fly direct to Nibiru?' said Ki.

'Yes.'

'But the Greys will sssee us, and they will attack.'

'That's the point. If the patrols witness one of their own ships under attack by the Greys wouldn't they lower the shields to help?'

'That isss extremely risky, and I must warn you we are only equipped with four point-defence lasers. Thisss isss not a warship. Our hull cannot take quite the battering I might have implied.'

'What other options do we have?' asked Cassandra. 'It could take years to find another way. Shalor is as close to

Nibiru as it's going to be. An attack is imminent, Dash said it himself. We don't have the luxury of time.'

'Nilah, how long before you can get a message through,' said Ki.

'A definitive answer will be reached in one point eight years.'

'That's insane!' cried Cassandra. Ki stared at her. Her first role to the Anunnaki was as a researcher, keeping an eye on a species set along the Star Protocol. This was military tactics, this was new. Ki nodded. 'OK we'll do your way. Nilah tell the crew to prepare for battle and plot a course to Nibiru.'

'Confirmed. Course plotted.'

Dash had finished screwing a suppressor to his assault rifle when Nilah called him into the cockpit. 'We are approaching the landing area, several miles out from our target objective.'

Dash looked down on the jungle landscape as it raced beneath them. Swathes of vibrant orange swirled above the vegetation. He realised he was looking at swarms of birds, gliding on huge feathered wings. Their tails must be three feet long. 'Good,' he said. 'Any sign our ship has been detected?'

'No,' said Nilah.

'They probably ain't expecting no attack here, what with the planetary shield still up around Nibiru,' said Will.

The Saucer hovered over a clearing in the jungle canopy. The instant Nilah opened the entry ramp doors, the humid air of the jungle hit Dash. He flicked the rifle's safety switch on and off, a ritual he'd not given up since his first proper forward recon mission. Even now after so many missions his heartrate increased; adrenaline still kicked in; he still had to fight his nerves. Will rested a hand Dash's shoulder. 'Ready?'

Dash smiled. The butterflies in his chest were his body's way of keeping him in check. He took one last glance at the orange birds, flickering flame-like in the distance. Treat the mission like it's your first. Every time. He nodded to Will and the two of them leapt from the ramp and ran for the tree line. Behind them, they were aware of the ship speeding away. They could only hope Nilah would find a location to keep it hidden.

Dash scanned the alien jungle. Trees wrapped in moss. Deep green leaves, a few inches long, dotted up the bark, flapping open and closed like butterfly wings. Thin branches twisted around themselves, creating delicate bridges lined with bright pink flowers the size of a hand. A dense overgrowth of multi-coloured plants and vegetation hugged the base of every trunk. A soft breeze swayed the vegetation and a small creature, thin and long as a corn snake, scurried past Dash's feet on eight reptilian legs. Other creatures howled from deep within the jungle.

Dash and Will activated their camouflage and blended with their new surroundings.

Soft earth concealed the noise of their footfalls. Dash glanced up at the weird banana-like tree tops where moss had peeled away in long flaps. The flora, and scuttling fauna, littered the area in in every colour from brilliant yellow to soft purple.

They forced a path through where they could, at times forced to track their way around an impenetrable tangle.

Progress felt painfully slow, but after an hour, Will stopped and pointed ahead. 'See that?'

Dash raised his assault rifle and brought his eye to the scope to take a better look. 'An old building or something? Well overgrown though. But it has a defined edge.'

'Worth checking out?'

'Well, we're here to recon.'

They clambered through more thick pockets of vegetation, coming closer to the structure the jungle was reclaiming.

Will stopped.

Dash sensed it, too. Something behind them had moved.

Both men spun round, ready to fire. The jungle stared back at them.

'What was that?' said Dash.

'No idea, but ah felt something.' Will scanned the tree tops.

A loud crack from their left.

Again they spun to face the noise, peering deep into the shadows where light couldn't break the jungle's cover.

'Anything?' Will said.

'I don't like this,' said Dash. 'Let's move … slowly … to that ruin.'

As they inched closer to old structure a low growl came from ahead.

A seven-foot-tall humanoid wolf strode out in front of them.

Dark, short fur waved in the slight breeze. A muscled, bare black chest heaved; a long snout sniffed the air. Within the creature's maw, razor sharp teeth gleamed. Its long tongue flickered, tasting the moisture around it. The beast stood on its hind legs, one arm against a tree, fingers clasped around the small trunk. Dash eyed the sharp pointed talons, but what worried him more was a hint of intelligence that gleamed within its eyes. Eyes that stared straight at them.

Dash and Will remained motionless. Was it the humid air sticking to Dash's forehead, or adrenaline fuelled sweat dripping down? Nothing to do but keep their assault rifles ready. This environment was as far from the Iraqi desert as it could be, and yet the same salty sweat was uncomfortably stinging his eyes again. And the creature waited. Some distance away a flock of birds rose into the sky, disturbed by something. The wolf creature sniffed the air again, then moved off into the jungle in search of prey.

It was minutes before the soldiers moved. Both had stayed as still as the rocks around them.

Dash was the first to speak. 'Tell me that wasn't a werewolf?'

'Dunno, but I think ah just wet myself,' said Will.

They picked their way closer to the ruined structure. Will was about to take a step when Dash grabbed his shoulder and pointed at the jungle floor.

A perfect circle of petrified plants and vegetation spread out around the structure. Will nodded to Dash, picked up a branch and tossed it into the circle. As soon as it entered, it started to wither; flakes of dust falling away from it. The bulk hit the ground with a thud. It had fossilized in a moment, literally turned to stone. It looked to Dash as if all its organic material had become quartz, bytownite and who knew what else.

'Let's move around,' he said.

They followed the curve until they came to an

untouched swathe, about ten feet long, of lush green plants that cut into the circle.

'Some kind of entrance?' said Will.

Not taking any chances, Dash threw another piece of branch. It hit the floor intact. 'I'll go first,' he said and stepped through the gap. Will followed.

They walked down an old stone path, clearly placed there, not a natural occurrence. Vines on either side climbed the ancient stone-built structure. At the end of the path, a stone wall blocked their way. Dash's eye was caught by a flash of sunlight reflected from under the damp leaves. He went up to the wall and brushed aside the overgrowth to reveal a black metal door. 'Not even a speck of rust,' he muttered after a quick inspection.

'Any way to open it?' said Will.

'Not that I can see.'

'I'll climb up.'

'That's about twenty metres or so,' estimated Dash.

'Piece of cake,' said Will and gave his assault rifle to Dash.

'Be careful.' Dash propped Will's rifle against the wall and then clasped his hands together to give Will a step up.

Will used the favour and grabbed a vine with the boost. Hand over hand, wrapping his legs around the vine for support he carefully made his way. It wasn't long before he managed to put a hand on the top and started to drag himself over.

About to haul his body up, a sound froze him. Right in front of him, a writhing mass of snakes snapped and hissed. The mass moved as one, rising upwards and turning.

A greenish-brown female face, almost human, turned to

regard him with the cold eyes of a lizard, her hair the mass of writhing snakes. She lifted herself into the air. Her upper body was that of a human woman with dark leathery skin; the lower half, an enormous snake marked with a diamond motif of browns, greens and a hint of yellow.

Frozen, staring the torso as it rose in front of him, Will risked lifting his gaze to meet her eye. She screamed before he did. Wide-mouthed and fork-tongued the snake-woman lunged towards him, arms outstretched.

With a cry of surprise, Will let go and plummeted downwards, snatching instinctively at a vine. It gave way, bringing most of the vegetation down from the side of the structure.

Dash's face was a mask of horror as his friend impacted hard on the ground. Then his jaw dropped in disbelief as the creature coiled its way after Will.

Will leapt to his feet, the rapid healing gene mending a broken rib and a gash on his cheek. The nightmare creature moved erratically as he watched it approach, staring as though in a trance, until the sudden crack of gunfire brought him to his senses.

Dash had fired two, three burst rounds into the creature. It turned as it howled in pain, then raced away across a lower part of the building.

Will, bruised but healing, picked up his assault rifle and was about to fire when the monster, as quick as a striking snake, turned its head and spat. A glob of red liquid sailed through the air, splatting down on a large plant next to Will. On impact, it smoked and hissed. The plant was instantly petrified, the effect spreading to the land around it.

With a quick flick of his thumb, Will switched the

assault rifle to full auto and depressed the trigger. 'Christ!' he exclaimed, with a disbelieving glance at the now stone plant, as his bullets ripped along the creature's fifteen-foot length.

The monster screamed in pain, and Dash also opened up. The half snake, half female crashed to the floor dead, riddled in bullets. Both men quickly changed magazines and exchanged perplexed glances.

'What the hell kind ah planet is this?' said Will. 'First a Werewolf, now Medusa?'

'Think yourself lucky.'

'How so?' said an exasperated Will.

'The myths back on Earth said she could turn you to stone with just a look.'

'The myths weren't far off.' Will pointed out the stone plant 'Medusa' had created with her venom.

'Come on, let's get out of here.'

'Roger that!'

As they left the circle, Dash turned to take in the ruins once more. Where Will had fallen, grabbing the vines to slow his descent, had revealed a much bigger part of the structure behind the jumble of leaves and flora.

Dash chuckled.

Will followed his eye and whistled. 'Bet the Professor would love to see that.'

Dash nodded. 'I bet he would.'

The two men turned and continued with their mission, leaving the face of an Egyptian Sphinx behind them.

Their target was in front of them. A small outpost which had several buildings scattered around a clearing in the jungle. One of the buildings housed a lift that would take them underground deep into the facility. The mission would be to determine the size of the occupation force, how big their fleet was and to cause as much damage as possible. The secondary mission would be to disrupt their communications. If they could stop reinforcements from arriving they might stand a chance.

Dash crawled through the undergrowth on his belly to get a view of the open compound ahead of him. Whilst looking through his scope he heard Will creep up alongside him. 'There are five single story buildings, dome-shaped, four an equal distance apart and the fifth in the middle.'

Will set up his sniper rifle. Through his scope he silently confirmed Dash's assessment. 'How do you want to play this?'

'I can't see any patrols. They probably think they have this planet to themselves. So, we either move now or wait until nightfall.'

'Once we're inside it won't matter about the time of day. We have a clear run at the moment … may not get a second chance,' said Will.

'Yeah and I don't fancy being out here at night anyway. Did you see the size of that tail?' Dash referred to the gorgon creature they'd encountered earlier in the day. 'How's the healing factor working out?'

'I feel like I've been punched, but that's about it,' replied Will.

'Would have been an embarrassing way to die. Falling off a wall.'

'Yeah, thanks.'

'Don't know what I would have told the guys back home.'

'I say we head for the complex now,' said Will, clearly determined to change the subject back to the mission. Dash smiled, satisfied he'd milked Will's slip long enough.

'OK, there are panels on the side of those buildings, hopefully they open up the doors. If this is an old Anunnaki base then we shouldn't have a problem.'

'I'll cover you,' said Will.

Kneeling up, Dash readied his weapon and then burst from the tree line heading for the nearest domed building. He made it without being spotted. But a moment later the door to the central building slid open.

'Hold position. Three Greys. Centre building heading your way,' said Will, holding his throat mic.

'Holding.' Dash leant against the wall, his assault rifle ready.

'They're heading my way now. Move left around the building on my mark,' said Will.

'Copy.'

Will waited until they were almost level with Dash. 'Mark.'

Dash moved around the building, coming up behind the three Greys. Not giving them a chance to respond Dash put two bullets into the first, one in the head one in the chest. As the other two spun around, Will fired twice in quick succession. Both Greys' chests erupted as the bullets tore through them.

'Ah hope our silencers kept the noise of gun fire down enough, but I guess we'd better bring these bodies to the tree line. I'll stay on over-watch,' said Will.

Dash grabbed the legs of the fallen Greys and dragged their surprisingly light bodies into the thick vegetation of the jungle. 'Hopefully the wild life will finish them off before they are noticed,' he said.

'Middle building seems a good place to start,' said Will.

This time, Dash made a run for the middle building and got there without incident. He knelt by the door and brought his weapon up. 'In position,' he told Will.

'Moving,' replied Will.

Will reached Dash and slung the sniper rifle over his back, then readied his assault rifle.

'Ready?' said Dash.

Will nodded, and Dash touched the panel next to the door. It slid open. Will peeked and then went in, closely followed by Dash.

Inside, was an empty room with a glass lift like the one on board Ki's research ship.

'Looks like we're going down,' said Dash.

It wasn't bright indoors, and the matte silver standard setting on their clothing suited the situation best, so they turned off their adaptive camo and moved into the elevator. Will pressed one of the only two buttons. Glass doors shut, and the lift began to descend.

CHAPTER 12

The modified flying saucer blasted out of the high density jump and into a binary star system, one huge star devoured by a smaller, hungrier beast over millions of years. The star map indicated there were two planets, both orbiting the larger of the two stars, and further out an asteroid field. The third, mystery planet was not on the charts.

John and the Professor stared, wide mouthed. Optical shielding through the front viewport meant they could study the colour spectrum of both stars without being blinded. One, a fiery orange, the other, yellow though much brighter than Earth's Sun.

A moment later the power to the saucer went dead. As the shielding failed, blistering white light flooded the cockpit. Both men clamped their hands over their eyes.

'Citalicue said this might happen,' said Kuan Ti and headed for an access panel towards the rear of the ship. 'The modifications to the ship have burnt out the central power grid.'

The Professor shivered, teeth chattering, the cold of space suddenly upon them. 'C-Can I help?' he stuttered.

'Nope.' Kuan Ti grabbed two wires from the panel.

'You're going to hot-wire a spaceship?' John stared.

'Yep,' Kuan Ti said and crossed the wires. One small spark later and the primary systems came back online.

'There is a proper way to get the power back online, but you two would freeze to death before it did. Citalicue showed me a shortcut. I thought it easier not to tell you.'

John looked over to the Professor who shrugged. They probably would still have come on this mission, but somehow ignorance really was bliss this time.

'Most of the main systems will be back up and running. Life support boots up first then Nilah will be back online. We are running on low though so no interstellar comms and we won't be able to scan beyond the local system.'

'Well, we're on our own for now,' said John. 'Where do we start looking?'

'The star charts indicate this is a binary star system, with two planets orbiting the orange star. There's an asteroid field further out and between the furthest planet and the asteroid field a nebula,' said Kuan Ti.

'Incredible,' said the Professor. 'It is most unusual for a nebula to exist like this inside a star system old enough for a yellow and orange star to form.'

John's puzzled face told the Professor he ought to elaborate. 'Stars form in nebulas. Dust, hydrogen, helium, they are the breeding grounds of stars. Nebulas are massive, containing hundreds of stars, not the other way around. A small one like this, inside a system ... well ...' He trailed off, even he was stumped. His first science was archaeology. Physics of this scale was a bit beyond him. 'I say we avoid the asteroid field. Navigating through that could be very dangerous,' he said, changing the subject. Focus on the mission. Someday, if ever possible, bring NASA back here.

'Agreed, that'll be the last place we look,' said John.

'That leaves the nebula,' said Kuan Ti. 'Or the two planets.'

'Nilah, you with us yet? Any clues as to where the third planet is supposed to be located?' said John.

'I'm here, John. I'm afraid long-range detection scans reveal nothing, although I can only get them operating at seventy six percent efficiency.'

'Citalicue estimated twenty percent,' Kuan Ti said, sounding impressed.

'I am picking up a single structure on the nearest planet however,' continued Nilah.

'Would appear to be a good place to start,' said the Professor.

Kuan Ti took control of the ship and guided it towards the planet. The Professor put his nose to the window, watching the green nebula in the distance. Boiling clouds of green gases broke off in arms of wispy string. The whole thing looked like a snapshot on a photo caught in time.

'Structure detected,' said Nilah as they approached the barren planet.

'Can we see it?' asked the Professor, seeing nothing but a big ball of rock.

'The structure is buried under sand but I will extrapolate an outline,' said Nilah and displayed a holographic image on the main console.

'That's an Egyptian Sphinx!' exclaimed the Professor.

'So, the Anunnaki *have* been here,' said John.

'That's not an Anunnaki design,' said Kuan Ti.

'Whatever do you mean?' said the Professor. 'I thought the Egyptian Sphinx was part of your culture.'

'When we came back to advance your civilisation and help the Egyptians build the pyramids, the structure you called a Sphinx was already there. We didn't take much notice as it didn't interfere with our plans,' said Kuan Ti.

'So, you don't know who built it?' said John.

'No, but as no other alien life forms put claim to it, we didn't bother with it,' said Kuan Ti. 'Up until right now, I've actually always thought you humans built the Sphinx.'

'Perhaps the Blood Princes built them,' said the Professor.

'Perhaps, but I doubt it,' said Kuan Ti. 'That said, the Princes did colonise a lot of other planets.'

'Other planets?' inquired the Professor.

'Yes, they were around a long time before they created us. We found some colonised worlds, but there might be many, many more. Space is a big place.'

'It's getting smaller,' said John. 'This mystery will need to wait. Anything out of the ordinary Nilah?'

'No John, both planets are barren and lifeless, and I detect no other structures,' said Nilah.

'I'd like to go down there, John, and study that Sphinx,' said the Professor.

'You and me both, Alex. We'll come back to it. For the moment we keep with the mission.'

'In that case, the nebula seems the obvious choice,' said the Professor.

Kuan Ti moved towards the green clouded nebula. To the layman it was massive, but to a trained eye like the Professor's it was small. Too small. As they got closer, the Professor noticed light glint off metal lazily spinning around the outskirts the nebula.

'My scanners are being jammed,' said Nilah before the Professor could point out what he'd seen.

'Is the nebula interfering with you?' said the Professor.

'No, this is an active attempt to jam my sight,' said Nilah.

Closer still and it was as mystical as it was beautiful. They entered the cloud of stardust and John, the Professor and Kuan Ti could all see broken, twisted parts of metal hanging in space.

'This isn't all Anunnaki tech,' said John. 'It's like ships have been torn or blasted apart.' Floating in the cloud, engine parts, small bits of ship hulls. Wrecks. Nothing discernible as a full, complete ship, mere bits of ships. A lot of ships. Alien ships.

'This is a graveyard,' said Kuan Ti. 'I'm getting us out.'

'Do it,' snapped John.

'I can't.' Kuan Ti tugged at the controls.

'Something has a hold of us,' said Nilah.

A cloud gave way. A huge ship was revealed. Drifting but undamaged. Dominating the bow were two gun barrels, diameters larger than their saucer. A long deck sported rows of launch bays, forward facing, the sort that shot small fighter craft out into space. The top deck was dominated by battleship-style turrets. Flecks sparkled along the length of the hull as the crew of the saucer sailed down helpless towards it. The hull expanded at its lower regions into a box-like section with massive engines. Separate hulls connected by bridges, perhaps just powerful engines. On top was a saucer section that dwarfed their ship. This vessel in front of them was easily several miles long, and bristling with antennae and spikes.

As they rounded the stern, a white beam of light shot out from the goliath, expanding to form a grid as it hit them. They had barely time to draw breath before it vanished.

'My sensors are back on line,' said Nilah.

'Scan that ship,' ordered John.

'Confirmed. Thirty-two decks, sixty-eight point-defence lasers, forty Ion batteries, twelve multiple missile ports, two fusion cannons, two high density jump drives, one thousand, four hundred and eighty-five fighter craft or other smaller vessels, no life signs, various sections unreadable.' said Nilah.

'Jesus Christ!' said John. 'What were these Blood Princes, explorers or conquerors?'

'We were led to believe they were explorers,' said Kuan Ti. He checked, but still had no control of the saucer as they edged towards the ship.

'What does that say?' said John. As their ship got closer he saw markings on the craft. Markings like those found at the temple in Ur back when he'd shot a Russian holding the Professor hostage.

'It's the name of the ship I think,' said Kuan Ti.

'What does it say?' said the Professor, 'The words are not similar enough to Cuneiform, I don't think. Perhaps 'Spear' and …'

'It's a hybrid language, a mixture of old and new Anunnaki. Loosely translated though, you are right, it says, *Tip of the Spear*, or *Spear Tip*,' said Kuan Ti.

'Because that sounds friendly,' said John.

Bright light engulfed them as an oval hangar bay door opened in the middle of the stern. Green clouds were blown away as atmosphere stored in the ship spewed out into the nebula. A landing bay now visible.

'John, I don't believe this nebula is entirely natural,' said the Professor.

'You don't say,' said John.

'We'd better get kitted up,' said Kuan Ti.

Their ship was swallowed whole as it entered the bay. They came to a halt and gently lowered, the saucer's landing ramp automatically activating as it touched down.

'I'll go first,' said Kuan Ti and shape-shifted into a hawk type of bird. Wings wide, he swept out of their ship.

'I shall attempt to interface with the ship's computer,' said Nilah.

'I don't think that's a good idea, Nilah,' said John, but there was no response. 'Nilah?'

'Nilah?' said the Professor.

'Great. This just gets better.' John cursed under his breath.

Kuan Ti appeared at the bottom of the ramp, back in his usual gecko appearance. 'All clear.'

John hesitated but could see nothing to contradict Kuan Ti's assertion. He followed the Professor down the ramp, listening to the echo of their footsteps. The Professor took a deep breath. 'Air.'

'Yeah,' John suspected that would be the case. He surveyed the area, it was bright and reminded him of the top deck of an aircraft carrier, empty but for a long line of crafts, similar in design to one of his favourite planes to fly, an American F-15 Eagle. But these had windowless canopies and were curvier, standing in a row, all made from of one sheet of black metal. The seamless hulls absorbed the light, the wings, slightly tilted downwards built for space and atmospheric flight, with two tail fins at the end of the fuselage sticking up at an outward angle from one another, weapons integrated on the tips. Large laser cannons John imagined. Where the wheels should have been on the landing gear, black claws replaced them. The whole craft appeared like a menacing, dark shadow.

'Explorers, my ass,' murmured John.

A movement from his right made him spin around. He stood still, holding his breath as an apparition of a human woman stood in front of him. Silver, electric blue, translucent. Her lithe body, ethereal. Her arm lifted to point at a door towards the other end, then she vanished.

John stood motionless for a moment. He'd drawn his gun without realising. It now pointed to an empty space. 'Please tell me you saw that,' he said to no one in particular.

'I saw her,' said the Professor with raised eyebrows.

'As did I,' said Kuan Ti. 'Human,' he acknowledged.

'Thank God,' said John and tucked his pistol in the back of his trousers.

'I think she wants us to go through that door,' said the Professor.

'She was human, Alex?' questioned John.

'Perhaps this vessel has the same technology that helped us understand the Anunnaki when we first met them,' the Professor said.

'Ti?' said John.

'Unsure,' replied Kuan Ti.

'I think we should continue on at any rate,' said the Professor.

'Not you Alex, I want you to stay with the ship.' John handed the Professor his spare sidearm.

'But ...'

'No buts, Alex. If this goes south you may have a chance to escape.'

'I'll set up the ship's communications so you can keep in touch with us,' said Kuan Ti, returning to their saucer.

'I would prefer to go with you,' said the Professor.

'I know, and if it's safe you can join us. Besides, Cassandra would have a fit if I knowingly put you in danger.'

'It's all done,' said Kuan Ti coming down the ramp. 'Just press the yellow symbol when you want to speak.'

The Professor reluctantly nodded. 'OK, but you tell me the moment you think it's safe.'

'I will,' said John. 'See if you can get Nilah back whilst you're in there, I'm worried about her.'

The Professor nodded. 'Me too,' he said, sounding glad he could be of some use staying behind.

John waited until the Professor had disappeared inside before turning to Kuan Ti. 'Let's go see where that door leads.'

Kuan Ti nodded and they both set off. Just before they reached the far door, John glanced back to make sure the Professor was safely inside the saucer. Then they left the landing bay.

All was now quiet. John and Kuan Ti had left and the Professor was alone in the saucer. The brightly lit surroundings started to fade and flicker, a pretence no longer required. This scene a mere hologram now switching off. A skeletal arm appeared beneath the dying hologram, a clawed hand reaching upwards as if grasping to a life it once knew. Another skeletal body appeared sprawled on the deck. More and more of the holographic illusion disappeared revealing the real hangar of the Spear Tip, a hangar deck riddled with skeletons of many strange aliens. Everyone had died attempting to board the mighty ship. In the apex of the now dispelled illusion, a lithe humanoid figure in white armour stood, its faceless helm showing only glowing green slits for eyes. It brought two slender fingers up to its long, white armoured, pointed ear and cocked its head to one side as if listening. Its gaze then rested on the saucer, the ramp still down. Bringing its armoured hand back down, a long elegant pistol appeared within its grasp as if crafted from the air around it. The figure moved towards the saucer.

The X51 Research Vessel wafted away from the Storm Clouds of Ion, leaving a triangular shaped hole in the blue and red behind it. Cassandra stood, staring out at their wake, the hole she realised was symbolic of her situation. The only human left on board. Dash, Will, John, her Dad, all away. And where was she, on a strange alien spaceship heading to the Anunnaki home world, Nibiru. An alien race her dad had tried but failed to convince the scientific community were real. An alien race she had no option but to trust now. A shadow fell upon her, another ominous sign? Are all Anunnaki as friendly a Ki?

The shadow was that of Apsu, a planet twice the size of the gas giant Neptune yet covered in ice and water. Citalicue, the head of engineering had suggested using the planet to cover their route to the home world; the threat from Grey attack ever present.

'We are about to leave the protection of Apsu,' said Nilah.

'Nilah, is it possible to fire up the FTL Injectorsss and jump to light ssspeed?' said Ki.

'No. Repairs to the damaged injectors are still underway, but we can get close to light speed.'

'Good.'

They had no choice but to pass Shalor, the jungle planet where Dash was performing recon and where a probable invasion force was waiting to attack Nibiru. Shalor was so close to Nibiru now you'd be forgiven for thinking it a moon of the home world, such was the remarkably similar orbits the planets took.

Cassandra was ready to breathe a sigh of relief – they were going to make it without incident –when from behind a small moon, two metallic, almost mirror-like, cigar shaped ships appeared.

'We have been ssspotted.' Ki's voice held a hint of panic. 'Full power to enginesss, Nilah.'

'Confirmed, full power to engines.'

'Now it isss a race to Nibiru. Let usss hope my people are watching.'

'Yes, let's hope they are,' said Cassandra biting her nails, something she hadn't done since she was young.

'Time to Nibiru, twenty minutes,' said Nilah.

Cassandra's legs were shaking so much she was forced to sit. 'It's been nice knowing you,' she said to Ki, who sat next to her on the command deck.

'It hasss been a privilege,' said Ki.

The ship shook violently as a powerful beam of bright green energy shot out from the leading pursuit ship. The beam burnt along the side of the X51 leaving a deep charred scar, but the triangular design of the ship was no mistake and deflected the worst of the beam.

'Missile incoming,' said Nilah.

The Greys had changed tack for the moment.

The missile homed in on its target, powered by the same alien propulsion technology which drove the Greys' ship, its deadly warhead packed with explosives.

'Activate point-defence lasersss,' said Ki.

'Already on it. Time to impact ten seconds,' said Nilah, spinning the ship around, pointing back at the gaining Greys whilst still travelling towards the planet of Nibiru.

The missile was within five seconds of impact when Nilah fired the defence lasers. Four beams shot out. Despite the missile's evasive manoeuvres, two beams hit and it exploded.

The Greys' ships closed the distance. They both fired green energy bolts. One sliced through the lower portion of the hull, the other missed its target.

Nilah now spun the ship back towards Nibiru and the planetary shield. Cassandra felt herself forced further into her seat as Nilah put everything into the engines.

'Time to Nibiru, ten minutes,' said Nilah.

'We aren't going to make it, are we?' said Cassandra.

'Internal force fields activated,' said Nilah.

'We can hope,' said Ki.

'Missile incoming,' said Nilah.

Lateral thrusters slew the ship sideways. The missile overshot, but at once started a sharp curve maintaining its target lock on them. Another green beam lanced out. The explosion as it hit one of their engines echoed throughout the ship.

'We are losing power to engines. Re-routing all remaining power to the starboard grid,' called Citalicue over the ships comms.

The ship lurched but carried on towards the planet. The front defence lasers this time missed the re-directed missile and it slammed into the side of their ship, exploding in the empty hangar bay. Flames shot through the deck, forcing an exit through the other side of the hull. A gaping hole appeared. Internal force fields were all that stopped the air from rushing out.

Like a wounded animal, the research vessel refused to die. The Greys' ships came up alongside and raked the upper section of the X51 with smaller, but no less deadly, secondary armaments, cutting open the hull with deep, searing gashes.

'All power rerouted to life support,' said Nilah.

The engines died, and Nilah steered the ship with the use of inertia only. The Greys could sense victory and lined up for the kill.

Cassandra was about to close her eyes, ready for the death she knew was coming, when she glanced at the digital window. Three holes had appeared in the planetary shield. From left and right, beams of intense blue light shot out. The Greys' ships vaporised in an instant and were gone.

The holes closed, leaving only the middle one on which they were already perfectly aligned. Their ship silently floated through, and it closed behind them.

Cassandra wiped tears from her eyes. Shocked. Terrified. Happy.

CHAPTER 13

Moisture dripped down the jungle rock that enclosed the dark room. Specs of light danced, blue and purple. Two Greys scrutinised a bank of monitors. A closed door faced them, two newly hewn corridors meandered into darkness behind them. The soft illumination from the screens created long shadows that emphasised the thin cracks that ran deep through the Greys' tough hides, where dead skin hung in peeling slivers.

One Grey leant close to a flickering image and beckoned the other. Had it seen two humanoid figures creeping down a corridor? Its long bone-like fingers played over the command console as the monitors pulled in live feeds from the surveillance cameras. They both looked closely, attention shifting from screen to screen. Then they saw it.

Two figures approaching a door, guns drawn.

The entrance in front of them burst open. Two humans, dressed in silver combat gear, stood framed in the gap. The Greys gaped. It was the last thing they expected to see. The humans' weapons spat fire and that *was* the last thing they saw.

Dash nodded towards the two passageways.

'Which one should we take?' said Will as he dragged the bodies of the fallen Greys into a darker corner of the room.

Dash studied the screens. 'Left,' he said and both men moved off into the newly constructed passageway.

They progressed deeper into the facility towards. At the far end of the rocky corridor a bright light flickered. Making no sound, Dash and Will approached an archway. Dash peeked inside.

A massive hollowed-out cavern met his gaze. Gantries led up and across, forming metal bridges leading to more chambers. He felt he was watching a giant ant's nest. The space was a bustle of activity, Greys strode here and there, inspecting consoles, watching computer equipment. He saw tall thin Greys in amongst the four-foot-tall creatures he'd grown used to. One area drew his eye and he silently signalled Will's attention to it.

Metal cylinders lined in neat rows. Huge missiles at least forty-feet in length. They reminded Dash of the old Polaris rockets, submarine-launched thermonuclear monsters of the deep.

'We need to find out how many of those they have?' whispered Will.

'Let's get up on to one of those bridges and take a look.'

They moved swiftly and silently. The scurrying Greys remained intent on their own tasks. No one looked their way.

Crouching at the top of the stairs at the lip of a metal bridge, Dash looked out across the cavern, and was awed by the sight. By his reckoning, it was well over a mile, an incredible feat of engineering. But, for as far as he could see, row upon row of huge metal missiles dominated the scene.

'Jesus Christ!' breathed Will. 'How many do you think there are?'

'Thousands, easily.'

'What kind of warheads, do you reckon?'

'Probably nuclear, depends on their tech, but a safe bet it isn't flowers.' Dash stared out across the landscape of weaponry as he spoke.

'Would this be enough to bring down Nibiru's shield?'

'Possibly, but from what Ki said I wouldn't have thought so.'

'So, what's the point?' asked Will.

'Well that's the million-dollar question isn't it?'

'Whatever the reasons we gotta get this information back to Nibiru somehow,' said Will.

'Yeah, I was expecting an army, an invasion force. This changes things, let's move out.'

'Roger that.' Both men eased back down the stairs into the rough, stone corridor and began to retrace their steps. They were halfway when they heard a swell of sound that could only be an alarm.

'Oh crap,' said Will.

From in front, a green bolt shot down the corridor narrowly missing Will. Military trained swiftness kicked in. Without conscious thought they took a knee, back to back; Dash's weapon aimed at the cavern, Will focused on the way out.

Three Greys burst into the corridor, green fire erupting from their palms. One bolt shot past Dash's face, temporarily blinding him, as he discharged his own weapon. He knew it more luck than good judgement when he saw two of the Greys fall. Behind him, Will stared in the direction of the exit, never flinching at the commotion behind him, knowing Dash had his back covered.

A speedy retreat was of the utmost importance now. He fired a burst of bullets to supress any possible enemy activity.

'Moving,' said Will and started up the corridor.

Dash fired to keep the Grey's head down and stop it from firing again. Convinced, for the moment, the Grey thought better of fighting and didn't want to join his two dead comrades, Dash began to walk backwards, his gun steady towards the missile room, his back to Will.

He heard Will's gun fire again, followed by the thud of a dead Grey hitting the stone floor. He couldn't help a brief grin. He supposed it had tried to dart across the doorway ahead of Will but instead caught one of his bullets.

Trouble doesn't take long to turn up, Dash thought, as two more Greys joined the one in his sights. He did his best to offer a warm Delta Force welcome and sent a steady stream of bullets their way until his gun emptied.

'Changing,' he yelled, releasing his magazine and slamming another one home.

Progress was slow. Firing shots at any Grey who dared pop their head out, this was going to be some extraction. They were way outnumbered.

Within twenty feet of the room which had access to the corridor with the lift, they paused.

'How many?' asked Dash.

'Don't care. Frag out,' said Will calmly. He already had a primed fragmentation grenade in his hand and threw it into the room. Dash and Will spun round and crouched down to cover themselves as the grenade went off, sending a wave of hot air over them. Dust was shaken off the ceiling above them.

'Move in,' shouted Dash over the ringing in his ears; the explosion had caused the pressure to change. That was reckless of Will, but probably still a good idea.

They ran in, green blasts from behind spraying randomly around them, searing the rock face by the door, boiling the condensation dripping down the sides. Six Greys lay dead or dying. Fragments from the exploded grenade had ripped through their small bodies. Dash covered the entrance behind them. Will stood ready at the exit that led back to the surface and to a hopeful extraction from Nilah in the Saucer, unfortunately grenade damage had jammed it shut.

'Ready?' said Will.

A blast knocked some rocks near Dash's face. He gritted his teeth and fired down the corridor. A Grey stumbled as a bullet caught its leg. 'Ready,' he huffed.

Will felt for a decent-sized gap between the solid metal panels. With grunts of effort and biceps straining, he pulled hard and forced the doors apart. At once, a green bolt of energy poured through, catching him full in the chest.

As Will thudded to the ground, Dash spun round firing a burst at the new threat, sending a Grey flying backwards. His rear was unguarded. Pain exploded in his shoulder. More fire came from the other passageway, the one they'd not explored. Trouble on three sides.

Dash heard Will's yell of agony; was aware of his friend desperately slapping at green flames burning his top, but before he could make a move, Will was up off the floor into a solid crouching position and firing into the corridor Dash had been shot from.

'Alright?' Dash asked.

He knew Will's chest must sting like hell, his clothing was charred black, but the rapid healing gene was at work stitching his wounds.

'We've got to make a break for that lift.' Dash shook off the damage to his shoulder.

'Cover me,' said Will and ran towards the exit. Dash followed, walking backwards in measured steps, facing the enemy and providing supressing fire to cover Will's escape.

Will made it to the lift. The door opened and there stood a Grey. He went to grab his rifle. The Grey stared, locking Will's eyes.

Will took his drink and raised a toast. 'To Wyatt and Shane.'

'Wyatt and Shane,' replied Dash and downed his shot.

They sat in silence. Only the flapping canvas of the tent, that was this makeshift bar, made any noise. Both had a fresh bottle of lager in front of them. Dash grabbed his and took a swig. 'It was my fault, Will,' he said.

Will remained quiet.

'We shouldn't have gone for that mortar emplacement.'

'We were ambushed.' Will tried to console Dash.

'It wasn't part of the mission though.'

'No.' Will took a mouthful of his lager. 'How many mistakes have you made, Dash?'

'Too many,' muttered Dash under his breath.

'And, how many times have you made the right call? How many lives have you saved?' Will stared at Dash, making sure he met his gaze. He wanted to say something about Wyatt and Shane knowing the job, he wanted to say something about following Dash to hell and back if he had to, but he was interrupted by their commanding officer entering the tent.

'Ladies,' the CO said, then must have realised it was the anniversary of Dash's defeat so softened his tone. 'I've got an easy babysitting job for you. Some British spy needs an escort to the old ziggurat.'

'Haven't got time for that,' said Dash. Two gun shots rang out.

Will was gobsmacked. How could Dash say that?

He turned to see his buddy just standing there, gun smoking in his hand. He glanced back at his CO only to find a dead Grey, slumped on the floor, two bullets through its brain.

'You OK?' Dash's tone was urgent.

Will shook his head to rid himself of the Grey's mind. The lift! He realised where they were, and dived inside with Dash.

He watched Dash's hand hit the *up* symbol. With a swoosh the glass door shut tight and the lift began its ascent. He knew this was far from over.

John's gaze followed the sight of his own cold breath, and he saw he was rubbing his arm; hadn't even realised what he was doing. 'It's getting colder,' he told Kuan Ti.

'This ship is an empty shell, nothing but death dwells here now.' Kuan Ti's sombre tone reflected the ominous darkness of the place. As if on cue, the silver spectre appeared, a mix of electric and wispy vapour. The ethereal being seemed to be guiding them through the star vessel, disappearing just as mysteriously as she appeared.

Everywhere in the ship stood slim white armoured humanoids. Motionless, permanently standing to attention for some long-forgotten Admiral. Curious, John approached one and studied it. Slightly taller than himself, it was faceless but for two eye-like slits. The detail on the torso and the rest of the armour was intricate, artistic even, serving no apparent purpose other than to look nice. The helmet had long pointed ears. John called them ears; Kuan Ti guessed audio-wave receivers. 'Same thing.' John grinned. It wasn't until he tapped one that he realised the suit wasn't hollow.

'That's not a suit of armour.'

'Some kind of robot?' inquired Kuan Ti.

'I don't know.'

'Well it would appear they are not active.'

'Batteries weren't included.' John grinned again, although saw from Kuan Ti's expression the joke was lost on him.

'Let's hope not.'

John took out the pistol tucked into the back of his trousers, checked a bullet was still in the chamber, and put it back. He looked at the statues one more time. Something wasn't right, but he couldn't put his finger on it. 'Come on, let's get going,' he said and man and lizard pushed on.

The moment John turned the corner, green eyes flashed within the resolute guardian, her head turned after John. Slender, gauntlet hands opened and above the palms two white, slightly curved, long-swords coalesced and appeared. The robot stood facing John and Ti's direction, long-sword in each hand, waiting. Then in the hands of another robot beside her, a white longbow rapidly grew to full length, the string glowing a luminous green.

Dash opened the door. A cool breeze from the evening air soothed his sweat ridden face. The tree line was within sight and the safety of the jungle was beyond.

'Have to make a run for it,' said Will.

Dash nodded. 'Go!'

They ran. The tree line came closer by the second. They were past the last domed building.

Then from out of the assumed safety of the jungle, a group Greys emerged, at least twenty strong. From behind them, more Greys were pouring out of the buildings. They were surrounded.

'So close,' said Dash.

There was no way of winning this battle, not out in the open like this.

'Drop your weapon and hold up your hands,' Dash siad. 'Hopefully that's a gesture known in this galaxy too.'

Both men slowly placed their assault rifles on the ground and raised their hands in the air. In response, the Greys placed their hands close together. Sparks and then green raw energy balls began to grow.

'Guess not,' said Will.

'Stop!' shouted a voice from the edge of the jungle. 'I want them alive!'

Dash recognized Anunnaki dialect and looked at Will, who shrugged. 'At least they've stopped.'

From behind the Greys, towering above them was an eight-foot gecko-type Anunnaki, his scales brown and gold, his eyes sharp, yellow and streaked with a strip of black, like a mask. The same Anunnaki Dash had seen in the hologram on Mars, the one Ki had called General Kraktus. The Greys were difficult to read, but Dash could sense confusion in them.

'Take them to the holding cells. I'll deal with them later,' said Kraktus.

And possibly a little annoyance.

John glanced over his shoulder convinced he was being followed. And if he was convinced it was normally true. But the silver phantom was ahead of them, floating by a large door which opened as he and Kuan Ti approached.

Cautiously, John stepped through and on to a massive command bridge. Banks of controls and consoles lined the walls, stairs swept in a wide arc upwards towards a mezzanine suspended above the command deck. The colour of the nebula outside flooded its green light into the room through the large rectangular windows. Pillars supporting the ceiling were carved with elaborate designs. John's eye was drawn to a cluster of eagle-headed serpent sculptures.

More of the white faceless figures stood around the vast room, silently watching as John and Kuan Ti entered their realm.

The phantom drifted on to the mezzanine so John and Kuan Ti followed. Within the middle of the deck stood a large circular plinth standing three feet tall with a four-foot diameter. A concave bowl at its centre sat surrounded by entwined snake carvings. The phantom stood on the plinth.

'Who are you?' said John.

The ghost smiled and then faded from view.

'She doesn't seem like a threat,' said Kuan Ti.

'That's what worries me.' John's MI6 training screamed caution at him.

'We should activate this plinth.'

John sighed and nodded. 'Agreed. It's what we came here for, but really this is Alex's speciality …'

Before he could continue, the plinth woke up.

Thin blue-white beams of light shot out from the bowl, creating a 3D holographic image of an Anunnaki man. The figure stood ten feet tall, covered from head to foot in purple light-reflective scales. A massive chest rippled with taut muscles. Its head looked almost human, yellow eyes more man than lizard. In fact, this Anunnaki looked nobler, more perfect than any John had seen so far. A prince.

'I am Commander Yazish of the Ninth Battle Fleet out of Zaos,' boomed his voice, the ominous tone echoing around the room. 'If you are watching this then all has been lost and our betrayal, complete. Listen to me very carefully whoever you are.'

He looked straight at John, or straight through him. John couldn't tell.

'You must be of Anunnaki descent. Our line must run through your blood for you to have entered this ship and been allowed to live. Know now that we have failed you. Our quest for black hole technology has been undone by a race calling themselves the Djinn.'

The hologram seemed to spit out the words as pain etched his face. White light shot from his mouth and eyes. The three-dimensional image of Commander Yazish struggled, clasping his arms around his own body, covering his mouth and eyes with his hands. For a moment he remained still, as though the recording had paused. Then he stood straight, the white light gone. The hologram flickered violently then seemed to reset.

'I am Commander Yazish of the Ninth Battle Fleet out of Zaos. Blood Prince of the first realm. Protector of the Anunnaki. If you've been allowed to live, then you are a descendent of Anunnaki and a friend. I leave the ninth fleet *Spear Tip* and everything it holds to you. With your help we will mount a defence against the Djinn.'

'The Djinn?' whispered John.

'An ancient enemy, long dead,' replied Kuan Ti.

The figure of Commander Yazish turned to leave then stopped and turned around. 'By now your own AI from the ship you arrived in will have integrated with our systems. It will be downloaded and merged within Spear Tip's battle mainframe. Your AI should already have achieved sentience. I tell you this because we found self-aware computers made our ships run better. We made them this way as we believe life is not just for the organic.'

The hologram winced, but the man still managed to retain his composure. 'So, the next time you see your computer, be nice.'

With that, the Commander turned and walked away. The hologram vanished.

A sparkle of light from behind caught John's eye. He turned to see the phantom, the silver female, the translucent human. Her eyes glowed an intense blue, flickers of lightning playing gracefully across them.

'Nilah?' whispered John.

'Yes John, I am Nilah.'

All around them the silent white-armoured guardians' eyes erupted in green fire.

CHAPTER 14

Cassandra stood on ground for the first time since she'd left Earth. Jelly legs shaking, adapting to real gravity again, but the warmth on her face from the sun was like a soothing comforter. A safe warmth, not the oppressive heat from the Iraqi sun she'd left behind so long ago. She closed her eyes and breathed. Soaking it all in, massaged by a fresh breeze, she told herself a secret; she didn't like being in space. This was where she, the archaeologist, belonged. On the ground, far from outer space. Safe.

Ki had somehow managed to land their crippled ship, the dark black triangular craft she'd first boarded back when its autopilot had taken them to the dark side of the Moon. It now rested on a huge platform. On an alien planet.

'She'll never fly again,' said Ki joining her on the platform.

They had escaped the Greys but not without incapacitating their ship. The landing platform had been cleared for them in case touch down went badly wrong. Due to the excellent crew and tractor beam technology it hadn't, but now their poor crippled vessel stood all alone on a massive landing pad designed for many more craft.

Citalicue had left the ship first and was standing at the edge of the platform. Beyond her Cassandra could see they were nestled between a snow-capped mountain range covered in rich green trees, and a large pristine lake. A city sprawled out in front of them. Elegant towers reached high into the air. Ziggurats of the Incas' ancient city Machu Picchu dominated one mountainside; an Egyptian pyramid sat in the middle of the metropolis and from its tip sprang a blue-white energy beam feeding power to the planetary shield. From her high vantage point Cassandra spotted a Mayan step pyramid taller than any she'd studied on Earth. All around her, flying craft as varied as cars back home flew in the hustle and bustle. A dramatic exciting place like New York, but the thing that made Cassandra's jaw drop when it dawned on her was the realisation that the city was built of gold. Purple tinted storm clouds in the distance amplified the effect; the sunlight here seemed so bright against the dark sky.

'Welcome to Manoa,' said Ki, with genuine pride.

'You mean the lost city of El Dorado?' said Cassandra, awestruck. It must be ninety percent gold, she thought. The planetary energy beam added to the wonder, highlighting the geometric lines of the pyramid buildings. If only her father was with her now.

'Our kind may have told talesss to your race about our capital city,' said Ki.

'No wonder no one ever found it. It was never on our planet.'

Citalicue called over from the edge of the platform. 'A delegation is coming.'

The other three Anunnaki survivors stayed by the ship whilst Ki and Cassandra joined Citalicue.

Descending the long flight of stairs from the landing pad, the three women found street level. Buildings lined each side with a main road leading to one of the Mayan-inspired temples, *or was that the other way around*, thought Cassandra. Coming towards them were three Anunnaki. Two males, each holding a silver spear and the third, a female, walking between them. She wore an ornate cloak made from feathers presumably from a very large bird as they were almost as tall as she was. The female gave a slight nod to Ki.

'Come with me please,' she said and started to walk back to the temple.

'So much for the warm welcome,' muttered Cassandra, but followed Ki's lead and stepped in behind them.

They were led up the street and through an open market of shops, flower and food stalls. Cassandra's stomach grumbled as wave after wave of spices, scents and the aroma of exotic cooked food splashed up through her nose. She'd been living of a diet of supplement pills for days. Anunnaki acknowledged their passing, some staring but most just glancing for a fleeting moment before carrying on their daily business, almost, it seemed to Cassandra, as if they had seen humans many times before. To her surprise she saw more than just Anunnaki. There was a tall alien with double-jointed legs and a long snout like a pharaoh hound. It was with a small child, playing on a handheld device, not looking where it was going. The adult's attention was all on its small charge. There was an ape-like creature buying what Cassandra hoped were noodles.

Ascending the steps of the golden Mayan temple gave her an even better view of the city below. It was one of the tallest building around, about two hundred feet she estimated. In the distance more temples rose well above the sprawling city. She imagined this was how ancient Egypt might have been in its golden age.

A square dark blue building sat atop the ziggurat, single storey with four wide-open doors, one facing the steps on each side.

Cassandra stepped into the only room, well-lit by balls of light suspended in mid-air, defying gravity. A long table dominated the space and hosted three more Anunnaki women, one of whom had an elongated head covered with a pale blue tapered headdress that immediately caught Cassandra's interest. It was flat on top with a slight flare rising from the base; a strip of precious jewels cut square across the middle and joined at the centre; a glistening golden cobra reared up from the front. It was a headdress Cassandra had seen before at the Neues Museum in Berlin. The Anunnaki's dress was made from looked like a sheer linen. Cassandra didn't notice her scales until the light hit them and they shimmered. Unlike Ki's blue and green, this Anunnaki sported scales of golden brown, from a distance like human skin covered in glitter. The other two women wore feathered cloaks.

The Anunnaki female who led them here bowed to the three at the table and left, taking her guards with her. The golden-tanned one at the head of the table broke into a wide smile. 'It is good to see you again, Ki.'

'It isss alwaysss a pleasure, Nefertiti.'

Cassandra's jaw fell open again. She knew that Nefertiti's body had never been found but to suggest that the ancient Queen of Egypt was an alien staggered even her.

'Who is this with you?' said Nefertiti.

'High Priestess of Nibiru, may I introduce Cassandra of Earth,' said Ki.

'Earth, ah yes, such fond memories of that world. I assume the Star Protocol has been successful then?'

'No, the third ssstage was not initiated. Instead we were attacked by the Zeta Reticulians.'

'I see,' said Nefertiti. 'Would you allow me to read your mind? I can hear your story quicker.'

'Of course.'

'And you, Cassandra, would you also allow me to enter your mind?'

'Um, I don't know about that.'

'It is perfectly safe, my child, I will do you no harm.'

Cassandra trusted Ki, who offered a simple nod.

Nodding reluctantly, Cassandra gave her consent.

The Sun was shining in a beautiful blue sky. Cassandra's gaze followed a jumbo jet's vapour trail high in the air, the plane no more than a white dot with long wispy clouds behind it. She wondered where it was off to? Australia maybe. Her father squeezed her hand with gentle kindness. They were standing at a burial. Though her dad was typically British with a stiff upper lip, the tear rolling down his cheek wasn't easy to miss. Cassandra was ten years old again. Her father put his whole arm around her and she burst into tears as a coffin was lowered into the ground.

The sabres clanged and clashed until Cassandra made a quick parry and struck with a riposte, hitting her opponent on the arm and scoring a point. Her father took her to his fencing lessons to help release stress for both of them. He preferred the foil, a more elegant sword and a gentleman's game, he'd said. But Cassandra shone with the sabre. There was more sword play and less foot movement which she liked, plus you could hit anywhere on the upper body and it counted as a score, even the arm. The foil was chest only. As the two swordsmen returned to their starting positions on the long mat, or piste as she'd learnt to call it, Cassandra heard her father clap; a slow clap and he was smirking. Her dad preferred chest hits.

'If this was real …' Cassandra smiled. 'He wouldn't be able use his weapon arm anymore.'

'I think his ego is taking more damage,' said the Professor. He winked at the man fencing his thirteen-year-old daughter.

'She hasn't won yet,' said the opponent. 'En garde!'

Cassandra showed her dad the doctorate in archaeology she'd worked so hard to achieve, and her happiness was amplified tenfold when she saw how proud of her he was. She was now in her twenties and bombarded with emotions.

What was Nefertiti searching for? Nefertiti? Wait … she was on Nibiru the Anunnaki home world. She just knew.

Another emotion, elation. Her father asked her to accompany him on expeditions around the world. Curiosity … being drawn in deeper with her father's theories on ancient cultures and their contact with aliens from outer space. Anger. Anger at the closed minds of others in their field, as they scoffed at her father with disdain. Anger with herself for not standing up for him enough.

Pain. She was with three soldiers and had just fallen into a cave whilst at the temple of Ur in Iraq. The discovery of a flying saucer. A proper, real-life flying saucer. Her father could be vindicated and yet she would be able to tell no one. Such a bittersweet moment.

A soothing voice calmed her thoughts, like waking reluctantly from a pleasant dream. Cassandra shook her head as the voice left her. The last thing she remembered was the shield opening allowing them to enter the safety of the planet, saving them all from certain death.

Nefertiti addressed the three lizard women sitting with her at the table. 'Leave us.'

They rose and left. Citalicue turned to go with them and Cassandra moved to follow.

'Not you, Cassandra. You have been through a lot, but I need to speak with you awhile longer.' Nefertiti gestured her to a seat at the table.

Cassandra slumped into the comfortable chair. The cushions moulded to her body, easing her tiredness.

'Wait for usss outside,' said Ki to Citalicue. Citalicue nodded and left.

Once they were alone, Nefertiti's face became grim. 'Your distress call from the Sol System never came to our attention.'

'Even if the Greys weren't blocking our signal from Earth, it would never have gotten through the planetary shieldsss anyway,' said Ki.

'You don't understand. The shields have only been up for the past three years, when the Greys occupied Shalor,' said Nefertiti. 'You sent the distress call two thousand years ago.'

'Ssso why wasn't my signal relayed to the High Council and aid sssent?'

Nefertiti leant forward in her chair. 'For a long time, we

have suspected there is a rebellious faction growing within the population. Some of our people say the Blood Princes have abandoned us.'

'Have they?' said Cassandra.

Nefertiti studied Cassandra's face for but a moment, maybe concluding that she deserved the truth. 'It's possible. I haven't spoken with them since the last hatchery cycle a hundred and fifty thousand years ago.'

'What doesss the other faction want?'

'To make their own way in the universe, to give up on searching for a cure to our infertility,' Nefertiti told her.

'But that would mean the extinction of your race,' said Cassandra.

'Yes, and the sad thing is they know that.'

'Hope, after all thisss time, isss fading,' acknowledged Ki.

'I try to convince them we should continue, not give up. But some of us view things a different way,' said Nefertiti.

'Ssso, my distress call was received but erased, so I couldn't warn anyone else.'

'And now with this new threat on our doorstep, the faction thinks the High Council are weak and if we continue to wait it out with the protection of the shield we will only die a slow, miserable death.'

'What's the plan then?' asked Cassandra.

'I don't know,' said Nefertiti, with a frank honesty that Cassandra had never heard of from any politician on Earth.

'You can't just give up,' said Cassandra. 'We need your help on Earth. There is a secret war being waged between your people left there and the Greys.'

'For now, there is nothing I can do,' said Nefertiti. 'Whilst the planetary shield is up, we wait out the threat. We estimate the Greys will give up after only a few hundred years.'

Cassandra put her head in her hands and was about to protest when Ki came to her aid.

'There may be a way,' she said. 'I can't bring a Blood Prince here but we might be able to sssupply the next best thing, if John and the Professor can find one of their shipsss.'

'Impossible,' said Nefertiti, but she looked at Cassandra as she spoke and seemed to see the pain in her eyes. Nefertiti once lived amongst us, Cassandra thought. She must understand something of our plight. But when Nefertiti spoke again, her only concession was a more tactful approach. 'If they did, it would buy us some time. If ... I'm sorry Cassandra, I'm not convinced they will. Even you are not sure from the thoughts I can read from you.'

'Summon the High Council. We need to convince them,' said Cassandra.

Nefertiti went to speak when alarms sounded throughout the city. Citalicue ran into the room. 'The planetary shield is down! We are no longer protected.'

A drop of water hit his forehead. Dash had been staring at it for a while, tiny droplets of condensation slowly coalescing on the stone ceiling above him. Clinging to the rock as much as they could, until one droplet too many and, splash, a wet forehead. Mesmerising as it was uncomfortable. Dash was pinned to an operating table, and it annoyed him. The more he got used to the existence of aliens who wanted to kill him, the more he was irritated by them. Will was stretched out on a table next to him.

The Greys had taken them to the holding cells and pinned them to these tables using their telekinetic powers, then with metal clasps locked them in place. Stripped of their gear and weapons, they had been poked and sliced. Another drop of water on his head brought back memories of passing out from intense pain. He had suffered at the hands of the Grey's medic. More than once. The rapid healing gene was no comfort here. It allowed the Greys to cut into them more than they could have otherwise. Dash felt his teeth grit, his fists clench. What really irked him was that the Greys had gone about their macabre work in silence. They'd asked no questions of him and Will. And he guessed they communicated with each via thought.

Splash. *We need a way out of here.* Will nodded back, as though he'd read Dash's mind.

The eight-foot Anunnaki shape-shifter with the black streak across its eyes entered the chamber. 'What do they know?'

One of the two Greys who was ready to operate again, on Will by the looks of things, communicated with the Anunnaki leader in silence.

'Interesting,' said General Kraktus. 'So, the humans know nothing about my team on Earth. They are all yours. The operation is about to commence. I'll be in the command station should you glean anything else of use.'

The reptilian left, leaving the Greys free to continue their torture. One hovered over Will. Dash smiled when his old friend whispered something to the villain. The Grey scientist peered at him then moved closer, a tiny hand at the end of a thin long arm reached up to pry open one of Will's eyelids. Both team members had worked out the Greys couldn't use their telepathic ability if you had your eyes closed. Why? Dash had no idea. It probably wasn't much use out in the field. If you had your eyes closed they would finish you off whilst you were effectively blind. Not much of a tactical advantage. But lying on a table here in this dank cave-come-torture-chamber, it was a different matter.

Will felt Grey trying to open his eyelid and fought against it. Then as it bent closer, he snapped open his eyes. Its face was inches from his, its stench strong in his nostrils. With all the strength he could muster, he head-butted it and heard a satisfying smack. The Grey reeled back, dropping its laser scalpel as it reached for a nearby console to steady itself. It lurched and fell to the floor.

The clasps holding Will snapped open.

Dash looked on as Will launched himself from the operating table, landing on top of the recovering Grey and punching it in the head. It went limp, pleasing Dash no end.

The engagement was so fast, the Grey standing next to Dash just froze. *Welcome to a Delta Force style mind game*, thought Dash. It would soon get a hold of itself and Will was too far away to do anything to stop it fleeing the room or injuring Dash.

Will took a different tack and slammed his palm on the control panel. Instruments powered down, the lights dimmed, another console slid from the far wall, and the restraints holding Dash clicked open. Dash smiled as his hand shot out to grab the remaining Grey by its throat. He witnessed the horror in its eyes as he snapped its neck.

'How the hell did you do that?' he asked Will.

'Dumb luck. Ah just wanted to give it a headache, something to remember me by. It must've hit a button releasing my restraints.'

Dash and Will strode to the table where the Greys had stored their equipment.

'Guess they thought we wouldn't be around to use these,' said Dash putting on his silver combat jacket.

'Their mistake,' said Will.

'Time for some payback?'

'Yeah, we need to capture that traitor Anunnaki. He has intel about Earth.'

Dash went to nod his agreement, when the floor started to vibrate. They heard a distant rumble of thunder.

'Now what?' said Will.

'That would be some extreme weather, or …'

'Missiles,' they said together.

Strapping on their equipment, they drew out their pistols and screwed on silencers.

Dash opened the door. 'Let's go,'

They intended to race to a lift, but saw other cells which held captured Anunnaki.

'We can't leave them like this,' said Will.

They raced along, taking one side each, opening all the cells, until they reached the lift doors. Anunnaki of all shapes and sizes, at least fifty of them, slowly made their way out of their cages.

'Either hide or attack, but we intend to help your home planet,' said Dash as he and Will stepped into the lift.

'Good rousing speech that,' said Will.

Dash shrugged. 'I thought so.'

He pushed the *up* symbol.

The doors opened on the ground floor. Two Greys stood on guard. One turned in time to see fire spit from Dash's pistol, twice. It fell to the ground, dead. Less than a heartbeat later, Will's double tap sent the other Grey to whatever afterlife it believed in. Both men moved to the door that led out of the cell block and, they hoped, outside.

'You didn't take any motivational seminars?' said Will.

'Did you?' Dash opened the door and peeked out.

'Well no, but I'm no leader type like you.'

'Really?' Dash watched two more Greys walking in the middle of the open compound. 'Could have fooled me.'

Bringing up his fingers, pointing to his eyes and then giving Will the victory sign.

'What do you mean by that?'

Dash and Will left the dome structure and crept up to the Greys, shooting them with two bullets each whilst still moving forward.

'You like to order me about a lot,' said Dash making his way to one of the outer domed buildings.

'Since when have I ordered you to do anything?' Will said as he followed Dash.

'You do it all the time. You just don't know you're doing it.'

Will hugged the wall and peered round the corner, seeing a single Grey on the opposite side. He shot it twice in the back of the head.

'You're full of crap you know that,' said Will.

Dash grinned. 'And you're not?'

From within the jungle there swelled another rumble

and the earth trembled. They stared up above the canopy of trees, as missile after missile streaked into the air.

'Launch site. We have to get there,' said Dash.

'No kidding,' said Will as they witnessed the missiles soar out of the atmosphere, towards one obvious target.

CHAPTER 15

In unison, the white armoured figures stood to attention facing John, stamping a foot each in perfect synchronisation. Impressive and intimidating, to say nothing of the discipline required for such a feat. The noise alone of ten troops stamping their feet on the metal floor at the very same time, to a nanosecond, was enough to make John's ears ring. He cursed himself for wincing, not the time to show weakness, however slight. Still, how was he going to get out of this one? Before he could react the door to the bridge slid open revealing the Professor and another armoured Guardian. Either the ringing in his ears was disorienting him or the Professor and the Guardian were deep in conversation. It took a few moments, and a gesture from the lithe white figure for the Professor to even realise where he was. 'Oh my! Here already. Hello, John.'

'Alex?' said John with a hint of disapproval.

'Oh, stop it, and you won't need that.'

John raised an eyebrow.

'I didn't mean it like that. I just … well you know.'

John relaxed and smiled at the Professor who obviously wasn't in danger. He released his grip on the pistol still tucked in his trousers behind his back and moved to the side to let Kuan Ti see what was going on.

It didn't go unnoticed to Kuan Ti that John had yet

again put himself in the danger zone should things have gone bad.

'So, who's your new friend, Alex?' said John.

The Professor's face beamed. 'This is Elindarial. He is extremely friendly John. Created by the Blood Princes in their Electronic Life Forms Laboratories, or Elf Labs for short. Think of a drone only a million times better.'

'Watch who you're calling a drone, Old One,' said Elindarial in a kind, soft voice.

The haunting, almost musical sound when the Elf spoke took John off guard. He had expected to hear something of a robotic noise.

'What's your purpose here, Elindarial?'

The Elf's head had no features other than a pair of eyes, which it turned to John. 'We are tasked to maintain this ship and assist the Blood Princes with whatever they need.'

John stepped back. This could be a potential situation. They had come for the ship and he wasn't about to leave without it. Elindarial also stepped back. 'I'm sorry, John, I didn't mean to upset you. Our appearance can be unnerving for some. Would this be preferable?'

The elf shimmered. An instant later an almost perfect human stood there, in leather-like armour with long moonstone white hair, slanted eyes and long pointed ears, skin as pure as ivory. Only green digital irises gave away its robotic origins.

Had the elf misread John's actions he wondered. 'That does look better. What do you think, Professor?'

The professor stared in awe. 'I think I've seen it all now. Space elves! How did you …?

'We control Zanites within us, robotic lifeforms on an

atomic scale created by the Blood Princes. We manipulate them to our whim. Observe.'

Elindarial held out his hand. Within moments black specks started to materialise, racing together out of nothing. A long elegant pistol appeared in the elf's hand.

'That's incredible,' said the Professor.

'The only drawback is for some reason the Zanites don't do colour very well. Black and white is our limit.'

'I would guess the Blood Princes wanted it that way. Your eyes are a vibrant green though.'

'The colour of our power core, yes.'

The green shone brighter, John was sure of it. Elindarial locked eyes with him. Good. That meant he was unaware that John's finger had edged back to the trigger of his pistol.

He gazed at the pure white elf before him. 'I intend to take this ship, Elindarial.'

'We know you do, John.'

'What's going on, John?' said the Professor.

A heartbeat. Damn those green eyes, impossible to read. Another heartbeat and the slightest of nods from Elindarial. The elf was with them. Finger off trigger and a gentleman's nod back to Elindarial. And thank God, too. John had only one bullet left in his pistol. He'd left a the box Citalicue had given him on the table in their flying saucer.

'Alex,' he said in a cheerier tone. 'You'd better see this.' He activated the Blood Princes' last message, and studied the Professor as he replayed the hologram. 'What do you think?'

'Fascinating. Absolutely fascinating. So, the Blood Princes and the Djinn, hey?'

'Do you know anything about them?'

'The Djinn? Only what ancient mythology tells us. They are supernatural creatures from Islamic mythology. Well, I say supernatural ... Obviously now we know they are, or at least were, real. The Djinn are mentioned frequently in the Quran. They inhabit an unseen world in dimensions beyond the visible universe and appear as dark vaporous entities. Sometimes scorching fire emanates within them. The word Jinn in Arabic literally means hidden from sight.'

'So, chances are they have been to Earth before?' said John.

'Given what we know now, I'd say that's a good assumption.'

'Both our peoples need to know about this,' said Kuan Ti.

'Agreed. I take it Nibiru has libraries? I would love to study everything you have on the Djinn when we get back,' said the Professor.

'Looks like we won't be going back to Earth any time soon,' said John.

'First, we have to get back to my home world,' said Kuan Ti.

'Nilah where are we with ship control?' asked John.

'The ship is at full power and under your command, John.' Nilah's voice echoed throughout the ship.

'Mine?' said John. 'I thought it would be under Ti's command.'

'No, John. The ship is yours.'

'Sorry Ti,' said John with a wink.

It was the first time they had seen Kuan Ti laugh. 'You think I want this responsibility? No thanks. Just tell me where you need me.'

It dawned on John the enormity of what he was about to do. 'I hope you know what you're doing, Nilah,' he muttered. 'I'm really going to need your help.'

'I'm here for you, John. I'm here for all our team.'

'As are we,' said Elindarial and he and the ten other elves bowed their heads and stamped their feet in unison again.

'OK, well, you're going to have to stop with the feet then.' John worked his finger in his ear to shake out the ringing.

Nilah appeared in her spectral form next to him. 'Shall we go and rescue the others now?'

The *Spear Tip's* exterior running lights sparked on, illuminating the green gaseous clouds outside. 'Did this ship make the nebula, Nilah?'

'Yes John,' she replied. John and the Professor smiled to each other. It was nice getting the confirmation of something they'd both worked out.

'Lord, may I suggest re-activating the galactic communication satellites,' said Elindarial.

It took a few seconds for John to realise the elf had spoken to him and not Nilah. 'Communication satellites?'

'Yes, the Princes developed long range satellites situated in deep space throughout this galaxy for quick communication.'

'How quick?'

'There is some lag of course depending on where the message originates from and where the receiver is, but the signal is sent from satellite to satellite using high density jump drive technology, then the correct satellite fires along a faster than light data stream to the intended ship or ships. So, it's rapid.'

'Yes, do it.'

The elf nodded, 'Yes, Lord.'

'I'm not a lord, but I do hold the rank of Commander if you'd prefer,' said John.

'Yes, Lord Commander.'

From the corner of his eye, John caught Nilah smirking, and knew he wasn't going to win this one. 'Never mind, just activate the satellites.'

'Lady Morrigan's first fleet is closest to Nibiru. If we only manage to contact them, it'll be worth it,' added Kuan Ti.

Elindarial stared at the now lifelike elves stationed around the bridge giving a silent command through the computer servers and suddenly it became a bustle of moving bodies as everyone found their place. Even the Professor took up a science monitor.

Across the room one of the elves acknowledged Elindarial who turned to John. 'Message sent. I will inform you when the galactic communications grid is fully operational.'

'Very good. One other thing, how many of you are on this ship?'

'Forty thousand five hundred and eighty, not including soldiers or pilots.'

John approved of that figure.

'We would normally be accompanied by fifteen thousand Blood Prince officers.'

'Understood. Take us out then, Nilah.'

Nilah stepped forward and addressed the room. 'Remove all gravitational anchors, plot a course for Nibiru, take us out of the system and prepare to jump.'

Kuan Ti, sat at the pilot's seat at the front of the mezzanine floor and followed Nilah's orders.

For the first time in thousands of years the enormous

ship began to move, slowly at first, then gaining speed out of the Nebula.

The chaos below gripped Cassandra like someone had grabbed her gut and wouldn't let go. She'd stepped into the temple on a peaceful, sunny day. Now the golden buildings of El Dorado were scorched and black. The storm clouds were closing in and the wind picking up. Anunnaki fighting Anunnaki. People fleeing into their homes like scared mice as groups of armed Anunnaki met each other. The tips of spears and hand-held weapons flared with energy bolts, reds, greens and blues, powerful and dangerous. Shooting out, cutting each other down. Saucer-shaped craft slewed through the air, dog fighting, their green lasers shining bright against the dark sky.

'We need to get to the council chamber,' said Nefertiti.

They were about to descend the stairs of the ziggurat when a missile streaked in from high orbit and impacted one of the golden pyramids. The explosion blasted the side of the structure clean off and a fireball leapt into the air. A wave flung debris and shrapnel out, cutting down those in its path. Giant boulders of gold thundering down, crushing everything in their path.

A dot in the sky grew into a missile. It hit another part of the city. Cassandra watched in horror as a plume of fire erupted and smoke billowed tall. Screams of pain and terror overlay the noise and chaos.

Cassandra felt someone grab her hand. It was one of Nefertiti's original three advisors 'We need to–'

A bolt of blue light cut off her words. Cassandra felt

warm blood splatter across her face. She froze, shaking, still holding the dead Anunnaki's hand.

Dazed, blood in her eyes, Cassandra stood as though frozen. The temple was alight with blue laser fire. Was the fire coming from behind or from the right? She couldn't tell ... couldn't focus. Another of Nefertiti's advisors fell. Cassandra could only grip tighter to the dead hand.

'Run!' Ki's voice was in her ear, soft but firm. Cassandra stared at her. 'Listen to me! Run!'

Cassandra let go of the hand.

They raced down the stairs. Then she saw what was coming at them and butterflies swarmed her stomach in a dance of death. A group of Anunnaki men, dressed like medieval knights of old, powered towards them. She barely took in the rearing red cobras emblazoned on their silver chests as they drew up their spears and launched a salvo of energy beams. Instinctively, she ducked but saw at once she hadn't needed to. The firepower was aimed at the assailants behind them.

The fight was over before Cassandra and Ki reached the base of the ziggurat, but dread was embedded in Cassandra's soul.

A knight in ornate armour gave a quick bow. 'I am the Captain of the Guard. We've been sent to escort you to the council chamber.'

'These people are with me,' Nefertiti told the Captain.

'Yes, High Priestess. Follow me.'

The knights surrounded them and led them into the city. Cassandra, Ki, Citalicue, Nefertiti and the last of her advisors jogged to keep up with the fast-moving men. The city around them burned as the missiles continued their rain of destruction.

'Damn it. We need ships in orbit to shoot down those missiles,' cried Nefertiti.

'Our star port was targeted in the first salvo,' yelled the Captain. 'But I've news it'll be operational soon.'

They took a corner fast, and were faced with a group of men with the crest of a swooping eagle-like creature with four wings. Nefertiti's escorts did not hesitate. From their spears, beams of red energy bolts cracked and lanced out cutting down some of the enemy. They then charged, some dropping their spears in favour of sidearms, others reaching for their swords.

Cassandra could only watch in horror as the fight raged. Then a new group charged from a side alley. Outnumbered, the knights were pushed back.

Citalicue grabbed two spears and threw one to Cassandra.

'Top button is kill, bottom one, stun. Use the top one.'

Next to Cassandra, Ki bent down to snatch a fallen sword as two attackers burst through in front of them. She held it out, clasping the handle tight and releasing a red blast of electrical energy that forked down the length of the blade, ripping out through the air. It hit one attacker, sending him reeling backwards as though he'd been hit by a swinging wrecking ball.

But the power of the beam was too much for Ki to handle. The sword recoiled high into the air allowing the second attacker to break through. He sprang at Cassandra.

She froze. A drum beat thumped in her rib cage as though her heart was trying to break its way out and escape. The enemy Anunnaki was almost on her, his arm in mid swing, his sword held high. Cassandra's hands tensed on the spear. She shut her eyes tight and waited to die.

After a moment it was clear she was still alive. She opened her eyes. Her arms were shaking violently. Her spear was jutting through the chest of her assailant, and a powerful energy wave still flowed through the spear tip as her vice-like grip clamped down on the trigger.

The assailant's eyes stared in shock, pain and anger, millimetres from Cassandra's face. She gasped for air. Her muscles eased. And she could no longer stop the spear from recoiling.

The energy beam sliced clean through her attacker from the point of entry to the neck and out.

Finally, she released the trigger.

'A killing move, no amount of rapid healing will save him. Impressive,' said Nefertiti as she helped Cassandra push the lifeless body away from her.

Cassandra felt sick. Nefertiti thought she had done that on purpose. Her hands still dripped with her victim's blood.

Of the knight escorts, only the Captain of the Guard remained standing. Six enemy Anunnaki had him surrounded. No words were needed. None of them was willing to leave the Captain, not even Cassandra.

Nefertiti drew out two beautifully crafted hand guns, ceremonial, but good enough. Cassandra drew up her spear. This was it.

A crow circled above. No, thought Cassandra, it must be the adrenaline. She risked a glance and there it was, a sheer black crow, a silent silhouette soaring down from the sky. The closer it came, the more humanoid it appeared.

A shape-shifter.

Short curved knives in each hand, it landed on one of the Captain's attackers, sinking its knives into its victim's head. As they stared, it launched itself over the Captain, flinging wide its arms releasing both knives, which sailed through the air and embedded themselves into the skulls of two of the enemy Anunnaki. Shape-changing into a winged serpent it wrapped a long tail around a fourth victim crushing the wind from its throat. The serpent's maw opened, and a jet of flame engulfed the Anunnaki's head. The Captain leapt into action and fell upon one of his attackers with his sword and electrical beam, twisting and burning the body until the eye balls exploded in a small puff of ash. The single attacker still standing, turned and bolted. He didn't make it to the alley. Citalicue's energy weapon cut him down.

The shape-shifter walked towards them, putting a hand on the Captain's shoulder and nodding to him in acknowledgement as he passed.

'Aliax, our Queen's Assassin at your disposal,' he said, bowing to Nefertiti.

'We are trying to get to the council chamber,' said Nefertiti.

'Myself and the Captain will ensure you get there.'

The shape-shifter pointed to the dead Anunnaki Cassandra had killed. 'Brave move. Held your ground. Brought him in close. I approve.'

The Captain passed the shape-shifter his two blades. 'Let's go.'

Cassandra wanted to say she hadn't done it on purpose and she had been scared out of her wits, but the Assassin and the Captain moved off in front of them.

Fire was now raining down from the sky. They approached what must have been a beautiful and elegant building. Now, its tall spires lay shattered and broken, craters lined the steps up to the entrance. It reminded Cassandra of an ancient Turkish citadel, imposing walls and domed roof.

They picked their way across the rubble-strewn streets and headed for the stairs into the building. The sounds of battle rang out around them. Cassandra's ears rang to the crash of explosions and howls of death. And over it all, the scream of incoming missiles. Would they be safer in a building? She had her doubts.

At the top of the stairs, next to the tall, but blown out double doors, Aliax stopped. 'I shall leave you here and go back into the city. I must help where I can.'

The Captain grasped his arm. 'Thank you and good luck.'

The Assassin leapt into the air and flew off as a black crow.

Cassandra followed the others down a grand corridor. Dust hung in the air, the elaborately carved golden walls had great cracks along their length. The sounds of war were muffled. It was almost peaceful.

They entered through a massive archway into the huge council chamber. Parts of the ceiling had already caved in. Chunks of stone and gold littered the room. On a large sweeping curved dais sat eight council members, ranging in size and shape, below them a contingent of guards readied themselves.

'These people are with me my friends and they helped me get here,' said Nefertiti.

The guards relaxed. One of them stepped forward. 'I'm glad you're here, Captain.'

The Captain looked around to Nefertiti.

'Brief these guards,' she told him. 'We will have need of them before this day is out.'

'We are all glad to see you, High Priestess Nefertiti,' said one of the male council members, a short stocky humanoid lizard with bright orange scales.

'The Queen?' said Nefertiti. The lizard dropped his gaze to the floor. 'The Queen? Quickly, where is she?'

'She was killed in the first five minutes of the attack. She now lies in state below us, tended by the priests of her order,' said a fiery red scaled female council member. 'Two of the others are missing. We do not know what has befallen them.'

'How has this happened?' said a green lizard.

'You know why,' said Nefertiti. 'Too long have we ignored our people and their concerns. For thousands of years we have deceived them. You know I have had no contact with the Blood Princes. Our hatcheries remain empty and the Star Protocol has yielded no results. This was inevitable.'

'You are also part of the lie,' said another one of the council members, a thin Anunnaki with dull brown scales who looked old.

'I know,' said Nefertiti. 'I should have spoken out when I had the chance.'

'Our city lies in ruin, and it's only a matter of time before the Grey ones take advantage of the situation,' said the female red scaled Anunnaki.

'We have doomed our race,' said the orange squat council member.

'Not yet.' Cassandra spoke up. 'There still may be a chance, but we will have to hold out, buy some time.'

'Who is this?' said the old Anunnaki.

'Her name is Cassandra,' said Nefertiti. 'She has come from Earth in Orion Arm of the Milky Way galaxy to help us.'

'To help us? I know that planet,' said the fat orange one.

'It's a backwater planet with next to no intelligent life, constantly at war with itself.'

'Well, my people are trying to help yours, seeing as you're doing such a good job yourselves,' snapped Cassandra, stress getting the better of her.

'Why you impertinent little …'

'If you finish that sentence I will kill you,' said Nefertiti. 'She and her friends have come a long way and willingly, to help.'

'How dare you speak to me like that, Priestess?'

'Captain, if this idiot speaks again shoot him.'

'Yes, my High Priestess,' said the Captain.

'Is there any way to get the planetary shield back?' said Cassandra.

'No. The pyramid shield generators for the planet have been destroyed, but we may be able to at least activate this city's own shields,' said Nefertiti.

'How do we do that?'

'I know where to go,' said the Captain.

'Cassandra, I can't ask you to do this,' said Nefertiti.

Cassandra smiled. 'You don't have to.'

'Take Ki with you then,' said Nefertiti. 'I will stay here with Citalicue and see if we can't think of something else to slow them down.'

The Captain turned to his men. 'You four with me. The rest of you keep the council safe.'

Cassandra followed Ki and the Captain out of the building and for the first time she saw the black shadow of Shalor dominating the sky above the clouds. And yet another salvo of missiles originating from that planet rained down. Some of these were blasted apart by ground defence lasers, finally manned.

'At least sssome of our weaponsss are operational at last,' said Ki.

'Come on guys,' whispered Cassandra staring up at Shalor. 'We need your help badly.'

CHAPTER 16

Dash spat out a wet leaf as he and Will crept over the brow of a small hill. At the apex, unmissable, a view of a huge missile silo. Rows upon rows of missile tips glinted through the open hatchways. Across from the silo, a flight control tower.

'That must be the command station,' said Dash. 'You think you can cover me from here?'

'Ah sure can. Clear line of sight for miles around. But ya know, once you're out in the open, how you going to get past all those Greys down there? I can only do so much.'

Dash had no chance to reply. Battle cries rose, louder than any beast on Shalor. From the tree line the newly-released Anunnaki prisoners burst out and charged the surprised Greys below.

Dash grinned at Will. 'Looks like my speech worked after all.'

Will sighed. 'And you call me lucky.'

Dash sprinted down the other side of the hill and into the open, casting a quick glance back at Will. Perfectly concealed in the vegetation, with the camo active he was all but invisible.

The Anunnaki were using claws and teeth to rip apart their oppressors.

Will set up the high-powered sniper rifle, nestling its little tripod into the vegetation until it rested solidly. Down the scope, he spied through the window of the control tower, seeing the gecko-type Anunnaki and four other Greys.

'You're lucky we want you alive,' he muttered to himself, itching to fire a bullet between the eyes of General Kraktus.

Down below, Dash zigzagged his way along, stopping twice to shoot a Grey who had lined up its palm weapon on an Anunnaki. This is perfect, he thought as he made a final slide to one of the silos. The Anunnaki were causing chaos among the ranks of the Greys. The few who had noticed him had fallen at his hand. He crouched next to the silo and took out a stick of C4. Wrapping two grenades around it, he popped the pins and chucked it down into the silo. Then he ran like hell for the control tower.

Ahead of him, the main door flew open. Greys spilled out, heading towards the chaotic fight with the escaped Anunnaki prisoners. Dash felled the first with a short burst from his assault rifle. Another doubled over as Will's shot took it in the chest. Another two Greys dived for cover, one letting out a blast from its weapon, a wild desperate shot, but enough to force Dash to duck.

Then, the ground heaved. Greys and Anunnaki alike lost their footing as Dash's C4 explosive roared.

As the blast ripped through the superstructure scaffolding, one of the missiles arced at the pull of gravity, and without its support structure, toppled back into the silo. Brilliant, thought Dash, watching the heavy metallic cylinder fall on to another missile which buckled under the weight. As both crashed to the ground, the payload inside detonated.

Flames erupted from the silos, multiple volcanic eruptions, a hundred metres into the air. Though the worst of the explosion was contained underground, Dash found himself tumbling as the shockwave took the air from his lungs and flung him helpless off his feet. As he crashed to the ground, feeling the crack of bones, he knew he'd been thrown clear of the intense heat. His rapid healing gene would sort out a cracked rib or two.

This was far from over. He struggled to find cover as a shard of twisted metal flew by, cutting into him. The tear in his clothes caused havoc with the adaptive camo. He watched it cycle through all its presets before settling on the desert colours.

Another explosion erupted. More missiles were detonating down below. The ground shimmered and vanished as a giant crater swallowed everything around the silos. The control tower toppled into a gaping fiery maw with a crash that raised a cloud of dust and sparked an electrical fire.

From his vantage point, Will looked on in horror. Desperately he tried to make out what was going on but could only focus on the plumes of smoke and swirling dust.

'Dash, you hear me?'

A groan came over the comms link.

'Hey buddy, you OK?'

'I'll be fine.' Will heard the lie but rejoiced that his buddy was able to speak.

Dash reached for a metal splinter, and pulled hard, groaning at the pain and the ripping of flesh. He was determined to stay conscious and to get on his feet, despite the blood and grime that covered him. 'Where's our target?' he managed.

'No way he survived that. There's not much left of the control tower,' said Will's voice.

'He has the healing ability, so don't write him off.'

Sure enough, crawling slowly from the side of the fresh crater, the traitorous Anunnaki dragged himself upwards.

'I see him,' said Will.

'Explain to him there's no escape whilst I try and get there,' said Dash. 'Nilah we need you now.'

'I am already en route to your position.'

Dash, face red with splatters of blood like a crazed Viking berserker, stood at the top of the crater pointing his assault rifle down at the Anunnaki, who had stopped climbing the instant a couple of carefully placed sniper shots almost hit him.

'You so much as blink, or try and shape-shift out of here, my partner will shoot you in the head,' said Dash.

The threat was unnecessary. General Kraktus was all spent. Having a building fall on top of him was enough and he put up no struggle. Luckily the gecko-looking humanoid didn't know how tired Dash was too.

Will joined Dash. The silver flying saucer appeared overhead and Nilah brought it cautiously to a safe landing spot. As they approached the ship, a group of Anunnaki prisoners met them. One stepped forward.

'Thank you for our freedom.'

'No problem,' said Dash. 'We have to take this one back, but I'll tell the High Council you're here.'

'No need, we have impounded ships here which will be easy to recover now. We will make our way back to Nibiru. We will not forget what you have done for us.'

Dash shook the Anunnaki's hand. 'Take Zofar here with you. He is also a shape changer. He will keep Kraktus under control.'

'You know this one?' said Will.

'Yes, he is the General of the Four-Winged Eagle faction. Why he has done this I don't know but the High Council will find out.'

'It's a safe bet the missiles we weren't able to stop are heading for your home planet,' said Dash. The Anunnaki could only nod in uncomfortable agreement.

The destruction could be seen from space as Dash and Will reached high orbit around Nibiru.

'Jesus, look at that,' said Will.

'Multiple ships have just entered the system,' said Nilah. 'Battle cruisers, with their support vessels.'

'Let me see,' said Dash.

Nilah displayed an image of a three-thousand-foot-long, cigar-shaped vessel with an array of antenna sticking out from its bow. The battle cruiser was flanked by several smaller but no less intimidating ships.

'Greys,' said Dash.

'An invasion force,' said Will.

Nilah entered the atmosphere and steered the craft towards what should have been a brilliant golden, capital city. They all stared appalled at the rubble-strewn streets.

'I will land just outside the High Council chamber,' she said.

The landing ramp extended, and Dash disembarked. The shape-shifter Zofar and the prisoner Kraktus came next, with Will bringing up the rear.

Despite the bomb damage, the glory of the city was apparent. Gold shone out from all around. Fires glinted from the shiny surfaces, giving a warm veneer to the carnage. Directed by Nilah, they sprinted into the council chamber, slowing to clamber over the fallen rocks. Inside, light filtered through shimmering gold dust that hung in the air, as though glitter had been sprinkled over everything.

'Dash! Will!' called Citalicue as soon as she saw them.

'Where's Cassandra?' asked Dash immediately.

Citalicue ran over and gave both Dash and Will a hug, which surprised them both. 'She has gone with Ki and some guards to re-activate the city's shield generator.'

'Can I leave these two with you?' said Dash. 'That's General Kraktus. He's the one responsible for the uprising, and Zofar was a prisoner of his.'

'What about the missiles?' asked Citalicue.

'No more should get through now,' Will told her. 'We destroyed their silos.'

'But you have an invasion force of Greys on the way,' said Dash. 'We saw them in orbit,'

'Go help Cassandra,' said Citalicue. 'Shoot anyone wearing a four-winged, eagle symbol.'

'Wait. Who are you?' said the fat High Council member.

'Earth Special Forces,' said Nefertiti, well-informed from her mind scan of Cassandra. 'They are here to help.'

Will flashed Nefertiti and big smile. 'Ma'am.'

Dash raised his eyebrows. 'Come on, show off. Let's go.'

Nefertiti watched both men disappear through the Grand Archway. She hoped they would come back alive. She owed these humans a debt she might never be able to repay. Then, she turned her eyes towards General Kraktus. 'I think we should talk.'

Dash and Will re-entered the saucer ship and Nilah took off.

'I have located the city's shield generator, and Ki,' said Nilah.

'Can you show me?' said Dash.

The metal beneath Dash's feet disappeared to reveal the ground below. After his initial shock, Dash realised he was standing on a large video display. Nilah brought up a holographic overlay to show detail. A central street ran from the generator. Cassandra and Ki were halfway along, nearing the target building. From two side streets, groups of enemy combatants were converging on their position.

'They ain't gonna make it,' said Will, embracing the video technology beneath his feet. It offered a huge tactical advantage.

Dash pointed to a building that sat on the crossroads. 'Nilah, we need to get on to that building. Do you think you'll be able to hover and deploy the ramp?'

'Yes, Dash.'

'Good. Head for that building. Full speed.'

Nilah threw the saucer forward knocking both men off balance. As they neared the deployment zone the ship lurched to one side. 'I have two enemy fighter craft on my tail,' she said.

'Can you make it?' said Dash.

'Yes. Drop point in five seconds.'

Dash and Will moved to the rear of the saucer. As the ramp came down they both jumped and rolled on to the building's roof. They watched as Nilah fired out the tractor beam. She'd used it to escort a Grey into deep space on their escape from Mars. It was enough to throw one of the pursuing fighters off course. With its aerodynamics screwed the enemy ship veered off and smashed into the side of a building.

The second fired laser bolts which hit their target, blasting through the left exhaust vent of Nilah's Saucer. Dash and Will could only watch as Nilah took the saucer low into the streets to shake off her pursuer. It didn't work. The Delta Force men witnessed an explosion on the ground and saw the enemy fighter craft fly off to join a dogfight further away.

Dash stared over to a distant mountain and saw a squadron of small attack fighters' race into orbit.

'Greys must be close,' said Will.

Dash nodded. 'Let's set up here.'

They crawled to edge, overlooking the side street and the route up to the target building. Will switched his camo to desert. It worked as a pretty good setting here. He set up his sniper rifle whilst Dash looked down the barrel of his assault rifle, picking possible targets through his scope.

'Call it,' Will said, nestling into the butt of his gun.

'Fifth house down on the right, three hundred metres, head shots only, otherwise they'll get back up,' said Dash.

Will took aim and fired. The Anunnaki's head snapped back and crumpled to the floor.

'Fifth house down, doorway, three hundred metres.'

The Anunnaki dodged into the house as Will fired. The bullet zipped across the door and impacted on the frame, sending shards of golden metal in all directions.

'Damn,' said Will.

'Centre, running east, one hundred fifty metres,' said Dash calmly.

Will acquired the target, leading his shot just in front of the Anunnaki and fired. Dash watched in grim satisfaction as the Anunnaki was lifted off his feet with the force of the shot, never making it to the far side of the street.

Dash was about to call out another target when a noise came from behind. Spinning around with the assault rifle up, he saw an Anunnaki with the eagle's crest emerge from the top of the stairs that led out on to the roof. The Anunnaki, clearly not expecting anyone one to be here, let out a cry and scrambled for his weapon.

Too late. Dash's bullets were already sailing towards him, one catching his throat, the other into his skull. 'Contact rear!' said Dash.

Will turned, snatching up his assault rifle scanning the area for hostiles. Seeing none he glanced back and reached for his sniper rifle, when out of the corner of his eye, he caught a movement. An Anunnaki in a building opposite was pointing his spear weapon. The energy blasted out.

'Incoming!' yelled Will and raced towards the stairs. Dash didn't need to be told twice and chased after him. Seconds later the spot where they had just been erupted, the ledge they had been firing over, melted away.

Will reached the landing first. An Anunnaki appeared through a door next to him. He tried to bring his weapon around but the Anunnaki was too fast. It snatched the gun and grabbed Will's neck, lifting him off the ground and throwing him the length of the room. Will hit the far wall with a sickening thud and didn't move.

Dash fired his assault rifle as the Anunnaki turned to face him. The weapon clicked, and nothing happened.

'Not good,' murmured Dash. Then the lizard lunged for him. He sidestepped, bringing his knee up into the Anunnaki's stomach. The Anunnaki backed off warily. Dash's close combat training took over. Feigning to the left, he punched the Anunnaki in its right side. It took the blow, then brought a fist up under Dash's chin, lifting him off the ground.

Dash cursed to find himself sprawled out on the floor. The Anunnaki advanced with clear intent to throttle. Dash let him get close then swung his legs.

Taken off guard the Anunnaki fell to the floor. Dash snatched out his sidearm, but before he could take aim, another Anunnaki burst in. He didn't hesitate. Two rounds saw the new threat drop to the floor. But it had taken his attention from his original attacker.

A scaled hand had him by the throat. The pain was intense. He felt his wind pipe starting to buckle.

A shot rang out. The pressure eased. The Anunnaki lay on the floor, half its head blown away. Across the room Dash saw Will crouching, looking groggy but with his assault rifle up.

'That was close,' Will said.

'You don't say,' Dash managed to gasp as he massaged his throat.

'Why didn't you just shoot him?'

'Thought I'd have a work out,' snapped Dash picking up his weapons.

'Work out huh?' Will watched as Dash changed his empty rifle magazine for a fresh full one.

'Had enough of a rest?' countered Dash.

'Not really.' Will grinned.

'Let's go.'

They ran down the four flights of stairs, found an outside balcony and took up positions that gave them a view down the side streets.

'I count at least eight coming this way,' said Dash.

'Ah count seven my way,' said Will.

'Yours wearing the eagles?'

'What else? You don't want this to be easy, do you?'

They lined up their targets and fired. Two of the Anunnaki fell to the floor dead, shot through the head. The others dived for cover.

'I think I've just found a shape-shifter,' said Will, as one of the Anunnaki grew into a ten-foot-tall demon, complete with bat-like wings, horns and hooves and the colour of bright red blood. It bellowed in rage and leapt to the skies.

'Jump successful. Now entering the Zaos system,' said Nilah, who now stood as an advanced sentient AI on the bridge of the *Spear Tip.*

Tactical displays fired up all over the command deck, system charts, enemy positions, damage states, troop movements on the ground, projected ship trajectories and so much more.

'Situation report?' said John. He was sitting in the captain's chair.

'Missile base on Shalor. Destroyed,' said Nilah.

'Well done, Dash,' John muttered to himself.

Nilah continued. 'Forty-One percent damage to capital city. Planetary shields no longer operational. Grey invasion fleet in Nibiru orbit.'

'A Grey battle fleet has just jumped in, two hundred and fifty miles from our position,' said one of the elves tapping a symbol on her holographic console, sending the image to John's station.

'John, things are going to start getting hectic. I can

inject you with a neural interface linked directly to me if you wish,' said Nilah.

John studied the movement of the enemy battle fleet, split second decisions might be all it took to be defeated or victorious. He stood up and turned to Nilah, who looked worried. She was offering him the chance to be directly connected with her and so effectively the entire ship. 'Don't worry, Nilah. Do it.'

She reached out her soft silver hand, hesitant. 'John, if I do this there will be no more secrets between us, not ever.'

John smiled. 'It's not me I'm concerned about.'

Nilah nodded and placed her hand on John's face. His head snapped back as tendrils of silver light wrapped around his body.

John was surrounded by billions upon billions of tiny dots of light, like pixels for a computer display, only in three dimensions building up a picture of the landing deck of the *Spear Tip*. He could see himself, the Professor and Kuan Ti exiting their saucer. The pixels glitched and raced around, disorientating him until the swirl created a massive image of his own face. It was disconcerting to see it so large in front of him. Then through him a swirl of harmless energy stepped forward. Spikes from the walls, floor and ceiling of the *Spear Tip* launched into the energy. It looked painful. A female hand and arm emerged and stroked the large image of his face. Was this the birth of Nilah? The spikes then shot out at John, piercing his skin all over, merging with him.

The pixels changed again. The dots formed a room from his memory, constantly changing the patterns on a carpet at his feet, as though he couldn't remember what the real pattern was.

'Traitor,' a voice said.

A painting of Margaret Thatcher hung over a fireplace. John remembered he didn't like it much. The pose was awkward and the colours washed out. Other pictures hung next to it, but they kept changing too, one from a house to a castle back to a house. His memory obviously wasn't as good as he thought it was. Though, small details matter. There was a cup of tea in his hand, almost real, dainty. Too posh for his liking. A solid white door in a Georgian style to the right of the fire place. He always had an exit strategy. Even here in the Prime Minister's study at number ten Downing Street.

'That's what they'll call you if you get caught,' said the Prime Minister.

He stared past the Prime Minister at Nilah.

'I'm accessing your memory banks, John,' said Nilah. He felt the urge to continue a conversation with the Prime Minister he knew he'd already had.

'Don't fight it,' said Nilah again.

'If the Russians get hold of alien tech it won't matter, and I'm telling you Majestic 12 isn't as secure as they think they are. The Russians have infiltrated their organization just as you had me do,' John said to the Prime Minister.

'When I learned Majestic 12 had given the cancel order on your first hit, I knew they must have their own operatives within MI6 and probably my cabinet too. Your undercover work is known only by me and a handful of others. Get caught and we will have to deny all of it.'

'I've seen aliens. I've studied their tech. So far Majestic 12 have kept it for themselves. Even the American government doesn't know the full extent. But MJ12 think the British archaeologist and his daughter are up for the biggest find of all, and the Russians know about it.'

'OK, go to Iraq. We'll set up a cover story with MI6 to get you there.'

He nodded. 'Yes, Prime Minister,' he said, and went to leave.

'John,' the Prime Minister added. 'The Russians and Majestic 12 cannot have access to whatever you find in Ur. Eliminate all knowledge if you have to.'

'Only if I have to,' he replied.

The light disappeared and Nilah withdrew her hand. John sank to his knees, raised a hand to stop Kuan Ti and the Professor coming to his aid. Gritting his teeth, he pushed the pain away until it evaporated, glanced up at the Professor who gasped. John saw the reflection of his own eyes as they faded from silver to their natural colour.

'That was more than just a neural link.' John stood up as he spoke.

'Yes, John, it was,' said Nilah.

'Well now you know everything about me, will that change things?'

'You know how I feel.'

John nodded once. 'Yes, I do.'

'I will help you with the dangerous game you're playing back on Earth.'

'If we ever get back.'

'We will, John. We will.'

'Lord Commander, a second Grey battle fleet has entered the system, six hundred and twenty miles from our current position,' said an elf.

'Why haven't they fired on us yet?' queried the Professor.

'They don't know who we are,' John said. 'We're an unknown to them. Target the first fleet's carrier.'

A three-dimensional holographic cube enveloped John and the Captain's chair, grid displays of enemy and friendly ships, their positions and headings displayed within the cube.

'Ti bring us on a heading two, zero, five.'

The *Spear Tip's* massive engines bellowed and roared as Kuan Ti manoeuvred the ship and pointed it square at the enemy carrier.

'Bring the fusion cannons to bear.'

'Target Locked,' said Elindarial.

'Fire.'

From their tip, two white-hot beams cut out into the vastness of space and smashed into the carrier's shields. The fusion beam splintered across the glowing shields for a moment, and then the shielding collapsed. The beam bored into the side of the carrier, cutting then bursting through. Six smaller ships were caught in the forked-lightning of its deadly wake. Multiple smaller explosions ripped through the ship tearing it apart from the inside out.

'Enemy fire inbound,' said one of the bridge crew. 'Second enemy carrier launching attack craft and moving away.'

'Shields up. Bring us about,' commanded John.

The Professor stared at the unfolding battle on his console. 'That's an awful lot of enemy vessels John. I don't know if we can stop them all, even with this ship.'

'You're going to like this, Alex,' said John. 'Deploy the ninth fleet.'

There was shudder all along the ship. The Professor instinctively grabbed hold of his console.

Nilah's soft haunting voice rang out. 'Destroyers one to four deployed. Battle cruisers *Armageddon's Reach* and *Sundering Void* deployed. Command and control frigate *Watchful Eye* deployed. Launching fighter wings and torpedo bombers.'

'I thought this was the only ship left of the Ninth Fleet,' said the amazed Professor.

'No Professor,' said Nilah. 'This ship *is* the Ninth Fleet.'

'Send a squadron of fighters to help defend the planet,' said John. 'The rest of us ... Let's go to war.' He nodded a silent order to Nilah.

Nilah's ethereal form disappeared from the bridge. John knew that she had reappeared deep in the bowels of the vessel, hovering at the computer core, her arms outstretched, her silver body shimmering as information from the computers on Nibiru uploaded to her consciousness.

The humans who had been so kind to her, treated her as part of the team, never doubted her word, called her friend, were now in mortal danger. She would not allow this. She lifted her head as her eyes turned from passive blue to raging red, electricity rippled through her body feeding raw power back into the *Spear Tip*. The Greys had brought this harbinger of death upon themselves.

CHAPTER 17

Cassandra stopped running. Mild stiches she'd had a mile up the road now felt like a thousand needles stabbing at her side. 'Sorry,' she gasped.

Following her mother's advice from when she'd been a small child, she brought her knee up to her chin on the painful side. She caught some confused glances from her Anunnaki comrades. Probably she did look a bit funny, balancing awkwardly on one foot, but it was working. If only her mum could see her now ... doing this trick on an alien world.

Her antics gave them time to assess the situation. In front, the domed building housing the shield generator stood undamaged. But between them and the building lay a torn-up street, battle scarred and smoking. Ahead was a crossroad intersection with a building lying in ruins around it.

Above, a saucer ship made smart use of its tractor beam, knocking the aerodynamics out of one of two pursuing fighters, forcing the vessel to crash and explode in a ball of flames. The other managed to damage the saucer's engines. To evade its pursuer the saucer ship banked sharply and dove towards street level, straight for them.

'Get down!' someone yelled.

They dived to the floor as the two ships sped overhead, so low Cassandra felt her hands scrabble on the ground for purchase, to stop her being swept away in the dust-laden push of air that hit them all.

It had been a valiant effort, but the saucer ship succumbed to another round of fire and crashed in a heap before bursting into flames. Cassandra, still lying on the ground, watched the enemy fighter craft fly off to join a dogfight further away.

'Keep moving,' cried the Captain, over the noise of battle all around them.

They had almost made the intersection when two shots rang out from somewhere up ahead. Two shots unlike any energy weapon on the entire planet. Shots like the ones she'd heard …

'Is it possible?' she gasped.

'Dash and Will?' said Ki.

'Only they use weapons that sound like that.'

Hope surged within her. Could Dash and Will be here, on Nibiru? Hope was enough. She felt the urge to push forward when the Captain pulled her down.

He pointed to a big red-winged demon beast. She froze. They all remained motionless. It was the stuff of nightmares, wielding a fire-engulfed sword. She stared terrified as it flew up to the buildings above. It hadn't seen them. Cassandra took the opportunity to wipe sweat from her forehead, though her hand shook so badly, it was all but impossible. She concentrated on letting out deep controlled breaths.

'Knew I'd find trouble if I followed you,' said a gruff voice from behind.

She spun round and there stood the Queen's Assassin, grinning. Aliax reached out and picked her up. His touch helped calm her.

'Captain, you have two groups of Eagles converging at the crossroads. Two humans are pinning them down from the building over there. I'll deal with the Demon.'

The Captain barked orders, sending men to assist the humans. Aliax winked at Cassandra, then sprang into the air. Huge white feathered wings appeared on his back as his body shifted into a pale, more humanlike shape.

With his long knives held outwards, the Angel sped towards the Demon.

'Captain,' said Ki. 'We need to get to that generator now.'

'Follow me and keep your heads down,' the Captain replied.

Dash ducked behind a wall, shaking his head in frustration. A searing bolt of energy had just singed his ear. The wind had picked up, throwing dust and debris everywhere. The sky was dark when it should still have been light; middle of the afternoon. Storm clouds boiled overhead but the air was humid and sticky. Sweat seeped its way into Dash's eyes. This was Iraq all over again, only weirder.

He rubbed his eyes ... but it wasn't because of the stinging, salty sweat. An Angel had risen from the streets below and shoulder-slammed into the Demon.

'Yeah, I saw it too,' Will said.

Both supernatural beings plummeted into a building, crashing through a window, raining shattered glass on the troops below.

'I think we've seen it all now,' said Dash.

His ear regenerated quickly but he was still annoyed he'd exposed himself to enemy fire like that. He peered over his cover. Four more Anunnaki, two on each corner opposite. Each adept at laying down suppressive fire, energy bolts lancing down spear shafts through the tip and launching out; the beam lasting for as long as the Anunnaki could hold the spear as the incredible power surged through it.

These four had changed their focus towards the other end of the street and away from him and Will.

'Who are you after then?' he muttered to himself.

As if in answer, there was movement from across the road. He saw one big Anunnaki with the emblem of a rearing Cobra on his armour … and then he saw Cassandra and Ki.

'I see Cass and Ki,' he told Will.

'Got 'em,' said Will.

'They're going to make a break for it,' said Dash. 'As soon as they do, open up.'

'Roger that.'

The air cooled. Hairs on Dash's arm stood up as a dark shadow engulfed him. Rectangular ships, basic containers really, dropped in from high orbit.

'Now what?' he muttered.

The containers slowed, just before hitting the ground, and landed. A door at either end slammed open, ejecting thirty Greys on to the battlefield.

'This is going to get a helluva lot busier,' said Will.

Not all the containers made it. One failed to slow and hit the ground with a devastating smash. The ground shook as a small earthquake rippled out from the impact. Nothing was left of the ship, but in its wake the eruption demolished the building where the shape-shifters had disappeared.

Rubble fell and metal clanged to the ground. They saw two of the Captain's guards crushed under falling chunks of gold and masonry, vanishing forever under a cloud of smoke. The Demon emerged, still alive, but with great rents down its wings and across its face. The Angel had fared no better. Both were fighting to the death.

Dash felt the floor wobble. Their building would collapse too. 'We need to get the hell out of Dodge,' he called. Will enthusiastically nodded.

The Captain took advantage whilst all sides were distracted.

'Now! Run for it!'

The Captain, Cassandra and Ki made it halfway across the rubble-strewn street when they fell into sudden shadow.

A huge cigar-shaped ship lumbered overhead, almost graceful in its movement. It jettisoned several egg-shaped pods which crashed their way into the battle. One of them landed on the street behind the enemy Anunnaki, behind the Eagles. Cassandra saw a narrow slit appear in the top half of the egg, whilst from the lower half two circular hatches opened allowing internal engines to ignite. The pods whirred into action, blue flames flaring beneath them, and hovered just off the ground. From each side, a mini gun deployed and started to spin up.

The enemy Anunnaki emboldened by these reinforcements from the sky, fired on Dash's location with renewed vigour. But it was nothing compared to the might of the Greys' egg-shaped tanks. Red bolts of plasma streamed from the mini gun, with no care for friend or foe.

A stream of fiery bolts tore through their already precarious building. With the damage sustained from the crashed container, Dash knew would collapse long before they reached the exit. He gritted his teeth and prepared for the worst.

'Get back! Get back!' cried the Captain and all but picked up the two women dragging them to the side of the street.

Cassandra looked at the domed shield generator. The storm had gathered momentum lighting the skies with cracks of purple and blue electricity. But the thunder was drowned out by the terrifying noise of four frantically spinning mini guns. Two pods stood unhindered at the base of the generator, blasting it apart. Cassandra's heart sank. There was no way so save the city now. The shield generator was destroyed.

'Main batteries open up on that ship,' said John. 'I want a full broadside. And for God's sake protect the fighters.'

He looked on as the elves told the *Spear Tip* what to do. It sounded like a simple command but required ten elves to fire separate manoeuvring thrusters simultaneously. Stamping their feet in unison seemed like a party trick when compared to piloting this beast of a vessel. The *Spear Tip* leaned ninety degrees anti-clockwise along it central axis bringing its full complement of imposing cannons to bear down on a Grey capital ship which had drifted carelessly beneath them. Along the *Spear Tip*, huge guns trained their sights on their target and thundered to life. Blue bolts blasted out, travelling two hundred miles in an instant, and smashed against the hull of the enemy battleship.

The Grey ship's shields flared to life deflecting a few bolts, which crackled around it like a spider's web, but the sheer might of the *Spear Tip's* port side main armaments pounded through its defences and cracked open the hull. Flames sparked up and were gone in an instant as the oxygen that fuelled the fire was sucked out into space, along with any hope of the battleship being useful in this battle. John wasn't about to finish off a helpless crew. He needed a more immediate threat to aim at. 'Give me a report, Elindarial.'

'Armageddon's Reach has engaged the enemy. Sundering Void in fire support.'

John pointed at a grid reference inside his holographic cube and the image expanded showing him real time telemetry. His link with Nilah gave him complete knowledge of the ship's systems. Armageddon's Reach had launched its small host of support fighters in answer to a squadron of enemy torpedo bombers. Even with knowledge of how these Blood Prince ships worked, it was difficult to make out how things were going through all the laser bolts and missiles flashing around as the two sides clashed. For as powerful as they were, John could tell the odds were stacked heavily against them.

'There are two hundred and twenty-four enemy capital ships, John,' said Nilah.

'You reading my mind again, Nilah?'

'I'm afraid I can't help it. Most of the enemy fleet is heading towards Nibiru, but three cruisers have broken off to form up on another battleship heading our way.'

John studied the battleship schematics. Shaped like a rugby ball, it was covered in rows of large guns stacked along the length of its hull. Formidable to say the least, but he'd already crippled one. Still, this one had cruiser support now.

'Request from Squadron Thirty-One to engage enemy fleet,' said one of the elves.

John expanded another grid, focused in on the twenty torpedo bombers hanging away from the battle in relatively safe space. 'Negative, await my go signal. Alex? Contact our destroyers. They've got the cruisers. We'll worry about that battleship.'

The Professor's knowledge of Cuneiform had been invaluable when they'd found this ship and now with Elindarial's help the Professor had all but mastered the *Spear Tip's* communication system.

The four destroyers moved to intercept the three cruisers and launched a salvo of long range missiles, a total of sixty streaked towards the enemy. The cruiser's point-defence lasers, both powerful and efficient, ripped through the missiles, destroying more than half, whilst close support fighters took out all but two which detonated on impact with one of the cruiser's shields.

The enemy ship found itself enveloped in a cloud of

tiny zanites, microscopic robots designed for one purpose, to eat away a shield. The shields flickered. Rippling, on and off. On board a destroyer, the space elf Captain targeted the computer core of the enemy ship, timed the volley of its forward armament to coincide with the flickering shields and fired.

With pinpoint accuracy, the volley hit a single area decimating the outer hull and pierced into the ship.

Within the command and control frigate *Watchful Eye*, an elf monitored the situation and noted the damage to the enemy cruiser's computer core. Using the powerful mainframe of the old Blood Princes' frigate she began to hack the enemy computer, dropping the security walls one after the other, working as fast as she could, knowing time was short and this was a rare opportunity. Only the joint skill of the other captains had made it possible.

'Watchful Eye has hacked the mainframe on one of the enemy cruisers,' cried the Professor, surprised and awed. 'The cruiser is lowering its shield and firing on its own side!'

John watched as the Greys were forced to destroy one of their own ships, moving out of position from the battleship they were escorting. From the melee of fighters two squadrons broke through and headed for the enemy battleship. John tapped a hologram of the elven squadron leader's ship to listen in.

'All wings align. Primary target on your screens.'

'Targeting input request accepted.'

'Enemy countermeasures active. We need a way through these mines.'

'Sundering Void accepts the challenge.'

John expanded the view further, as the battle cruiser

Sundering Void joined the fray and launched a withering volley of blasts clearing a way for the fighters.

As the first fighter cleared the minefield, the enemy battleships defences sprang to life. Three fighters were destroyed, but the rest were upon it.

'This is squadron leader to *Spear Tip*. We're targeting the shield cells now.'

The Greys' battleship hadn't forgotten the *Spear Tip*. It fired all the weapons it could, thumping the flagship.

'Nilah?' said John.

'Fusion cannon at thirty three percent Tritium and Deuterium levels.'

'That'll have to do.' John felt a moment's amazement that he knew what Nilah was talking about. 'Ti get us into a closer firing position. I want to hit him as hard we can. Once the fusion cannon is depleted, pull right up alongside them and bring our starboard guns to bear.'

The *Spear Tip* closed on the enemy battleship and fired its powerful forward-mounted beam cannon. White hot fusion blasts lit the darkness and almost took down the enemy shields before the cannons ran dry.

Kuan Ti engaged the rear thrusters, lurching the *Spear Tip* forward.

A hail of counter fire blasted the *Spear Tip* as she moved. This must work, thought John.

More and more of the main battery cannons flared to life as they were brought to bear on the enemy ship. Secondary armaments from both ships spat searing hot energy bolts at each other.

Then finally the battleship's shields failed under the torrent of *Spear Tip's* rain of death.

The fighters, who had been waiting for this, raced

towards their primary target, missile after missile hitting the same place.

'Squadron Thirty-One, you are a go. Remove that battleship from my space.'

'Acknowledged Lord Commander.'

'Elindarial, concentrate fire on the two remaining cruisers.'

The twenty bombers of Squadron Thirty-One carrying high yield torpedoes accelerated to beyond light speed and, at almost point blank range, unloaded their deadly cargo. Some torpedoes were shot down by point-defence lasers, but nowhere near enough and they impacted all along the ship. Blinding bright flashes tore the craft to pieces as the warheads detonated inside the rugby-ball-shaped vessel.

As the battleship was destroyed, the *Spear Tip* turned to face the two cruisers.

John had to admire the enemy Captains, for the two cruisers turned and sped towards the *Spear Tip* and, with undiluted anger, opened in revenge. Laser bolts scorched his mighty ship, but the shields held firm. 'Return fire,' he ordered.

'The Galactic Communications network is up at last,' said the Professor, looking at his console.

'Excellent!'

'But another enemy fleet has entered the system.'

'That's a tad inconvenient,' said John.

Elindarial turned to the Professor. The Professor shrugged. 'British understatement.'

'Use the Galactic Comms. Hail all available Anunnaki ships wherever they may be. Tell them their home world is under attack by the Greys.'

'Already done,' said the Professor. Elindarial gave him a nod. The space elf seemed impressed with the Professor's robotic efficiency.

'Show me the new fleet,' said John. His holographic displayed changed, showing a huddle of enemy ships. One stood out, a cruiser identical to the others except for extra armour plating.

'Nilah, scan that ship.'

'John, it's a biological weapon, origin unknown.'

'They're going to fly into the planet,' said the Professor, worry etched on his face.

'Look how they are configured,' said Nilah. 'That ship is in the middle. It intends to get to Nibiru.'

'All ships to Nibiru maximum speed. Ti engage the FTL Injectors.'

Dash grabbed Will's vest and helped haul him out of the rubble. It was all about survival now. They must team up with Cassandra and Ki.

He looked out across the intersection. The Angel was stuck between the Demon and a Grey attack pod. With mechanical precision, the mini guns turned and clunked into place, aiming at the Angel. The Demon came up behind him, its sword ready to thrust.

Instinctively, Dash went to call out a warning, for what little good it would do, then stopped on a gasp. The Angel leapt high in the air. The Grey pilot in the pod tank opened up the full might of its mini guns. He narrowly missed the Angel, but ripped the Demon to shreds.

'We gotta go for it,' said Dash.

Will nodded, setting up the sniper rifle. 'I'll cover you.'

'On your mark.'

Will lined up the sniper rifle on the Grey pod. 'Mark!'

Dash raced into the open. The Angel flying high above threw both his knives at the Pod. The Grey ignored the Angel, electrical discharge from the knives not troubling the Pod's armour. The pilot lined up on Dash. The mini guns once again clunking into position.

Will zoomed in the scope. He saw the pilot's eyes through the small slit and fired. A high-velocity bullet whistled across the battlefield true to its mark, instantly killing the Grey. The pod, with no one to control it, remained motionless.

Will grabbed the sniper rifle and started to run, vaulting over a small ruined wall and out into the street.

Dash made it to the other side and skidded to a halt, turning to see Will sprinting across the street. Then to his dismay, he saw the pods that had destroyed the shield generator fire at his buddy.

'Covering fire!' he yelled, and fired his own rifle at one of the pods. Sparks flew as his bullets ricocheted. The three remaining Anunnaki along with Cassandra and Ki added their fire power but the weaponry bounced harmlessly off the attack pods armour.

Red energy bolts ripped up the ground around Will. One glanced off his leg making him stumble, then fall. He dropped his sniper rifle, whipped out his sidearm and let off of a few shots. Then, horrified, he watched one of the pods launch a small missile. The deadly projectile wobbled in the air as it found its target, then streaked towards him.

Dash watched as the missile struck the ground, missing Will but lifting him off the ground in a shower of debris, and throwing him several metres to land with a sickening crunch.

'Will!' cried Ki and ran out into the street, oblivious to danger.

'Wait!' shouted Dash and moved out, firing at the pods to give them another target.

The Angel flew down to the motionless pod, threw out the lifeless pilot, and shape-shifted into a small boy who grabbed the controls and aimed squarely at one of the other pods.

Seeing what the Aliax was up to, the Captain and his men fanned out, firing at the pods, distracting the enemy from the real threat of the Queen's Assassin.

'Air support inbound, your location, five seconds,' came Nilah's voice over their comms.

'Friendly in the field,' Dash called back. He didn't want the Angel shot at.

'Affirmative,' replied Nilah.

'Wait ... Nilah?' It dawned on him. He thought he'd lost her when their saucer had been shot down.

The Queen's Assassin spat a barrage of laser bolts at the enemy pods, damaging them both.

They spun up their mini guns, taking aim at the assassin's pod, an easy slaughter now they'd identified the threat.

'Down!' yelled Dash, as he heard airborne fighter crafts.

Everyone dived to the floor as fighters came in low over their heads, strafing the pods with their cannons, blowing them apart. As they rose into the air they split into two groups and came in low again this time strafing the two side streets. Dash could hear explosions as more of the enemy were hit. He watched as the fighters reached the intersection and barrel rolled, narrowly crossing each other.

His thoughts were on his fallen comrade.

It was Ki who reached Will first, lifting his lifeless head on to her lap. His skin was charred and burnt, and remained so. The healing gene no longer worked its magic. Cassandra's face was already wet with tears when Dash reached them.

The Captain of the Guard set up a perimeter around the group, whilst Aliax took the pod away, looking to avenge the death of a fallen human.

Dash looked down at Will. He had seen dead soldiers before, but this soldier, this man, his closest friend, his brother. It took all his willpower not to cry, yet a single tear made it through.

Then Ki opened her mouth wide revealing two sharp snake-like fangs.

CHAPTER 18

The *Spear Tip* slowed three hundred miles above Nibiru, flanked by her support vessels which took up defensive positions. Twin planet Shalor loomed close. John took stock of the tactical displays.

'It's a full-scale invasion,' said the Professor, staring past the view port, his eyes as wide as John had ever seen.

'Cassandra is OK,' John said, in his best reassuring tone.

'The wing of fighters we sent when we arrived in this system have confirmed human sightings,' said Nilah appearing on the bridge close to John.

'*We* might not be OK though,' said Kuan Ti from the pilot's chair on the mezzanine above John.

Six Grey battleships had stopped their orbital bombardment. They turned to engage John and the *Spear Tip*, and were flanked by eight super quick corvettes and ten more cruisers. It was enough to cause a serious problem.

'The Greys underestimated us before,' said John. 'They won't this time.'

The two Grey fleets entered the contested space along with the remnants of the first. The prize was Nibiru, the Anunnaki home world.

'We make our stand here,' said John. 'This is the line the bio weapon does not cross.'

'It's the right thing to do,' said the Professor.

'It's the Human thing to do,' from Nilah.

'Elindarial, could you please take a battalion down to the planet, find Dash and protect the Capital?'

The elf nodded and left the bridge. John ignored his holographic cube and looked beyond the main view port at the space battle above Nibiru. Friendly defence forces were badly under-powered but putting up a valiant fight. Multi-coloured beams of light played out in front of him, occasionally a bright flare marked the destruction of a ship.

'Orders?' asked Kuan Ti.

John studied the tactical displays. '*Armageddon's Reach* and *Sundering Void* intercept those cruisers. Destroyers, I want those battleships disabled. *Watchful Eye*, you're going to have to get your hands dirty and engage their carrier group. We'll take on the Bio Ship.'

John felt a slight twitch on his left shoulder, like a brief shock of static electricity. It was Nilah's hand. He caught her eye. Was it worry he saw?

'And Alex … Give the order to launch all remaining fighters.'

His orders were obeyed without question or hesitation. A thousand *Spear Tip* fighters fanned out in an arrowhead. The tip of the spear, thought John as he watched the two sides meet a hailstorm of missiles and energy weapons.

'Lord Commander, *Watchful Eye* has engaged the enemy carrier fleet.'

Watchful Eye, the brave little frigate, just a small blip on his display compared to the mighty Grey carrier vessel.

'Permission to help *Watchful Eye*?' came a voice over the comms.

John smiled as he murmured, 'Permission granted, Wing Commander,' to the request that was clearly a formality. The hologram already showed torpedoes streaking out from at least twenty of Squadron Thirty-One's ships. The rest of the wing of over a hundred bombers followed suit as he watched. He liked their squadron leader.

John switched his view to the corvettes in front. Green beams of light added to the bright fireworks over Nibiru. Energy surged out. The shields flickered and rippled as they absorbed the fire power, but he could see them weakening. Grey fighter craft whizzed past the corvettes and engaged fighters from the *Spear Tip*.

John fell back into his seat. The *Spear Tip* had physically shaken when missiles from the corvettes slammed through its shields. John caught the Professor's eye.

'We're just going to have to plough on through this lot,' he said through gritted teeth. The *Spear Tip* was a big ship, a massive ship, but was it big enough to withstand this?

'Strike cruisers have turned to intercept our destroyers,' called out an elf.

'Destroyer zero one, shields down to sixty five percent. The other one down to fifty five percent,' said the Professor.

'*Sundering Void* has broken engagement to pursue the strike cruisers,' called out the elf again.

'Should we open fire on the cruisers?' said the Professor.

'Negative. The Captains know what they're doing.'

'But John, they'll be destroyed.'

'No, they won't. If we open fire on the enemy now, we'll split their formation. I don't want that and neither do our destroyers. We can help with the battleships though.' John switched his comms to address the crew directly. 'Gunners, concentrate fire on those battleships.'

The enemy strike cruisers sensed an impending victory and launched a barrage of missiles. The point-defence lasers engaged. Lightning-fast laser bolts ripped the incoming missiles apart. John saw the Professor's amazement, in truth he shared it, as they watched each dot wink out on the holographic screen.

'They are ignoring the *Sundering Void* and its fighter wings,' said Kuan Ti.

'Of course they are,' said John. 'They want to protect the battleships from our destroyers.'

As if hearing him, the strike cruisers fired their destructive beam weapons. They drained the shield on their target destroyer and ripped into its hull. The destroyers were now upon their foe, sailing silently, one enemy ship between them and two to either side.

John smiled and murmured, 'Open fire, guys.'

Sundering Void's fighter wings peeled off, cut power to their engines and swivelled, letting inertia carry them down the length of the two outer strike cruisers. Their weapons roared to life. As the fighters strafed the hulls, the destroyers gave each enemy ship a broadside at point blank range. Raw power ripped apart the enemy hulls. Gashes opened where high-yield missiles slammed into them.

By the time the destroyers had passed, the enemy strike cruisers were shieldless, floating hulks of debris ready for *Sundering Void* to finish off. The battle cruiser left nothing of the enemy before it headed out in support of the ever-valiant *Watchful Eye*.

'Our destroyers lured them in,' said the Professor.

'Now it's our turn,' replied John.

An Anunnaki pilot, flying a smaller, fighter variant of the saucer ship, lined up an attack run on a cigar-shaped Grey battle cruiser. A hopeless gesture, most of his squadron were dead, but in defence of his home world, he would give his life.

To his surprise, eight black fighter ships appeared. Marked only with a *Spear Tip* emblem on their swept-back wings, they formed up on either side of him.

He banked left and started his attack run. The mystery fighters banked with him. A shower of defensive fire shot out from the enemy cruiser, taking out one of them. Then they were upon it. As the Anunnaki fired, raking the top of the hull, the black fighters also fired.

Bay doors opened underneath them, missiles launched from each ship and slammed into the cruiser. Multiple fires sprang up along its upper hull.

It banked away in a graceful arc, but the fighters followed its every move. With growing optimism, the Anunnaki lined up for another attack run. Five larger black ships, with that same *Spear Tip* emblem, raced past down towards the planet.

His comms unexpectedly crackled to life. 'This is the battle cruiser *Armageddon's Reach*. Your ship is damaged. Please dock in bay six. Another fighter is waiting for you.'

He turned to see flash after flash of blue bolts slam into the Grey's ship, then banked away, followed by his escort of black fighters. With renewed hope he headed for his saviour.

Ki sank her fangs into a vein extruding from Will's neck. Dash wiped the tear from his eye, spreading dirt and grime across his face. So wrapped up in what Ki was doing, he ignored the gun fight going on around them.

The Captain knew his business and kept a safe perimeter around the humans.

The burns on Will's faced slowly ... minutely ... began to heal. His eyes opened.

'What'd I miss?' he croaked, looking up at the beautiful lizard woman.

'What just happened?' gasped Cassandra.

'I injected him with a ssstronger dose of healing.' Ki's fangs, dripping with blood and clear mucus, started to retract.

'We need to be more careful,' said Will softly, feeling at the two needle-like holes in his neck.

Ki lowered her head and kissed Will on the lips, then abruptly pulled away not meeting anyone's eye. Will, though for once speechless, managed a big smile.

'If I knew that's what it would take to shut you up, I'd have kissed you myself a long time ago,' said Dash.

'Time to go.' The Captain ordered two of his men to help Will.

'Captain,' Dash acknowledged. He could appreciate rank on any world. 'Where to?'

Cassandra grasped Dash's hand. 'We need to go back to the council. We've failed to protect the city's shield generator.'

'Report,' said John.

'Group One are currently engaging the enemy carrier group,' the Professor called out. 'They … um … they …' He stuttered, searching for information. 'They're winning but have taken heavy damage. The *Sundering Void's* shields are OK. No, sorry … *Sundering Void's* shields have completely failed. One destroyer's dead in space. Two crippled but still fighting … um …'

John knew the Professor was doing a remarkable job operating the communications system of this ancient ship. But now was not the time for delay. Perhaps an elf should take over.

'Alex!' he demanded.

'Um … Group Two has fared a little better. *Armageddon's Reach* has crippled four enemy cruisers. It's holding position should we fail. One hundred and forty-seven fighters out of action,' the Professor gabbled out and fell silent with a huge sigh.

'Bio Ship coming into range,' said Kuan Ti.

They were outnumbered, outgunned, and now surrounded.

'Keep ploughing, Ti,' said John, immediately cursing himself for sounding so lacklustre.

Kuan Ti nodded. The Professor leaned back in his chair.

John glanced up at Nilah. 'You'll think of something,' she whispered.

'Four enemy cruisers on intercept course,' from one of the bridge elves. 'Bio Ship taking evasive action, trying to get out of weapons range. Six escort vessels following it. Enemy fighters attempting to break out of the dogfight.'

'Enemy battleship has just jumped into the system,' called another elf. 'Wait! Make that two.'

'Oh dear, this just gets worse,' mumbled the Professor.

'Fusion cannons at one hundred percent,' intoned Nilah.

Enemy battleships and four cruisers fired everything they had. The *Spear Tip's* shields erupted in a fiery glow, and drained at an alarming rate.

'Bring us around,' commanded John. 'Lock fusion cannons on to the Bio Ship. Main cannons return fire on the lead battleship.'

As the *Spear Tip* swung towards the Bio Ship, the enemy cruisers launched a volley of missiles. John watched their point-defence lasers lash out at the oncoming projectiles. Most were destroyed, but a few streaked through, impacting on the shields that erupted in brief fireballs before the cold vacuum of space extinguished the flames.

'The Bio Ship is getting away,' said Nilah. 'Shields to forty percent. Enemy battleship shields collapsing.'

'Keep on the Bio Ship. More power to thrusters,' ordered John.

The *Spear Tip's* thrusters ignited at maximum power, slewing the massive ship around. But there ahead of them, the Bio Ship came into view.

'Target Locked.'

'Fire!'

Fusion cannons blasted out across the void. John stared intently as they smashed into the Bio Ship's shield.

'Enemy shields to eighty percent and falling,' said an elf from one of the bridge consoles. 'Seventy percent … sixty percent …'

'Keep it up.'

'Rerouting power from auxiliary engine output to fusion chamber,' said Nilah.

John expanded the sector in his cube. Tactical data streamed in front of him.

'Enemy shields at thirty percent.'

Alarms sounded within the bridge. 'Our shields have collapsed. One enemy battleship crippled. Do we re-route power to shields?'

'Negative. Stay on target.'

The *Spear Tip* shook violently. Without shields, the Greys' energy weapons ripped into her hull.

'Bio Ship shields at zero percent,' cried an elf.

John allowed in grim satisfaction as he saw the beam start to eat away at the enemy's hull. Then he stared in disbelief. An enemy cruiser sailed into the path of the fusion beam, soaking up the destructive force.

The *Spear Tip* rocked as Grey weaponry raked her hull.

John could only watch as the fusion cannon was depleted. It was no consolation to know that the enemy cruiser's shield was no longer operational.

'We failed. We can only hope that *Armageddon's Reach* can slow it or stop it. Main batteries fire at will. I'm not going down without a fight.'

Like predators sensing an injured animal, the enemy ships pounced on the *Spear Tip.* John saw escort vessels move from the Bio Ship to engage *Armageddon's Reach*. The Greys' biological weapon was going to reach Nibiru and there was nothing he could do about it.

'Incoming message,' said the Professor.

'Inform the ground we have failed to stop the Grey advance.'

'It's not from the ground.'

'What?'

'It's not from the ground,' repeated the Professor.

'Nilah let's hear it,' said John.

A voice sounded throughout the bridge. 'This is Morrigan of the *Rearing Cobra*, First Battle Fleet of the Anunnaki. We have been monitoring the situation. Stand by.'

CHAPTER 19

Three sunburst yellow energy bolts, bright and mesmerising against the dark storm clouds above Manoa, arched overhead with a crackle of lightning behind them, and disappeared beyond golden buildings in front. Three loud explosions followed that drowned out the best thunder-cracks nature had to offer.

'High energy mortar rounds,' said the Captain, answering Dash's question before it had been asked.

'Where are they aiming?'

The Captain thought for a moment, getting his bearings. 'The market district, hotels, tourist area. It's not the High Council. We're OK.'

'Oh my God, they're going after the non-Anunnakis,' said Cassandra remembering the child playing with its alien Gameboy. 'They must have been stuck on this planet when the shields went up?'

'They'll be evacuating that district now,' said the Captain. 'But if the High Council is destroyed then truly, all is lost.

Dash unclipped his half-empty ammo mag and refilled it with the silver bullets Citalicue had provided. Why did it have to be a mortar emplacement?

Will unslung his weapon. 'Your call.'

'Dash, there are children there,' said Cassandra.

Dash closed his eyes, drowned out the sound of battle

and dove into his own thoughts. He could see the Taliban mortar. It would be firing on a small village whose only crime was helping an American soldier get back to health. He could see his friends, Shane and Wyatt, and he could see the Stars and Stripes folded neatly on their coffins. Given a second chance, would Dash attack the mortar emplacement again.

Damn right he would.

'You feeling better?' he asked Will.

'Right as rain.' Clearly Will was lying.

'You can't be ssserious!'

'Ki, you once said the Anunnaki were afraid of humanity's capacity for violence.'

Ki turned to stare at Dash.

'Well, they were right to be afraid.'

Ki replied with an audible gulp.

'Will, give the Captain your sniper rifle. Captain, find a high vantage point then act as over-watch for me and Will.'

The captain nodded. 'I don't need your weapon though.'

'Yes, you do,' said Will. 'Your beam weapons are lethal but give away your position.'

'Fair point.' The Captain took the offered rifle. 'I'll do what I can, but it's been awhile since I used such a ... primitive weapon.'

'You are in no ssshape for another battle, be careful,' said Ki.

'What can we do?' said Cassandra.

Dash studied the two women. Both brave, standing in a war-torn city, discussing how fit the men were, forgetting about themselves. 'These people need our help. We are the ones who fight so others don't have too. You follow the Captain and his remaining men. Me 'n Will will neutralise the mortar.'

Dash didn't like to give orders to civilians. Cassandra was an archaeologist not a soldier. But his commanding instincts had kicked in. He and Will raised their suppressed weapons and headed towards danger.

The Captain watched them disappear into the ruins of his once shining city, and shook his head. 'Why do they put themselves in harm's way for a people they don't even know?'

'It'sss the bessst of human nature,' said Ki.

'I'd hate to see the worst.'

Cassandra gazed down the alley where her men had gone. 'I have a feeling you're about to.'

The mortars fired again. The Captain glanced around to pick out the best spot. He saw a perfect one, a building overlooking the square where the mortars were set up.

'Follow me.'

Will peeked round a corner. 'All clear,' he said. 'I liked your speech better than the last one.'

'Really?'

'Yeah, I had me a tear and everything.'

'That's just because you're a big baby. Get a few scratches and you faint.'

'I was hit by a missile.' Will broke into a run and sprinted across the road on Dash's nod.

'It hardly touched you.' As they reached the other side, Dash crouched against the wall spying for enemy targets.

'Yeah right. I died you know?'

Dash signalled to move out. 'Oh, stop exaggerating. You might have …' He held up his hand as he turned down another street.

Will stopped, took a knee and scanned all around. 'What you got?' he whispered.

'Alleyway. Opens into a square. Could be a market. Lots of movement within.'

'Copy.' Will moved to the other side of the alley entrance.

An Anunnaki soldier wearing the enemy emblem, the four-winged eagle, rounded the corner and took up position at the far end of the alley. Over the comms link the Captain's voice said, 'In position.'

Dash cursed himself for sweating. This was hardly the roasting desert of Iraq. In fact, it was cold. The temperature had dropped significantly in the last few minutes. He cursed again, this time for thinking *rain* was sweat. The storm clouds were finally upon them and a few droplets soon turned into a downpour. He drew his silenced pistol as Will took out his combat knife. The Eagle must be taken out quietly or their cover would be blown, making their mission a lot harder. He aimed down the sights of his pistol, focus sharp and precise. His left hand supported his right, holding it steady

A small piece of rock chipped off the alley wall in front of his target and a bullet ricocheted harmlessly away. The Anunnaki jumped just as another bullet hit the ground near Dash. The Eagle turned and saw him. Human and alien stared at each other.

'Will,' he muttered. 'Don't let anyone borrow your sniper rifle again.'

The Eagle pressed buttons on a device on his forearm and raised his arm. Half a heartbeat later some kind of static electric pulse fired from the device. The next heartbeat saw the Anunnaki drop to the floor dead as Dash's pistol spat fire. The pulse had caused no injury, but their adaptive camo flickered before reverting to its matte silver setting.

Dash confirmed that his camo was OK, seeing Will patting himself down to check for injury. 'What was that?' Will asked.

Dash shrugged.

They heaved the dead Anunnaki into the alley and peered out. Three mortars sat in the middle of the opening, surrounded by six Anunnaki and forty or fifty Greys. To their left, a hulk of thick armour made its way towards the square on wide caterpillar tracks. It was topped by a large cannon embedded in an angular turret.

'Oh, wonderful they have a tank,' said Will.

'That's a big tank. You'd think it'd hover or something.'

'How do you want to play this?'

How did he want to play this? He thought out loud, working through their options. 'Time precious … Odds? Well, if we've met worse, I can't remember when … Lots of cover from here to the mortars … Half the buildings have collapsed …'

He gestured towards the heaps of rubble. 'Full assault. No mercy. Disable the mortars and get the hell out of Dodge. Although, I don't know if we're coming back from this one, buddy.'

'I hear you. Ready when you are.'

Dash held his throat mic. 'Captain, we're going to be

using cover to get as close as we can to those mortars. Shoot anything that moves.'

'You got it,' came the reply.

The Captain of the Guard groaned. He'd just given away Dash's position. Fortunately, his intended target had fired a defensive short-wave pulse, designed to disrupt energy weapons but ineffective against Dash's Colt. He scanned the area. Most worrying was a large Grey tank. They had fifty enemy troops down there too.

Dash's voice crackled over his radio. 'Captain, we're going to be using cover to get as close as we can to those mortars. Shoot anything that moves.'

'You got it.'

Ki stared on to the battle ground below, but directed her comment at the Captain. 'He meansss hit sssomething.'

'It's this damn weapon,' the Captain said and aimed at a Grey soldier. The bullet sailed past it. The Grey didn't even notice. At least that part of the plan worked, the sniper rifle wasn't giving away their position.

'Was I at least close that time?' he asked.

'Not even close …'

He fired again. 'Well how do I aim with this damn relic?'

'Wind speed, velocity … Gravity,' said Ki.

Dash and Will crept out into the square, weapons nestled into their shoulders. Two Greys were the first to die from their bullets. An Anunnaki cried out in alarm as he saw the Greys fall. Dash fired and the Anunnaki's head snapped back from the force of the bullet through his brain. The two Deltas carried on without stopping, searching left and right. Two more Greys met their maker as they climbed on to the debris straight into the path of the Special Forces team. Then a small Grey came out behind them, a green ball of energy already in one of its hands. It had circled to outflank them and was about to unleash death when a line of sniper bullets impacted the ground around it, one bullet finally hitting its mark. The alien's body lurched forward with a crack of bones and it lay lifeless behind them.

They made it to the first mound of rubble and covered each side. 'So far so good, but that tank over yonder gonna cause us some trouble,' said Will.

'Yeah, and I think the element of surprise has been lost.'

An energy beam blasted apart the stone work. 'You don't say,' responded Will.

They raced for the next set of cover, shooting at two Anunnaki who tried to engage. Their assailants were knocked back, but without a killing shot the Anunnaki's healing gene had them back in the fight in moments, though not before Dash had settled behind a solid block of gold.

The rain fell heavily now. The dust from the fire fights, missile attacks and fallen buildings mixed with the water, sludging up. Will crouched behind rubble a few feet from Dash.

They were inching closer to the mortars, but with every passing second the Greys were moving in on their position. One Grey got close, but was hit in the leg by a flurry of sniper shots from the Captain's concealed position.

'It's better than nothing,' murmured Dash seeing Will's eyes roll.

The Grey clutched its leg and was out of the battle.

'Our priority has to be those five Anunnaki's–' began Dash, when a massive energy bolt obliterated the surrounding area, lifting them both off their feet. Dash felt himself fly helpless through the air until he landed with a thump in some kind of ditch, aware that Will was nearby.

His head pounded, like something was trying to punch its way out through his skull. An ill-advised attempt to shake off the headache caused his eyes to water, blurring his vision. He felt the wobble of a broken jaw, then warm blood poured from his mouth. His nose felt sticky. His hand came away from it stained red.

He closed his eyes tight, clenched his fists and willed the healing gene to kick in. Why did it choose now to take its damn time? When he could manage words, he put a hand on Will who was hunched over. 'You OK, buddy?'

It was obvious Will was in some pain. His earlier wounds had re-opened, staining his fatigues red. But Dash needed him mobile.

'Buddy?' he asked again.

'Ah, damn dirt in my eye,' said Will, who proceeded to remove his glove in an attempt to get a more tactile approach to dirt removal.

Dash thought about Will's predicament then chuckled. Dirt? He chuckled again.

'It's not funny,' said Will, but then began to chuckle himself.

Both men lay in the dirt laughing at the absurdity of it. For all they've suffered, dirt in the eye *was* a pain in the neck. Coughing, spluttering and still part-laughing they hauled themselves up, and peered over the rim of the ditch.

Through occasional breaks in the smoke, they saw the huge tank cannon aimed at them. Rain bounced off the armour with a ping, ping, ping, underlining how useless their weapons would be against the brute.

They stopped laughing.

A battle cry went up. Dash let out an audible breath as the Anunnaki and Greys charged their position. This was it. Their last stand.

He flicked the setting of his rifle to a three-round burst and engaged the enemy. From the corner of his eye he saw two welcoming beams of light shoot down from the Captain's building and perhaps the scream of a woman hitchhiking on the wind. The tank, so ready to kill them a moment ago, now swivelled its imposing cannon towards the light. But it was small respite for the enemy troops were now upon them.

Cassandra shook her head in horror as the blast from the tank sent Dash and Will flying into a shallow ditch. Relief at seeing them alive was short lived when all the remaining Greys and the five Anunnaki headed towards their position.

The Captain put another round down range, but huffed as he missed his target again.

All the while, the tank rumbled with a steady monstrous pace, towards Dash and Will. The cannon, the eye of a Cyclops, stared down at Dash with extreme prejudice. Death, the only thought it was capable of.

The Captain threw the sniper rifle on the floor and glanced at Ki. An unspoken communication ran between them. They grabbed their spear energy weapons and opened fire. Powerful beams of light scorched the rain drops as it seared through and smashed up the ground below.

Dash rolled away from three approaching Greys. His movement distracted them enough for Will to take full advantage and kill all three.

'So much for keeping their position a secret,' yelled Will as another beam of light fired out from the Captain's building.

'It's working,' said Dash, aware the support from the Captain had stalled the Greys' advance a little.

He shot one Grey but saw the five, eagle-crested Anunnakis racing for the Captain's building. He managed a reflex shot and hit one of them in the back of the head, but as it fell, the others disappeared into the building. The tank's cannon fired. The roar seemed to explode in Dash's head as a giant energy bolt flew over their position and smashed into the building behind them.

The devastation was complete. And the rain beat down.

Cassandra risked popping her head up to witness the battle first hand. She saw Dash shoot a Grey, then her attention was caught by something closer to home. Anunnaki entering their building.

Her heart thumped, pumping adrenaline around her body. Four enemy Anunnaki would reach them soon, but Ki and the Captain couldn't stop providing covering fire for Dash.

Then she saw the handle of the Captain's sword extruding from its sheath strapped to his hip. Memories rushed back. The joy of the fight that Nefertiti had uncovered when she'd read her mind. Fencing was one skill where she surpassed them all. She could do this.

With a steady hand, Cassandra took the sword. He didn't react, maybe didn't notice.

The black handle felt like soft leather. White straps crisscrossed it to provide extra grip. She had room to hold it with two hands, but was surprised to find it as light as the sabres she was used to handling. She swung it one-handed and found it comfortable to hold. The white pommel had a black sphere set inside, which clouded as she gripped the sword tight. She scrutinised it and saw a miniature storm, bolts of lightning flashing inside tiny swirling clouds, brightening the edges so the darkness in the centre made it look like an eye. Cuneiform script carved into the matte white blade lit up a whitish blue. This was more than a mere sword. Power surged through it.

She composed herself, steadied her footing and waited. And waited. The door in front of her remained closed.

She changed her stance and held the sword with both hands.

The door crashed open. An Anunnaki wearing the crest of the four-winged eagle stood in the entrance, his own sword already drawn, the Cuneiform on its edge glowing a pale shade of lilac.

Cassandra charged. If she could keep him there, he would block his comrades from coming through. Before their blades met, lightning from both edges cracked and hissed, drawn towards each other, dancing, fighting, whitish blue and lilac burning the air around them.

Attack! The best form of defence she'd learnt from her many lessons. Cassandra lunged. The Anunnaki, looked surprised.

He brought his long-sword up to meet hers. The weapons clashed.

She twisted her white blade around the steel edge of his, then pushed his weapon away, exposing his chest armour. With that, she drove her sword forward.

The armour stopped her weapon from penetrating skin, but with a clap of thunder, the power from the sword itself pushed the Anunnaki and two behind him to the floor.

The one left standing came at Cassandra, sword drawn, standing on his comrade as he lunged towards her. He charged with such force, her instinct had her step out of the way.

Now he was inside the room. Ki spun round and fired her spear. A direct hit from point blank range. The eagle did not survive.

'Behind you,' Ki shouted.

From the corner of her eye Cassandra caught the flash of a lilac blade. She spun with her sword and met the edge, parried, beating the blade away with hers, then coming down hard, cleaving the enemy's sword arm off at the wrist.

The Anunnaki screamed as his hand, still clutching his weapon, fell to the floor.

Another of the recovered Anunnaki fired a shortwave

pulse from his forearm contraption rendering all their energy weapons ineffective. The now one-armed Anunnaki took advantage of the brief commotion and lashed out, grabbing Cassandra by her throat and lifting her into the air.

She kicked and flailed her arms, trying to stab at her captor, but felt life draining from her, darkness encroaching on her vision.

The Captain thrust his spear low, jabbing the one-armed Anunnaki in his leg. Still holding the spear, he rammed it deeper into the Anunnaki's thigh. The Anunnaki let out a low growl.

Cassandra recoiled at the stench of its breath, but its grip on her neck did not weaken.

Another of the Anunnaki staggered forward to help his comrade, bringing his sword down on the spear, cutting it in half. Lightning bolts shot out from both ends, one slamming the Captain back into the wall; the other racing up the leg of the Anunnaki who held Cassandra.

He dropped her with an enraged cry and swung out with the back of his hand. The blow smashed into Cassandra's face and threw her across the room.

Ki stepped forward and thrust her spear through the one-armed Anunnaki's head. It fell to the ground as she withdrew the weapon. In front of her an Anunnaki held a long-sword cracking with powerful electricity. One other remained standing. It pulled out its power spear.

Behind Ki the Captain groaned, his hands blackened where the lilac bolts had burnt him. At least he's still alive, noted Cassandra still on the floor, back up against the wall. She felt blood trickle from her mouth, determined to stand, but for the moment the pain was too much.

She hated to feel so helpless and tried to lift the long-sword but could barely move her arm. Blood splattered on her hand and sword as it fell from her lips. She watched the sword soak up the blood as though it was a sponge. Then the storm in the pummel gathered force, flashing red. The Cuneiform script lit up, and as she stared, the sword changed shape.

The matte white blade thinned. The cross-guard morphed into a D-shape around her grip. The long-sword was now a sabre. Red lightning forked up Cassandra's arm, caressing her, energising her. She stood up.

The Anunnaki with the spear turned and fired the beam from its tip. Instinctively, Cassandra held up her sabre. It rattled in her hand. She narrowed her eyes and held tight as her blade split the beam, bending it harmlessly around her. The red light in the Cuneiform letters outshone everything, the sword drew power from the beam as well as deflecting it.

Cassandra met the eyes of the Anunnaki. He stopped the beam, maybe realising she was stealing its power. Too late. Her sabre, held upright, directed a tight ray of raw power along its blade, slicing the enemy in two, vertically.

At once, Cassandra positioned herself for the final confrontation. One Anunnaki remained alive. She bent her knees, placing her sword-side foot forward and her left hand on her hip. The tip of her blade pointed to the Anunnaki. She was ready, focused, prepared. Long-sword versus sabre.

The Anunnaki clutched his long-sword with both hands as he came forward. Cassandra sensed his trepidation.

Their blades touched and scraped. Lightning hissed between them. Her edge was below the Anunnaki's when he tapped her blade down.

She recognised it as a nervous move either to feign an attack or try the double bluff. It was obvious to her that he was planning to strike.

As swiftly as the battle had started, it was over. The Anunnaki lunged. Cassandra kept their blades touching, guiding his away from her body, drawing him in closer, before stepping aside, twisting her torso, bringing her sabre around and flicking her wrist. Her blade slashed the Anunnaki's head. Red lightning did the rest.

She stood motionless keeping hold of the sabre but letting her arm hang and the tip touch the floor. The glow of the blade dimmed. Four dead Anunnaki lay at her feet. She let out a giggle, which turned to laughter, which turned to tears. She wept. The enormity of what had happened was terrifying her.

'It's not over yet,' said the Captain who stepped away from the window and picked up one of the dead Anunnaki's powered spears.

'Your sword.' Cassandra held out the blade to him.

'It's your sword now.'

'It changed?'

'That sword is Blood Prince technology. It adapts to the user. For me it became a long-sword. Once your DNA activated it, the sword knew what it needed to become for you.'

'But I can't take it.'

'The sword has been passed from Captain to Captain, but there have been no more Anunnaki births for a hundred and fifty thousand years.' The Captain picked up another spear and tossed it to Ki. 'Besides, the sword chooses its master, and it chose you.'

Cassandra wiped tears from her cheek, smearing blood over her face like war paint. She admired the sword. In truth, she wanted it. This was historical.

'You'll need this too.' The Captain unbuckled his belt with the sheath attached. When he handed it to her, the black and white belt conformed to her size and the sheath morphed to fit the sabre.

Ki gave Cassandra her old spear. 'I have reset the power cell. It will run on half ssstrength for now, but more than enough to despatch the Greysss. Dash and Will …'

Ki was cut short by a blinding flash. They were all thrown to the floor as half the room was blown open by a bolt from the tank, leaving them exposed to the elements. Had they been standing by the window, they would all be dead.

Forty capital ships of the Anunnaki First Fleet dropped out of light speed and opened all guns, blazing fire on the enemy. Beam weapons and thundering bolts of energy ripped into the Grey armada. Fighter wings launched from the Anunnaki carriers and hundreds of saucer-shaped fighters supported the *Spear Tip's* own fighters, irrevocably changing the balance of power.

But it wasn't enough. The Bio Ship was now using Shalor, Nibiru's twin planet, as cover.

John left his chair, stepped away from his tactical cube and walked, slow, reserved to the main windows of the bridge. He needed a clear view of the Bio Ship, away from the off-putting glow of the holograms, almost as if he wanted to catch it with his own hands. As the weaponised vessel disappeared behind Shalor, a faint smile grew on his otherwise stern face. 'Oh, what an idiot I've been!'

'You've got a plan, haven't you?' Nilah smiled.

'Yes, I think so. Patch me through to Lady Morrigan in the *Rearing Cobra*.'

'Done.'

'Lady Morrigan, this is Commander John of the *Spear Tip*. Are you in a position to bring the remaining shields down on the Bio Ship?'

'Yes,' came the reply. 'But we won't be able to stop it in time.'

'You let me worry about that. Just bring its shields down.'

'Whatever you're going to do, I hope it works.'

John turned to the Professor. 'You're in command. I'll be back soon.'

'What are you up to?' said the Professor.

'I'm going to board the damn thing.'

John raced to the nearest docking bay and kicked himself for the third time on this ship for not reloading his pistols when he had the chance. He had one bullet, and had to hope he wouldn't need any.

He burst into the hangar and couldn't help but spare a few heartbeats to admire the black fighter. Its vicious, talon-like landing gear, its graceful swept back wings ending with two imposing laser cannons. The back tails poked upwards like a shark's dorsal fin allowing stability in atmospheric flight. A black, giant eagle.

He approached the underside of the plane which opened. The cockpit chair swivelled down to meet him.

He sat and it gracefully rose into the fighter, locking into place. A joystick and thrust control configured like an F-15 Strike Eagle materialised before him, whilst holographic displays lit up the cockpit with a soft, pale green glow.

'Zanites?' enquired John.

'To a configuration you're used to.'

'I actually know how to fly this ship.'

'Of course, you do. I do, so you do.'

'Good.' John could feel Nilah beam with pride within him. 'I notice you didn't try to talk me out of this.'

'It's a good plan. Our only plan,' she said.

John activated the power core and the giant eagle lifted from the flight deck. The talons retracted, and he eased the craft out of the hangar, plotting an intercept course to the Bio Ship.

He was immediately flanked by the remnants of Squadron Thirty-One. 'My Lord, permission to provide escort cover,' asked the Squadron Leader.

'I'm guessing you're going to do it even if I say no.'

John turned to his right and could see the Squadron Leader in the cockpit of his damaged bomber. The reply to his comment was a salute. John saluted back and engaged the afterburners.

As he approached the Bio Ship, energy beams from the massive triangular command ship of Morrigan's personal battleship lit up from over three hundred miles away and disintegrated what was left of the Bio Ship's repaired shields. Now all he had to do was get past the remaining cruisers and fighters.

John had flown an F-15 Strike Eagle back on Earth, and this one flew no differently. In fact, it flew better. The on-board computer compensated dynamics for the vacuum of space giving the illusion of atmospheric flight for John's benefit, and the fighter soared through space as graceful as ... an eagle.

A wave of fighters came his way. He blasted his cannons, forcing them to spread apart. Now a cruiser blocked his path. Missiles from the bomber squadron flew past him, converging on the blocking cruiser blowing a hole clean through the ship.

He continued full pelt, flew straight for the fresh hole and straight through the cruiser. There in front of him was the Bio Ship. No escape.

'Squadron Leader, I'm through,' he called, full of renewed hope. 'Squadron Leader? Are you there?'

'Squadron Thirty-One has been destroyed, John,' said Nilah's voice.

He said nothing.

The Bio Ship presented a damaged section of its hull which he made wider with every weapon as his disposal. He felt Nilah almost fearing his anger. Almost.

The Bio Ship had a forcefield membrane. From his neural link with Nilah, John knew it was a safety net designed to keep oxygen and heat in place when a space-faring vessel experienced external hull damage. He could fly right through it and it would reform behind him. He did just that, and landed the Eagle on board the Bio Ship.

The enemy ship was dark, and quiet. 'No one's home?' John muttered as he left his craft.

He then found himself surprised by the low ceilings, so used to the *Spear Tip*, he had forgotten the Greys were only four-feet tall. He could stand, but with only a foot of space above his head. He removed his pistol from its shoulder holster, checking that his single bullet was at least still loaded.

He crept forward cautiously, ducking under low support beams. 'What do you need, Nilah?'

'Any computer attached to the AI Core. I do not need to be on the bridge.'

He reached a door. It was locked. The keypad symbols were in an alien language he didn't understand.

Nilah reached for the pad. Her hand sunk into the bulkhead where the console was situated and seconds later the door slid open. The corridor was empty. Some of the walls were missing. He could see through to the rooms beyond, also devoid of equipment.

'This ship is only half built.'

'Looks like they weren't intending to use it so soon,' agreed Nilah.

He stared down the corridor feeling the emptiness of the ship. 'Have they a skeleton crew aboard?'

'Yes John.' Nilah's electric ghostly hand dug deep into the pad, zapping an occasional spark from the interface, connecting to the Bio Ship's main computer. 'I've located the server room. It's not far.'

Nilah lit the route on the heads-up display inside John's visor, and John ran. To hell with stealth. With no time left, they must take control of this ship before it crashed its deadly virus into Nibiru.

***

The tank fired at Cassandra's building blowing away a portion of the wall, including the area where Dash's allies had been firing their beam weapons in support. As the cloud settled Dash could make out Cassandra standing there, along with Ki and the Captain. For the first time, he experienced a gut-wrenching feeling of helplessness. If … when … When the tank fired at the building again, Cassandra would be dead.

He glanced back at Will, who put another Grey into the ground, only for two more to take its place. They were being overrun, but at least the Greys remained dead. The Anunnaki, unless it was a critical wound, just got back up.

A blinding light flashed in front. The shockwave hit, taking the air from their lungs and slapping both Dash and Will to the ground.

The tank had exploded.

Dash lay on the floor. Above him clouds meandered across the sky throwing down their heavy rain to splash his face. For a moment, he thought he was on Earth. A split second later, the peace was shattered as two jet black fighters in formation sped overhead. One launched a missile from its belly at a target Dash couldn't see. The other fired a missile at the tank. Dash braced, ready for the second shockwave. That tank was out of action indefinitely.

Following the fighters came a ship five times their size. As it swooped overhead, it fired multiple lasers, disintegrating every alien they hit.

Dash turned his head to Will, who was also lying on his back. 'Ready?'

'Ready.'

While confusion reigned, they stood up and raised their assault rifles. Once again the supressed weapons spat in anger, felling two Grey still staring up at the sky.

Moving fast but carefully, they advanced towards a large mound of rubble and debris which overlooked the mortar position. Four more enemy soldiers died by the time they reached the base of the mound.

John almost banged his head when he ducked under the door into the server room. The place was lined with display consoles and towering computers. At one console, a Grey was frantically pushing buttons and symbols. It didn't even see him as he strode up behind it and cracked it in the back of the head with the butt of his gun.

He pulled aside the body, smearing the console with black blood from its nose. 'Is this what you're looking for?'

Nilah floated forward and interfaced with the console, her delicate hands resting just above the symbols. 'Yes, this will do.'

She paused, cocked her head to one side, as though she'd heard something. 'John, a silent alarm has been triggered. There are Greys on the way to stop us.'

'How long do you need?'

'Not long.'

'That's not an answer, Nilah.'

The sound of running feet pounded down the corridor. John could see the reflected green glow from energy balls that must already be growing within the approaching Grey's hands. Ducking out of sight by the door, he put out his arm as the Grey rushed in, causing it to fall to the floor.

A green bolt flew down the passage. Another Grey appeared, followed by another. Then a green flash. John picked up the fallen Grey and used it to block the enemy fire. The Grey he held was dead, but its hands were still energised with power. He lifted the dead arm and yanked back its wrist, causing the palm weapon to fire. It missed, but it slowed his assailants.

'Anytime now, Nilah.'

'Almost there. Setting the coordinates.'

The Greys gained courage and attempted a frontal assault, leaping down the corridor towards them. John downed the first by hurling the body of its dead companion at it. The second was caught in mid-jump by lightning, shot from Nilah's outstretched arm, that encased its slim body. All that was left when it landed was a black smouldering husk.

'Thanks,' said John.

'Anytime.' Nilah smiled.

John caught a movement. The Grey he'd downed was scrambling out from under its colleague's body. It stood, clutched its fists and prepared to fight. John punched it in the face knocking it out.

Four more Greys ran in.

'Nilah?'

'It's all done John. Ten seconds to jump.'

The Greys prepared their final assault. All four generated large green power balls between their palms.

'Five seconds to jump.'

John remembered when they'd first travelled via High Density. Such a powerful manoeuvre. Ki had waited until they were past Pluto before activating it. Something about being too dangerous to jump in a star system.

The Greys were at the point of firing when all the servers lit up like it was bonfire night, before immediately shutting down. The jump had begun.

A quantum rainbow appeared, identical to the first time. John made his move. For what had confused the hell out of Dash, John now used to gain the advantage. He appeared next to all four Greys and shot every one with his last remaining bullet. In the next instant, everything was back to normal and four Greys slumped to floor.

'Impressive,' said Nilah.

'Yeah, I thought of it a while ago when we first jumped, the idea of being everywhere at once, but nowhere at all, like the cat Alex went on about. Dead and alive. All the possibilities. Wondered if I could be everywhere at once. That would be a manoeuvre which might come in handy.'

'Most impressive,' said Nilah again.

'And the best bit, I didn't even use a bullet.'

Being linked to Nilah the way he was probably helped, but John was glad she didn't mention it.

'I've set a course for the sun in this system,' said Nilah. 'We need to get back to the fighter. The remaining Greys are trying to override my command from the bridge, which they might be able to do if they had the time, but they don't.'

John nodded a strong affirmative and set off. The path back towards his fighter was free of the enemy. The bird dropped the pilot chair as John approached.

'Whilst I was setting the coordinates, I came across some disturbing information,' said Nilah.

'Of course, you did. Come on then let's hear it.' John strapped into the chair, whilst it rose back into the cockpit.

'This Ship isn't carrying a biological weapon, although it would have certainly still killed most of the lifeforms on Nibiru.'

'So, if it wasn't a bio-weapon what was it?' As he spoke, he took off and guided his ship out.

'It was a terraforming gas.'

'For the Greys? I didn't think they needed to do that on a world like Nibiru.'

'They don't, which is what worries me. If it wasn't for the Greys, who was it for?'

'Good question.' John watched as the Bio Ship sped into the Sun. Even with the visor of the fighter compensating for the glare, he couldn't stare for long. The silhouette of the ship disappeared, gobbled up by a consuming glow. The blip on his radar screen vanished soon after.

'At least it was quick,' he said.

'I programmed it that way.'

His attention was drawn to a strange artefact not too far away, a kind of spherical object. Then realisation dawned. Realisation of the power of the HD Drives. He envisaged a tennis ball size chunk out of a football. 'That's part of Shalor!'

'And that's why we don't jump inside of star systems. But we didn't have a choice, John.'

'But what about the life on it.'

'I put it at the same orbit and distance to this sun as it was in the Zaos System, so in theory it should still be OK, and besides I was in a bit of a rush.'

'I know, but we destroyed half a planet. I'm so screwed when I get back.'

Nilah appeared in the cockpit, sat on John's lap with an arm around his shoulder. 'And how, oh great leader,' she teased, 'are we supposed to get home?'

John stared at her, knowing the fighter didn't have jump capability. 'I didn't think that far ahead.'

What happened next stayed with the Captain until the end of his days. He couldn't believe what unfolded in front of him. Later he would liken it to the tales of legends, when perfect harmony and awareness engulfed the heroes of old.

Observing from his high vantage point he saw a wave of Greys surround the mound. This had become all about stopping the two humans. The mortars had stopped firing. Focus was on Dash and Will.

He stared as Dash and Will, with the enemy crashing down upon them, covered each other in perfect motion. When an enemy broke through their deadly dance, a combat knife or pistol added the enemy soldier to the body count which mounted in their wake. And all the time they moved forward up the hill.

Cassandra, terrified for their safety, still glowed with pride. They reached the top bloodied but unbowed, and were somehow still alive. She watched as they lobbed small objects that she could only presume were grenades, until the explosions that followed confirmed her guess.

They had completed the mission, against all odds.

She turned to see the Captain and Ki gazing at her, and all she could do was shrug with a smile on her face.

The Captain nodded at her. 'So, that's what Death looks like.'

Dash was sitting on the mound, a large ship hovering above him and Will. He held his hand up to cover his eyes as its rear door opened. Out jumped elves, he counted twenty-five.

One landed near him and he watched a white recurve bow materialise in its hand. The bow string and arrow were a mix of green fire and energy. The elf immediately shot a Grey who was trying to flee.

Another elf ran up to the first. 'Perimeter secure. Package two secure and on route. Secondary target eliminated.' Then as if noticing Dash and Will for the first time added, 'And package one secure.'

'Good, muster the men and be ready to move out.'

The elf nodded then left. The one who seemed to be in command, walked toward them.

Dash hobbled to his feet, in no position to fight. The rapid healing gene was only just keeping up with the damage he'd sustained.

'General,' said the elf to Dash. 'My name is Elindarial sent by Lord Commander John of the *Spear Tip* to assist you.'

'Did he just call you General?' said Will holding his red-stained stomach, his face spattered with black blood.

'Must be a field promotion,' joked Dash, then turned back to Elindarial. 'How is John? By your presence, the Professor was successful in locating the Blood Princes' ship.'

'John is battling several Grey invasion fleets and attempting to stop a biological weapon from reaching Nibiru, and yes he found the *Spear Tip* with our kind on board.'

'Your kind?'

'We're robots.'

'I think you're a little more than that.'

'Well, ah for one am grateful for your timely appearance,' added Will.

Elindarial nodded. 'With your permission, we shall help re-take this city.'

'Please do,' said Dash. 'We're on our way to the High Council.'

Elindarial smiled at Dash. 'Your way is clear. We shall meet again soon, I hope.'

And with that he led his men off into the city.

The Greys were on the run, their fleets were all but destroyed. With the intervention of the First Anunnaki Fleet, the tide of the battle had turned.

The Professor stood on the bridge of the *Spear Tip*, some of the shielding had been restored but not before several parts of the ship had been damaged. The true toll would be counted later. He adjusted the holographic image before him, contemplating whether or not to open fire on an enemy cruiser that was attempting to leave the sector, when the *Spear Tip* crashed to one side, as though hit by a massive wave. Systems went down throughout the ship.

'What was that?' gasped the Professor, grabbing hold of the command chair behind him.

Kuan Ti, from his pilot seat, gazed out of the large window. Ships on all sides floated aimlessly in space. Emergency lighting powered on. Systems re-booted. The same must be happening on the other ships, as he could see the vessels powering up.

Many of the Greys took the opportunity to ignite their main engines to full power and flee the system at faster than light speeds.

'Professor take a look.' Kuan Ti's voice had the tremble of awe.

The Professor stood right up to the window on his

command deck. Slowly spinning were the remains of Shalor. A huge sphere had been ripped from its side leaving a crescent. The Bio Ship was nowhere to be seen.

'They did it,' breathed Kuan Ti.

'But at what cost, and where did they go?'

Kuan Ti understood the Professor's sad tone. 'I'm sure they made it.'

One of the elves turned to the Professor. 'I have an incoming message from *Watchful Eye*.'

'Well, let's hear it then.'

A holographic image of the frigate's Captain appeared on the bridge. 'Just before the Shalor incident a short beam transmission was sent to us with the coordinates of the Bio Ship's destination.'

'Yes!' cried Kuan Ti.

'Let's go and get them,' said the Professor.

'Unfortunately, we can't. The high density drive chamber took a hit and damaged both units,' said one of the elves.

The Professor thought for a moment. 'Put me through to Captain Morrigan.'

The elf manipulated the controls and the image of Lady Morrigan's face floated on the bridge.

'I need a favour,' said the Professor.

Several beeps and warning lights lit up in Johns cockpit, as a large ship entered the system. His communication channel flared to life. 'This is Morrigan to the Destroyer of Worlds, do you read me?'

'She sounds annoyed,' said John.

'She touches you, I'll fry her brains,' said Nilah.

'Let's see what she has to say first.' John laughed.

'This is John, and technically I didn't destroy a world. I just kind of cut it in half, a little bit.'

Morrigan broke into a laugh. 'Do you require a lift?'

CHAPTER 20

The rain stopped, and the evening sun was doing its best to part the clouds. Dash was reunited with Cassandra and the Captain gave Will his sniper rifle back.

'Sights are off, or it doesn't work properly,' Dash had heard the Captain say.

'Really?'

Dash watched Will check over his beloved weapon, before holding it up and taking aim at a small can on a market stall. The can vanished under the perfect precision of the shot.

'Hmm,' murmured Will. 'Maybe that was too close?' He aimed at a bottle further away. It too vanished with a single shot.

'Seems OK,' Will said to the Captain.

'Well, you're just shooting up someone's livelihood there.' Dash smiled as he heard the fake disapproval in the Captain's muttered comment.

Things were changing for the better, but the withdrawing Greys were desperate and dangerous. Elindarial had ordered two fighters to stay with the beleaguered party on over-watch. And on their way to the High Council, Dash felt relieved to have black guardians hovering above, ever vigilant.

They stopped once to let one of the *Spear Tip* fighters deal with some Greys holed up in building to the east. It unloaded its deadly payload into the structure then spiralled away, arcing back and swooping low over Dash. The elven pilots made sure nothing came close.

The rest of the journey was trouble free. They had made it.

Even damaged by bombardment, the Council building impressed Dash. They passed under a grand arch into a walled courtyard. On either side of the wide path, trees with deep red bark and white blossom stood unharmed. The area was strewn with boulders of masonry, chunks of gold and chrome, but such was the place, they could almost have been put there on purpose, artistically. Dash allowed himself a brief chuckle upon seeing a long set of steps leading up to the main building at the end of the courtyard. They reminded him of the temple of Ur. The ziggurat he and Will had climbed back on Earth, which led to the discovery of the flying saucer, and ultimately led them here. He wiped dry blood off his cheek. A circle of men from the House of the Rearing Cobra stood guard at the base of the stairs, snapping to attention when they saw the Captain of the Guard.

Cassandra called his attention to a figure emerging from their left. 'That's the Angel,' she whispered into Dash's ear. 'The Queen's Assassin, Aliax.'

As Aliax approached he gave Cassandra a wide grin. 'Hello, trouble maker.'

'It's good to see you too,' said Cassandra.

'Call me Aliax,' he said to Dash.

They all shook hands and introduced themselves, then climbed the stairs into the council chamber.

Dash took in the grandeur of the main chamber hall. It was wide with a polished floor. A round table stood at its centre, set with nine seats, though only one Anunnaki was sitting: an overly large Anunnaki covered in orange scales introduced to them as Lord Toogar. A raised dais stood at the end of the hall; chrome pillars lined the side walls. Clusters of people stood deep in conversation.

'Dad!' Cassandra broke through the hum of chatter.

The Professor had been engrossed in conversation with John, but on hearing his daughter's voice he spun to face her. She ran to embrace him, tears flooding down her face. The Professor hugged her tightly.

Will looked at John then muttered to Dash. 'Not a single God damned scratch on him!'

They all met, shaking hands and embracing, talking about the events that had led them here. Dash overheard Kuan Ti and Aliax.

'You are not going to believe what we've found,' said Kuan Ti.

'Trust me old friend,' responded Aliax. 'At this point I'd believe anything.'

'I will interrupt,' came Nefertiti's voice from the dais.

Everyone looked up at her and unconsciously stood in a line.

'I have some matters of state to deal with first,' she began.

'Yes,' said Lord Toogar. 'Like the reparations these humans *will* start paying. For the damage caused to this planet, and our twin.'

Nefertiti looked at him incredulously. 'The humans? They saved this planet.'

'She arrived,' he said, pointing to Cassandra. 'And in the first five minutes, destruction rained down upon us.'

'Are you serious?' demanded Nefertiti.

'Yes, I am. Guards, arrest these humans.'

The Captain of the Guard glanced at his troops and very slightly shook his head. The guards remained where they were.

'I am a member of the High Council and you will do as I say!' Toogar almost screamed.

'Not any more. You are hereby stripped of that honour,' announced Nefertiti.

'You are *not* the Queen. Only the Queen has that authority.'

Aliax stepped forward. 'I can remedy this,' he said looking at the fat orange lizard. 'Lord Toogar, and assembled High Council, if you would like to arrange your champions I shall fight them. The last champion standing will confer the right of King or Queen to the respective Lord or Lady.'

An old brown-scaled Anunnaki looked down at Aliax. 'And who exactly are you going to champion?'

'My allegiance is with *Queen* Nefertiti,' said Aliax.

The old Anunnaki laughed. 'Ha, well played. I for one will withdraw my challenge.'

So, it went down the line. Each of the High Council members withdrew their challenge until it came to Lord Toogar, his orange face ashen. 'Bah, I withdraw. You have not heard the last of this, Nefertiti.'

The speed with which Aliax threw his knife was unparalleled. Dash had never seen a knife fly so fast. It was as though Aliax hadn't moved at all. The blade flew through the air and embedded itself in the head rest of Lord Toogar's chair, a millimetre from his head. 'That's Queen Nefertiti. Do not ever threaten her again, or you'll have me to answer to.'

Lord Toogar leapt to his feet, gripping his ceremonial staff with uncontrolled rage. 'You are but one man!' he screamed levelling the staff at Aliax.

Aliax was about to move when Lord Toogar relaxed the grip on his staff and backed away. Behind Aliax, everyone – Dash, Will, John, the guards and even Cassandra with her new sword – everyone had their weapons pointed at the Lord.

'None of my friends ever stand alone,' said Dash. 'You'd do well to remember that.'

Queen Nefertiti stood tall and proud. 'Guards remove this snivelling wretch from my sight.'

As the guards removed Toogar from the chamber, Nefertiti looked at the men and women below. 'I will have the coronation a week from today, and you shall all be guests of honour. Please, do you accept this invitation?'

Dash and the rest bowed. 'It would be our honour.'

A week on Nibiru was five days not seven.

It was the morning of the coronation and Dash was enjoying another bath, reflecting on the last few days. He and Will had healed well thanks to the rapid healing gene. Will was, at least in Dash's opinion, spending a lot of time with Ki. She was taking him out on personally guided tours of the city, well ... what remained of the city.

The restoration work had begun in earnest the day after the war ended. Large diamond-shaped craft helped lift the huge blocks with the use of tractor beams.

John had told his story, where and how the Professor had found the *Spear Tip*. The Professor himself had kept true to his word and was busy studying everything he could in the vast libraries of Nibiru. Anything he could find on the Djinn, the Ninth Fleet ... and he was now convinced more secrets were locked away in the *Spear Tip's* mainframe.

The bath would easily accommodate four people. Dash reached over the side and grabbed another bright purple fruit the size of a plum. It was juicy and tasted a bit like apple cider. He sighed the sigh of a man relaxed, before deciding it was probably time to get out of the bath. Two floating metal balls emerged from the ceiling and began to spin around him, letting out a warm flow of air, drying him off. He walked over to his clothes, laid out ready to wear. A design for his dress uniform had been given to the tailors by Ki. The new uniform was of course from the same silver twill most of the Anunnaki wore, but then dyed so it was almost identical to his original ones on Earth, except if caught by light the cloth would shimmer like oil in water.

As he started to dress, he couldn't shake off a nagging feeling. This was just the beginning of something ...

A knock at the door cut off his thoughts. 'Come in.' He did up the last of his buttons and reached for his tie.

The door opened and in walked Cassandra. She wore a long gown shimmering a dark blue in the light, with a low-cut V-neck and a slit up the left leg. On her feet were matching high heels. Her long hair cascaded over her shoulders. She'd said she wanted a dress more Earth culture than Anunnaki, to match Dash's uniform.

Dash stood gawking at her.

'Shall I do your tie for you?' she said. 'They're all waiting for us downstairs.'

Dash nodded, letting her put her arms around his neck.

As she pulled the tie up into a knot, she gently kissed him on the cheek. 'Thank you,' she said.

'What for?'

'For keeping us all alive.'

Before he could respond, Will appeared at the door, face grinning. 'You two ready yet, or should I tell the new Queen to wait a few minutes?'

They made their way downstairs. Ki came up to him wearing ceremonial dress and long black cape which had the emblem of a rearing cobra emblazoned on the back.

'Before we begin, the Queen would like you to know that, ssshould you choose, ssshe will provide an Anunnaki crew for the *Spear Tip*, yoursss to command in case of further attacksss.'

'I have to get back to my world first,' said Dash.

'The Queen thought you might sssay that. A ssship has already been dispatched to Earth to keep an eye on the Greys for you. Ssshe wished ssshe could sssend more but considering what's happened …'

The Captain of the Guard came and stood next to Ki. 'It's started.'

Queen Nefertiti stood resplendent in a white iridescent gown that flowed gracefully in the light behind her. The crown was made up of four golden cobras each with eyes of glowing jewels.

The speeches were ending when the Queen turned to the huge crowd that filled the streets and grounds. Thousands upon thousands of Anunnaki had come out to see the Queen crowned.

'Finally,' she said, her voice amplified so everyone could hear. 'There are special guests I would like to recognise. Without their help our city and this very planet would have been destroyed. Their personal acts of bravery, for a people they never knew existed, are unparalleled and as such they are awarded the Andromeda Star.'

An audible gasp rippled through the gathered crowd. Will whispered to Ki. 'What's the Andromeda Star?'

'It'sss the highest award a ruler can confer. One hasn't been awarded for the last two hundred thousand yearsss.'

Will was prevented from asking more when the voice of the Queen's speaker boomed out. 'Would Dash, Will, Cassandra, Alexander and John please approach the Queen.'

They got up from their seats and made their way down the aisle the Queen had walked along earlier, thousands of Anunnaki eyes upon them. Then from behind, the glowing form of Nilah appeared, ribbons of white-gold light snaking out of her, forming a canopy above the team. The crowd erupted in cheers, a deafening roar lifting the city up in joy.

'Don't overdo it,' muttered Dash.

'That comes in a minute,' whispered Nilah.

They reached the Queen and each in turn bowed as she placed a ribbon over their head with the diamond Andromeda Star hanging from it. They turned to face the crowd. A deep rumbling sound caught Dash's ear, almost drowned out by the cheers of the Anunnaki. The timing couldn't have been more precise, for as Dash and his friends started to bow to the assembled crowd, eight *Spear Tip* fighters roared overhead, trailing multi-coloured smoke which hung in the air, then exploded in a dazzling display of energy, bathing everyone in sparkling colours. The crowd erupted again.

Dash was filled with pride.

EPILOGUE

Lord Toogar approached General Kraktus' cell. Sounds of the Queen's celebrations reached even here. The General stared up and shook his head. 'It's over. What are you doing here?'

'Nonsense. It's just begun,' said Toogar.

'We have been defeated. Your plan has failed.'

'*My* plan? Oh no, General, it wasn't my plan.'

'What do you mean? You've been stripped of your place on the Council and I'm in here.'

'The intervention of the humans was unforeseen; however, the result has been the same. I was never going to stay on the Council. I had to act like a moron to make sure of it. We don't want any unnecessary suspicion falling on the rest of the council members, one of whom planned this for years.'

Kraktus narrowed his eyes. 'I thought I was working for you alone.'

Toogar opened the cell doors and indicated for the General to come out. When he did, he saw two sleeping guards.

'They will be asleep for at least four hours, which is enough time. Come on, our ship is waiting.'

'Where are we going?' said the General, shape-shifting into one of the guards.

'You'll see,' said Toogar, ushering him down the corridor.

The End

ABOUT THE AUTHORS

A child of the 70s, Simon Marett grew up with good old fashioned sci-fi like Flash Gordon and Buck Rogers. Qualified as an electronic engineer and a competent table-top gamer, his sense of adventure comes from years of dungeon mastering countless games of traditional pen and paper role playing games.

Ramon Marett is the Creative Director of a successful advertising agency in the Southwest of England. He is an experienced writer and has authored many commercials for over two decades.

His first published work from Fantastic Books Publishing was *The Easy Way Out* a short story in the Elite: Dangerous tie-in anthology *Tales from the Frontier*.

Read more on the Star Protocol website:
www.thestarprotocol.co.uk

If you have enjoyed this book, please consider leaving a review for the Marett brothers, Ramon and Simon, to let them know what you thought of their work.

You can read about the Marett brothers on their author page on the Fantastic Books Store. While you're there, why not browse our other delightful tales and wonderfully woven prose?

www.fantasticbooksstore.com

Printed in Great Britain
by Amazon